# CUT-THROAT

An absolutely addictive crime thriller with a huge twist

# BILL KITSON

*DI Mike Nash Book 13*

Joffe Books, London
www.joffebooks.com

First published in Great Britain in 2021

ISBN: 978-1-78931-995-8

*For Val*
*My all-round superstar*

# CHAPTER ONE

In a remote area of countryside, near the small port town of Silloth on the banks of the Solway Firth, the natural divide between Cumbria and Scotland, stood the large detached house. The area was quiet enough during the daytime, in the early hours of the morning even more so. It didn't take much sound to disturb one of the inhabitants.

'John! John, wake up.'

'Eh? What . . . ? What is it?'

'Wake up! I think there's somebody in the house.' She was shaking his shoulder.

'What?' he mumbled again, still unsure if he was awake or dreaming. He opened his eyes, blinking in the light of the bedside lamp his wife had switched on.

'I heard a noise. It sounded like somebody moving about downstairs.' Alice's voice was little more than a whisper, but the meaning louder than a shout.

They listened, barely able to breathe. After a minute, they began to relax, albeit marginally, almost convinced that Alice had imagined the noise she claimed had woken her.

The lamp was extinguished and John was drifting back to sleep when he heard a sound. This time he knew it was real, and no figment of Alice's imagination. The sixth step on

1

the staircase leading to the first floor always creaked. It had done so for many years. Without conscious thought, as Alice relit the lamp, John leapt out of bed, stuffed his feet into his slippers, and opened the bedroom door.

He shivered, not because the pyjamas he was wearing afforded little protection from the cool night air, but mainly out of fear. He had only taken one pace onto the landing, his form illuminated by the bedroom light behind him, when that fear was justified. Out of the darkness, an arm gripped his shoulder. He felt the point of a knife at his throat.

Alice screamed as she saw her husband fall backwards into the bedroom, blood pumping from the open wound as he collapsed on the carpet. Her screams intensified as the burglar strode confidently into the room, stepping over his victim's body. Within two strides he was at the bedside and grabbed Alice, hauling her from the bed.

'Where's the safe?'

Alice continued to scream.

'Shut it. Or you'll be joining your husband. I won't ask again. Where's the safe?'

She pointed to the dressing room, and was dragged unceremoniously by the hair towards it. The intruder kicked the door wide and, with the knife, indicated the safe. 'Open it!'

With trembling hands, she keyed in the code on the panel. As the door of the wall safe swung open, the burglar yanked her head back. Seconds later, Alice was as dead as her husband.

As the burglar emptied the safe, a wide smile spread across his face. He removed several thousand pounds in cash, and jewellery cases with necklaces, rings, earrings, and brace-lets he knew to be highly valuable. Best of all, matching Patek Philippe watches, which would themselves be worth well into six figures.

Ignoring the couple he had just murdered, the intruder began rifling the bedside cabinets before turning his attention to the dressing table. He spotted an engagement ring and various other items of jewellery, which he swept into his bag. This was proving to be a highly lucrative night's work. There was the silverware he'd seen in the dining room as he made his way through the house, and the L. S. Lowry painting in the hall didn't appear to be a print.

He took his time. He knew there was no chance of the woman's screams having attracted unwelcome attention. The nearest house was over a mile away — the only likely listeners a fox or an owl.

Before leaving the bedroom, he turned his attention back to the couple. It took only seconds for him to add a trademark signature on both corpses. He smiled slightly as his knife traced the outline of a letter of the alphabet on their foreheads.

* * *

Craig French had been made redundant. The traumatic news of his job loss had been delivered by his employer in terms that were as gentle as possible, citing his ill health and inability to sell the company. As the firm's newest employee, Craig was aware that eighteen months' service wouldn't entitle him to any redundancy pay. And the amount he earned as a seasonal beater for shoots on the local estates wouldn't go very far either. The news had been bad enough, but when he arrived at his girlfriend's place that evening, her news made the situation worse. As gently as possible, Tiff announced that she had bought a pregnancy test, which confirmed she was pregnant.

With unemployment in the area well above the national average, Craig's chances of finding a job were slim. Allied to that, another hungry mouth to feed was the last thing he needed.

A few days later, Craig was acting as a beater for the Winfield Estate's prestigious shoot. It served as an antidote to his depressed mood, but more than that, the result of a chance encounter created a possible solution to his financial crisis. The opportunity involved a huge gamble, but if Craig's actions proved successful it would yield a sum of money far in excess of anything he could have dreamed of. If he had severe doubts over the legality of the scheme he had been invited to participate in, those misgivings faded in the face of the enormous potential reward.

Three weeks later, at the end of the last drive of another day's shoot, the gamekeeper, Barry Dickinson, had instructed Craig to take three brace of pheasant — Barry's allowance from the day's bag — to his house. 'Hang these in the outbuilding, will you? You'll find the spare house key on a hook in there. Go into the kitchen and help yourself to some sandwiches and cake. There's some beer in the fridge as well. Shirley's out, but she left food ready. I'll be along later, once I've seen this lot settled.' He'd indicated a group of Sir Maurice's distinguished guests who had formed the shooting party, before adding, 'When I return I've an idea I want to put to you. I think it's something you might like — just don't eat all the grub.'

The planned conversation had never taken place, nor had Craig been able to help himself to any of the refreshments. He'd finished hanging the pheasants and was about to retrieve the house key when he received a panic text from his mother, demanding that he return home ASAP. Craig headed for the main road, cadged a lift from one of the other beaters, and soon reached his mother's house.

Knowing how house-proud his mother was, and of the trouble he would be in if he muddied the new hall carpet, Craig went to the back door, removed his boots, and entered the kitchen. He expected his mother to be alone. That wasn't so. The door to the lounge-cum-diner was open and he saw two men facing his mother, their body language making it clear to Craig that this was no social visit.

The older of the visitors looked at the new arrival as he simultaneously produced a warrant card. 'Craig French?' It was more of a statement than a question. 'I am arresting you on suspicion of—'

Craig didn't wait to hear the remainder of the sentence. Panic caused him to overreact, with disastrous consequences. Mindful of what he had concealed in the loft, and the dubious source of the huge amount of cash, he flung the two pheasants, his bonus for the day's work, at the nearer of the men, turned and bolted through the kitchen and out into the back garden.

The senior of the detectives signalled to his colleague to give chase. Unfamiliar with the layout of the property and the topography of the area surrounding the house, the officer was also hampered by being older, heavier, and less fit than the fugitive.

Craig seemed to be on the verge of getting away when calamity struck. As he tried to leap the fence at the rear of the garden, a dangerous act at the best of times, his sock caught on a nail. Unable to control his fall, Craig tumbled over.

There had been more rainfall than usual over the winter. The area beyond the gardens of the houses in that row had once been operating as a stone quarry. Although now worked out, the crater formed by the extraction of thousands of tons of sandstone still remained. The rain had rendered the embankment at the rim extremely unstable. Craig's weight, combined with the shock wave created by his impact on the soft soil, was sufficient to trigger a landslide and carry the instigator with it. Craig's last memory was of sliding, and of excruciating pain as his head, arms, legs and torso came into contact with rocks.

Almost sixty feet above him, the detectives who had travelled to Helmsdale in North Yorkshire from Cumbria to arrest Craig French for murder stared down at the apparently lifeless form below. Although they summoned emergency medical help, the officers were convinced that when the recovery team and paramedics arrived it would be too late. The only service they could provide for the young man was to confirm that Craig French would never stand trial for the double murder he had undoubtedly committed. You cannot prosecute a dead man.

\* \* \*

Several hours later, following emergency admission to Netherdale General Hospital, the neurosurgeon leading the team treating Craig brought his mother and the detectives up to speed. 'Mr French is in a critical condition. His skull is fractured and he is on his way to theatre for surgery to relieve the pressure on his brain. At this stage it is much too soon to assess the full severity of his internal injuries. He has a broken arm, a broken leg requiring more surgery, and several broken ribs. At present, he is in a medically induced coma and being ventilated. I am unable to give you any guarantee regarding his chance of survival. Even if he does recover physically, it is far too early to speculate as to his mental condition.'

It was at that point that Craig's mother, Brenda French, generally acknowledged to be one of the strongest women on the Westlea estate, having become fully aware of her only child's slender hold on life, collapsed in tears.

# CHAPTER TWO

The lights were bright, their neon intensity sufficient to hurt his eyes. His vision was slightly blurred and Craig attempted to focus. That didn't work. He tried to move his head. That didn't work either. He blinked and relapsed back into the coma from which he had only just begun to emerge.

Although he was unaware of it, his brief period of consciousness had not gone unnoticed. The nurse picked up the phone and reported to the physician in charge. 'It's Sister Pearce on ICU. I was checking on your patient, Mr French, and he woke up. It was very fleeting, only a minute or so, and he's unconscious again, but I thought you should know.'

The physician was mildly surprised. 'With his injuries I thought it wouldn't happen, and we might have to pull the plug eventually.'

The nurse winced at the allusion to euthanasia, but concentrated as the specialist continued issuing instructions.

'I still need him under constant observation and wish to be informed immediately should there be any further change.'

Sister Pearce wanted to protest, to mention staff shortages and constraints on her team's time, but knew it would be of no avail.

* * *

Although Craig was unaware of the passage of time, and continued to open his eyes more frequently, it was some days before he was aware of someone alongside him.

'Oh, Craig, love. You're awake. How are you feeling? Craig? Craig, answer me.'

He saw the woman's lips move, but didn't hear anything.

Questions flooded his mind. Where was he? What was this place? The room seemed vaguely familiar — he could make out banks of machines, but had no idea of their purpose. Had he been here before? He was confused and couldn't remember. There were two women standing close to where he was lying. The younger of these was dressed in some kind of uniform, while the older one, whose lips had moved, was in ordinary clothes, and appeared to be distressed for some reason.

He could see three men, two of whom were wearing white coats. All of them were staring at him. Perhaps they knew him, but he couldn't recall having met any of them before. It was at that moment when he realized that he couldn't remember anything. It was all too baffling, so Craig resorted to his previous defence mechanism and drifted back into unconsciousness. Had he been able to hear and make sense of what was being said, he would have been deeply disturbed.

'Now that he's waking up I want him moved to a hospital nearer to where he will be tried,' the detective stated, taking it for granted that the medics would approve.

'That's not going to happen for a long time yet,' the neurosurgeon snapped. He glanced at his colleague, and the orthopaedic specialist alongside him nodded agreement. 'Apart from the broken bones, Mr French has sustained a severe head injury, which required surgery to relieve the pressure, and he has been in a coma. Just because he has opened his eyes doesn't mean he is "waking up", as you put it. His skull fracture needs time to heal, and I believe he may be suffering from aphasia and possibly traumatic amnesia.'

'What does all that mumbo-jumbo mean?'

'He fails to respond when anyone speaks to him, even after repetition. That could indicate deafness, a common by-product of brain damage.' The specialist gestured towards Brenda French as he continued, 'His mother is constantly at his bedside, but he gives no sign of recognizing her.'

'You're trying to tell me he doesn't know his own mother?' The detective's disbelief was evident from his tone.

'I do indeed.' The neurosurgeon paused for effect and then added, 'There is also a strong chance that he doesn't even remember his own name.' Seeing the police officer's continued scepticism, he drove his point home. 'One thing I can tell you for certain — there is no way I will allow you to attempt to question Craig French until I am completely satisfied that his cognitive state is good enough for him to understand what you are asking.'

The detective turned to walk away. 'Well, it better not take too long. I want him where he belongs — behind bars.'

On hearing this, Brenda French, her face a mask of distress, turned to the nurse. 'My Craig wouldn't do anything like he says. I just know he wouldn't.'

Sister Pearce put a reassuring arm around her shoulders. 'Come on. Let's find you a cup of tea, then you can come back and sit with Craig again.'

Despite the pessimistic forecast, Craig's recovery began a few days after this meeting. His hearing returned first, to a constant bleeping sound which continued day and night. To some it could have been an irritant; to Craig, in his confused state, it was like a lullaby. Although he was able to hear what was being said to him, the words were scrambled, leaving him to wonder if he was in another land, and the speakers were foreigners. His own attempts to communicate were limited, as if the injury had impeded his vocabulary and damaged his pronunciation ability.

Eventually, his speech improved and his vision cleared. Those were the first positive signs. Others took longer and were far less complete. His understanding, even of simple sentences, was at best patchy, and his memory was non-existent.

His mother visited him every day, hoping for some sign of recognition, knowing he had no idea who she was, or why she came. The casts on his arm and leg had now been removed and he was enduring daily physiotherapy sessions. The results were good, but he needed constant reminders of the movement and exercises.

After waiting impatiently, the Cumbrian detective leading the case obtained a warrant, eventually allowing him to transfer Craig to a hospital closer to the scene of his alleged crime. There, his treatment would continue, along with the aid of occupational and cognitive therapists. No expense was being spared to get Craig French to court.

\* \* \*

Seven months after his abortive attempt to flee from the detectives, when Craig acknowledged that he could remember his name, and that he recognized some people, such as his mother, he went on trial for murder.

Having listened to the overwhelming evidence pointing to his guilt, the judge and jury hearing the proceedings were in no doubt that Craig was guilty. He hadn't provided an alibi and was unable to say anything to refute the allegations. This was hardly surprising, for Craig had no idea whether or not the verdict was correct. He was unable to argue his innocence, because he couldn't account for the damning presence of some of the stolen Cumbrian property found alongside the murder weapon on a shelf in his lockup garage. Neither could he give any explanation for the items from earlier burglaries, also found in his garage. Nor the forty-five thousand pounds in used banknotes in a holdall stored inside a large suitcase concealed in the loft of his mother's house. The huge sum of money and the suitcase both bore his fingerprints.

Hearing of this discovery, the jury had no trouble accepting the prosecution's assertion that the money was proceeds from the sale of the more expensive items stolen from the dead couple — items that had not been traced.

In his closing address, prosecuting counsel cast doubt on the claim made by Craig's barrister that his client was unfit to stand trial due to a condition known as post-traumatic amnesia. Having pointed out the disparity of opinion in the medical evidence presented by both sides, he stated, 'It seems to me that this so-called amnesia cited by my learned friend occurred at a highly convenient time, resultant from the fall suffered by his client. Might I remind the jury that the incident in question arose when the defendant was attempting to escape from the police officers who had gone to arrest him? That, in turn, raises the question why the defendant deemed it necessary to try to run away from those officers? He certainly wasn't suffering from amnesia, feigned or real, at *that* point in time, and would definitely be fully aware of what was happening. Fleeing headlong from the police is the action of a desperate man — and, I venture to suggest, a guilty one.'

He waited for the jurors to absorb the impact of his final sentence before sitting down. He was confident that they would bring in a guilty verdict. His confidence was merited when, after less than an hour's deliberation, they found Craig French guilty of both murders.

Following his sentence, he was transferred to the maximum-security wing of Preston Prison in Lancashire, the nearest category A facility. Fifteen minutes after Craig was escorted into the cell which would become his new home, his son was born.

* * *

During the first few weeks of his time on remand prior to the trial, Craig's confusion had increased rather than diminished. His bewilderment was largely due to the unfamiliar surroundings and unusual regime of prison life.

A slight change in his circumstances reversed this downward trend, albeit providing only a very gradual improvement. It came about following his first meeting with the physiotherapist appointed to assess his physical injuries. A recommendation of regular sessions in the gymnasium to strengthen the muscles that were wasted following disuse during his long, slow recovery was the result.

Craig had entered into the exercise programme willingly, and even if his brain was showing little sign of healing, his physical condition was improving beyond expectations.

Following his conviction, and later transfer to Felling Prison in North Yorkshire to allow his mother to visit, he was allowed to continue and increased his exercise regime. The effect became noticeable.

Craig had also become aware that his memory, although still far from complete, was beginning to return. In many instances, he was uncertain about the accuracy of his recall. Incidents from his childhood were the first signs of this improvement, but with one drawback. To confirm that it was his memory rather than his imagination that was conjuring up these images, he had to wait until his mother's next visit to check their accuracy.

One subject that was *definitely* not discussed during those visits was his former girlfriend. When Craig had been taken into custody, the police officers had delighted in telling him the name of the woman who had informed them of his crime. The lead detective had sneered as he'd said, 'She identified herself as Tiffany Walker and claimed to be your girlfriend. Said she was terrified in case you turned on her, once she knew what you were capable of.'

At the time, this statement failed in its objective, because Craig had no idea who the woman was they were talking about. Sometime later, when he remembered the conversation, he'd been forced to ask his mother if she knew who this Tiffany Walker was.

Brenda, distressed by this additional evidence of her son's debilitated mental condition, and furious about what she regarded as a betrayal, vented her spite on Tiffany.

One thing Craig could not grasp was the fact that his mother kept trying to make him understand that he was father to a baby boy. It was ten months into his incarceration before some enlightenment emerged regarding what, until then, had been to him a mystery woman. He was in the prison library, searching for something to read, when he came across a book entitled *Uncle Tom's Cabin*. Staring open-mouthed at the spine, a memory came flooding back. The recollection had nothing to do with Harriet Beecher Stowe's anti-slavery classic. The word *cabin* and its personal association were what provided the spur.

That night, he pondered the information his brain had regenerated, now recalling every minute detail of Tiffany Walker. Every intimate moment they had shared during their passionate love affair, consummated whenever and wherever possible, and on many glorious occasions in a log cabin set in remote woodland. The affair had been far more than merely a physical expression of lust — certainly as far as he was concerned. Tiff had been the girl of his dreams, and he thought there was an unbreakable bond between them.

Then she had betrayed him, her treachery heightened by the knowledge that she was carrying his child. Even as he considered her action, and despite his mother's vitriolic tirades about her, Craig sought to excuse Tiffany. He knew she had informed the police of his crime. However, if he really had committed a double murder, he could understand why she had given him up.

Although he was now able to recall many parts of his life prior to his arrest, he could still not remember the key incident. He didn't recall ever being a burglar. And had he really committed such an horrific murder? The evidence certainly suggested as much. However, he had no recollection of the event, or anything surrounding it.

He had served almost twelve months of his life sentence when chance provided a huge spur to his recovery. On this occasion, Craig was again in the library browsing through some old magazines, his interest minimal, until he saw a man's photograph on the cover of one of them. He stared at the image as he recalled an event a short while before his accident. The consequences of Craig's intervention that particular day were so dramatic that remembering them sent him dizzy.

He leaned against the wall waiting for his head to clear. He then studied the photo and the date of the accompanying article for a long time. '*Birch Delighted by Test Results on Slowcoach*', the headline read. The text described how Sir Lionel Birch, owner of the racehorse Slowcoach, had been pleased and relieved when he learned that his horse, which had won a prestigious steeplechase almost eighteen months ago, only to be disqualified after a doping test, had been found to produce extra cortisol. The Equine Research Station's lengthy investigation revealed that, in common with some other animals, Slowcoach had an over-active adrenal gland, and the extra hormones he produced had mimicked the performance-enhancing steroid betamethasone in the test results. This had absolved both the owner and trainer, and Slowcoach was reinstated as the winner.

The news may have fascinated many readers, but to Craig French it was sensational. As he read the article, he remembered what happened on the day he met Sir Lionel, and also Sir Lionel's unique way of repaying the debt he owed him. It explained the huge sum of money in his mother's loft, money that had nothing to do with the proceeds of a robbery in Cumbria, or elsewhere.

That meant there was a huge hole in the allegations made against him. Although he could still not find an explanation for the items in his garage, knowing that there was nothing illicit in the source of that cash caused Craig to believe that he was innocent of murder. Believing it was one thing; proving it to the satisfaction of others was a different matter entirely. Now he had to try to remedy the situation. That would take time and planning.

# CHAPTER THREE

*Six months later*

Detective Inspector Mike Nash was listening to the radio as he drove to work at Helmsdale Police Station. Or rather, the car radio was on, but Nash wasn't paying much attention to the Helm Radio breakfast show. He was reflecting on the past month and thinking about how swiftly his life had changed for the better — and that was wholly due to the woman who had kissed him goodbye a few minutes earlier.

His reverie was interrupted by the radio announcer reading out the local news. The lead item puzzled him, as he had only heard the last part. A prison escape was obviously newsworthy — that of a convicted murderer even more so — but as the offence and trial had taken place elsewhere, Nash couldn't understand why it merited such close attention from local media.

It was only when he was greeted by their uniform sergeant, Jack Binns, that he learned of the connection. 'You'll have plenty to occupy your time today,' Binns told him by way of a greeting. 'Not much chance for skiving with one of our worst villains on the loose.'

'Are you talking about that piece on Helm Radio? I don't understand why it's making the headlines here.'

'Don't you remember? Craig French got life for a vicious double murder over in Cumbria. French is a resident of Westlea estate — or he was until he got put away in Preston Prison. Then at the request of his family — that is, his mother — he got moved to Felling.'

'When did that happen? Was it a long time ago? I don't recall it.'

Binns' reply was a reflex one, and he regretted it as soon as he spoke. 'No, it was less than a couple of years back, but I'm not surprised you missed it. You were too busy at the time fretting over the loss of a beautiful *señorita*.' Binns winced, knowing how badly Nash's relationship had ended. He waited for the rebuke and inevitable sad response.

He was surprised when, rather than looking downcast, Nash gave him a wide smile. 'You're dead right, Jack. Every time I looked into her eyes, I'd forget everything but her.' He turned on his heel, and Binns heard the sound of happy whistling echoing down the stairwell as Nash made his way to the CID suite.

A few minutes later, when seated at his desk, Nash heard the general office door close. He looked up to see his second in command, Detective Sergeant Mironova, enter the room. The good-looking blonde was removing her jacket, grinning as she spoke. 'Morning, Mike. I think you've been rumbled.'

'What do you mean, Clara?'

She came into his office. 'Jack Binns was asking questions about you, said you're more cheerful than he expected now Daniel's back at school. He suggested it might be because I've been back from holiday for a few weeks. Or that it's been a bit quiet.' She paused for dramatic effect. 'And then he threw the name of your house guest into the conversation.' She raised her eyebrows. 'I wasn't sure if you wanted everyone to know yet, so I played dumb. My lips have been sealed.'

'I don't mind who knows; we've kept it quiet long enough. If it hadn't been for you and David convincing her to return, she might still be in Spain.'

'You're wrong. It was all down to Daniel, remember?'

It was nearly two years ago, while in Spain on Viv Pearce's stag party, that Nash had become involved with Alejandra Torres, a successful artist with an international reputation. Preferring to be called Alondra, she came to live with Nash and his son Daniel, who adored her. The relationship had ended in somewhat tragic circumstances, and although Mike Nash was known to be a ladies' man, there had been no other women in his life since — until Clara and Daniel had found a way to bring Alondra and Mike back together.

'Yes, I'm sure it was all Daniel's idea.' Nash laughed. 'By the way, you've got it wrong. Alondra isn't my house guest now.'

'Oh, no, I'm so sorry. Hasn't it worked out?' Clara was crestfallen.

He grinned, an expression that Clara had not seen for a long time. 'It certainly has. She's a permanent resident now. Besides, I don't think Daniel would ever speak to me again if she left.'

Before she could congratulate him, the phone rang. Clara automatically picked it up. 'DS Mironova,' she greeted the caller. Then, 'Yes, he's here.'

She passed the receiver to Nash, raising her eyebrows as she told him, 'It's Superintendent Edwards for you.'

Nash blinked with surprise. He knew Ruth Edwards, a senior officer in the IPCC, the Independent Police Complaints Authority, having worked with her on one or two previous occasions.

'Good morning, Ruth. How are you? What can I do for the IPCC this morning? It's a long drive from London, so I hope we're not due an official visit?' Nash slanted the receiver so that Clara could hear both sides of the conversation.

17

'You're out of date, Mike. It's the IOPC, Independent Office for Police Complaints. And I'm not in London, I'm in Netherdale at HQ. I guess that means you haven't opened your emails yet,' Edwards suggested.

'I never have been good with acronyms, and no, I've only just this minute arrived. Is there something I should know?'

'I can see your deductive skills are as sharp as ever. I've been seconded to take charge in the absence of Chief Constable O'Donnell while she's on compassionate leave, and while Superintendent Fleming is still off with her injury. You must tell me about that incident when we meet. I've seen the report, and apart from the horrors you uncovered, it reads like a shootout from an old western movie.'

'I know. I was there,' Nash responded. 'It was the stuff of nightmares.'

'Anyway, back to business. The powers that be felt it unfair for you to be landed with the admin as well as the detective work. Either that, or they wanted to ensure you behave yourself, but that would be asking too much of anyone.'

'That's the best piece of news I've heard for a while — your appointment, I mean, not the slanderous remarks.' Nash paused and then corrected his statement. 'Actually, I'm wrong. It's the second best bit of news.'

'I guess the other one might have something to do with the young woman who answered the phone when I rang your house? In which case, I gather congratulations are in order?'

Having thanked her, Nash suggested he knew the reason for her call. 'I'm guessing you wanted to speak to me urgently because of the escaped murderer?'

'You're dead right. I've already had the chief constable of Cumbria on the phone, jumping up and down. He seems to think we'll be able to arrest this Craig French character before lunchtime. He wasn't happy when I suggested that the last place French would head for is here, where he stands more chance of being recognized than anywhere else. So I'm following protocol, by letting bad news obey the law of gravity. In other words, it's down to you and the team, Mike.'

'I haven't got much of a team at present. Viv Pearce has taken time owed before going on holiday in a day or so to Antigua. He wants to introduce his grandparents to their great-grandson, and he's not going to be back for three weeks. Can I have Lisa Andrews for backup?'

'I'll send her over. I've already got the troops keeping an eye out while they're on patrol. I've got his details from the PNC and sent a car to watch his mother's house on the Westlea — her house has been searched — although I doubt he would be stupid enough to try to go there. But you never know.' She gave Nash the details. 'Just keep me posted.'

When he'd ended the call, Clara asked, 'What did she mean about the law of gravity?'

'She was referring to an old, rather embittered attitude that shit rolls downhill. Now, all we have to do is find Craig French and get him tucked up back in his nice warm cell. To do that, we need to know something about him. We need background. It's a shame that Viv's off, because we could set him to work on the PNC. See if you can find anything, and also contact Netherdale HQ and ask them to source a hard copy of his record. It might also be worth talking to Tom Pratt at the same time. In the meantime, I'll have a word with Jack Binns and find out what I can about French. If he's from round here, Jack should know about him.'

Clara thought it was a tiny example of what Nash referred to as Sod's Law. It was more generally referred to as Murphy's Law, but she reckoned Nash's version — as he interpreted it in the context of their job — was more appropriate. The law referred to the likelihood that the thing you least wanted to happen would do so, and it would take place at the most inopportune moment. DC Viv Pearce was their IT expert, and had the knack of unearthing background. At least Tom Pratt, who had been a senior officer with the force and now worked as a civilian support officer, might be of help. Between them, his and Jack Binns' local knowledge was hugely valuable to the small team of detectives in the sub-station where they worked.

At one time, the original Helmsdale Police Station had operated round the clock in an old Victorian building. Having been relocated to a new site, occupied by all the emergency services, they now worked mainly office hours unless demand required overnight accommodation for prisoners.

\* \* \*

'French was convicted about eighteen months ago,' Tom told Clara when she called him. 'It was notified to Netherdale. As you said, he was tried and convicted elsewhere, so there would have been minimal involvement from here.'

'Jack Binns told Mike that French used to live on the Westlea, and I was wondering if he's got more family in the area, and if so, could he be heading for home?'

'I don't know anything about him myself,' Pratt admitted, 'and I can't seem to find any previous on the PNC, not even petty crime, which seems a bit unusual to me. But we should discover more once I've ordered the file from Cumbria.'

She reported this to Nash, who agreed that there was little they could do until they received the file. 'When Lisa arrives, see if you can discover where he worked, so we can check out his former colleagues, if he ever had a job.' Nash raised his eyebrows in question. 'And if we get some photos printed — they might just jog a memory somewhere. We might be called on to lift every stone in the district to see if this guy's hiding underneath it. It's as well there isn't much happening at present.'

Clara wondered if Nash had just invoked Sod's Law, but refrained from commenting.

\* \* \*

Elsewhere in Helmsdale on the Westlea estate, the news of Craig French's jail-break was received with alarm. Tiffany Walker had heard the same bulletin as Nash while she was preparing breakfast for herself and Noel, her eighteen-month-old son. Tiffany, known as Tiff since her second day at school, had been about to pour warm milk onto cereal when the announcer gave the escapee's identity. The glass jug shattered on the tiled floor as Tiff stared at the radio, her face drained of all colour.

The squeal of dismay from Noel as he banged his spoon on the highchair brought her attention back with a jolt. She stared at the child for a second before attending to the broken glass. Tiff's thoughts were preoccupied with the terrible news. Why had Craig escaped? Was his intention to come to Helmsdale? If so, Tiff knew exactly where he would head. He would come looking for her, to meet the son he had never seen, and even more chilling, to take revenge on her for — as he believed — grassing him up. That had been Craig's threat, the message conveyed to her by his mother in the menacing and embittered diatribe she'd spouted in the street. In the early days after Craig's conviction, Brenda had vented her spleen on Tiff several times for what she considered Tiff's disloyal conduct. Those insults were accompanied with some bloodcurdling threats as to what might have happened to Tiff had she not been carrying Craig's child.

Now she knew Craig was capable of murder, her fear went into hyper-drive. Tiff hadn't been the one who had betrayed him. How could she? She didn't know. Worse still, why did he think it was her?

While Craig had been in hospital, her brother had also been arrested, charged as accomplice to Craig in earlier burglaries — substantiated with evidence found at his work premises. He'd been convicted of robberies she couldn't believe either of them capable of committing. Christened Robert, he had always been referred to as Bobby. Once he opened his construction business he had become known as Bob the Builder after the children's TV show, and had even used that nickname in his advertisements.

During Craig's trial, it had been revealed that a witness had seen him at Bobby's house overnight when Bobby was working away. Rumour of an affair had spread — everyone knew there was no smoke without fire.

The question she'd debated many times was, would she have grassed Craig up had she known the facts? Tiff loved her brother and could always turn to him for help, but now that wasn't possible. Bobby's crimes were bad enough, but at least he hadn't been with Craig when he'd committed that unspeakable act of murder.

If only Craig had delayed his escape for a few months. By then, Tiff hoped to be able to leave England to join her parents and sister who had emigrated to Australia. Tiff felt a shiver of fear run through her. Perhaps that was precisely why Craig had chosen this time to make his jail-break. His mother must have got wind of her plans and told him. Was he going to try to stop her? Either that, or snatch Noel from her?

Tiff glanced down at the boy. Who could she turn to for help? There was one person, but she was unwilling to go down that route, knowing the price that would be expected for the assistance — a price she was not prepared to pay. Her other alternative was to ask for police protection, but she wasn't going to do that either, knowing that such an act wouldn't go down well on the Westlea.

Perhaps she was panicking over nothing. With luck, Craig would be found long before he got near the town of Helmsdale. Tiff had read somewhere that prisoners still had to wear uniforms unless they'd earned the right to their own clothing via good behaviour. Fat chance of Craig qualifying for that, she thought. Even in solitary he'd struggle to behave himself. No, she was worrying needlessly. Craig hadn't the nous to stay clear of trouble. That much was obvious by the way he'd stored the murder weapon and jewellery in his lockup, and kept that huge sum of money in his mother's loft. There would probably be a piece on the radio within a few hours saying he'd been recaptured.

Despite her confident prediction, Tiff listened to every news bulletin. She remained inside the flat, the doors and windows locked, with the curtains drawn even during the hours of daylight — in essence as much a prisoner as Craig had been. Next day, with still no word of Craig being recaptured, she realized that she too had to make her escape, if only to go shopping. Dismissing her fears as best she could, she dressed Noel in his coat, added a bobble hat, and got ready. Fortunately, she'd secured a ground-floor flat, courtesy of Helmsdale Council and Social Services. That meant she didn't have to struggle up and down stairs with the awkward buggy.

Once outside, Tiff headed to the road at the top of the cul-de-sac and set off in the opposite direction to the supermarket. Having walked fifty yards or so she turned left down the ginnel that connected her street with the one behind. Another left turn brought her on course for her destination. The route was one she'd used many times. The subterfuge enabled her to reach the shop without passing the house occupied by Brenda French. There had been several acrimonious exchanges between the women in the weeks before and after Craig's conviction. This simple diversion reduced the chance of a repetition. She was also keen to avoid other local inhabitants eager to discuss Craig's escape. Some might be well-meaning; others she felt sure would be less than friendly. Tiff would prefer to do without either confrontation.

She was relieved when she reached the door of Good Buys supermarket. Having parked the buggy securely, she sat Noel in a trolley and began selecting the provisions she needed. Price was as much a consideration as quality. Her benefit money was hardly sufficient for a lavish lifestyle.

Her apprehension only subsided when she returned home, where she locked and bolted the door before attending to Noel and storing her meagre provisions. She had just placed her son in his playpen when she heard a knock at the door.

Tiff's fear returned in full measure, escalating immediately into panic. She waited, hoping and praying that it was nothing more sinister than a neighbour in need of sugar. When the knock was repeated, she knew she would have to act.

Using extreme caution, she lifted the edge of the curtain sufficiently to identify the persistent caller. Her terror subsided as she recognized the man standing on the path, the only person she had thought might help her. Although she didn't actively dislike her visitor, who had been a neighbour when she lived with her parents, she was certainly nowhere near as keen on him as he had been on her. His pursuit of Tiff had ended when she met Craig, and from that point the relationship declined even further.

She opened the door.

'I was worried,' he told her. 'I was passing by and I saw that the curtains were closed and wondered if you or the little one were poorly. Either that, or you'd someone else here.'

'No, I'm keeping them shut because I don't want anyone peering in. They'll stay that way until Craig's back inside. I was terrified when you knocked on the door. I thought he'd come after me.'

She invited him inside, locked the door, and offered her visitor a cup of tea. Despite her reservations about the caller, she was glad of the company, and to have someone to talk to. As they waited for the kettle to boil they resumed their previous topic of conversation.

'I think you're worrying unnecessarily. I doubt he'd show his face on the Westlea. Too many people would recognize him, and most of them wouldn't hesitate to grass him up, given what he did. He might be a bit dim, but even Craig isn't stupid enough to risk being caught by coming here.'

'I wouldn't put it past him,' Tiff retorted, 'especially if he's as angry as his mother said. Still, I suppose you're right. It would be too much of a risk, certainly in daylight.'

'Does he know you've moved here? You didn't get this place until the little lad was born, and that was well after he was arrested.'

'He will do, because that harridan Brenda will have told him.'

'I wonder if she knows where he is, or if she's hiding him? Mind you, the coppers have turned her place upside down and there's a cop car parked outside. That'll be going down well.' He laughed. 'No, I reckon someone must be helping him, or he's found somewhere too remote for the police to catch up with him. Have you any idea where he might have headed?'

It was a question Tiff hadn't given any thought to, but as he mentioned the word 'remote', she suddenly realized where French might be hiding out. 'I didn't, not until just now, but there is one place I think he might have gone, and it's somewhere the police wouldn't know to look.' She smiled ruefully as she added, 'It was a place that had a special meaning for us once. But nobody would know that he's aware it exists.'

Tiff explained the location and its special meaning. Later, after her visitor had left, she mulled over their conversation and wondered if her guess had been accurate. Would Craig have headed for the cabin in Thornscarr Forest? If so, how would he survive out in the wilds, with no amenities to rely on? Admittedly, he was accustomed to the rural life, having worked short-term on various estates. But with no means of cooking, heating, or washing, she couldn't see him lasting long there. She shook herself mentally. She despised him for the vicious crime he'd committed, detested him for the way he had betrayed her, especially when he was aware that she was expecting Noel — so why was she feeling the slightest concern for his welfare?

She was pondering another remark her visitor had made when a cry from the lounge caused her to hurry through. The crisis that had made Noel call for help was that he had dropped his feeding cup out of the playpen, where it had rolled out of reach of his tiny hands. As Tiff returned it to the infant, she forgot her puzzlement over her caller's opening remark. He'd told her he was passing by and had noticed the curtains were closed, but Tiff's flat was at the end of the cul-de-sac and the windows wouldn't have been visible from the road. It didn't seem important. So she put it out of her mind.

# CHAPTER FOUR

Mike Nash was reading the file on Craig French's conviction. The document made interesting reading, and it didn't take Nash long to begin listing several questions he would have liked to ask those involved in bringing about the prosecution.

Eventually he called Clara and DC Lisa Andrews into his office. 'Did you read this before you gave me it?'

Clara shook her head.

Nash turned to Andrews. 'Have you seen it, Lisa?'

'No, Mike. I don't even know what it is you're looking at.'

'It's the Craig French file.'

'Is there something wrong with it?' Clara beat Lisa to the question by a short head.

'I'm not commenting, because I've read it and I'd like you both to look through it and give me your opinion. While you're doing that, I'll make coffee.'

'I actually met Craig French a few times,' Lisa told them. 'As a teenager he used to go beating on the Winfield Estate and some of the others nearby, to earn extra pocket money. I encountered him when Alan and his mate Barry Dickinson were short-staffed and dragooned me into service. I met him again as an adult and I must admit I didn't have him down as a cold-blooded killer — seemed a nice bloke. But I suppose people change over the years.'

'That's certainly true,' Clara responded. 'Take Mike, for example. Nobody in their wildest dreams could imagine him settling down to a life of domestic bliss.'

Nash responded with a grin, then went out, returning a few minutes later with the drinks. He found the two detectives bent over the paperwork, perusing the final sheet. After a few seconds, they sat back and looked at Nash.

'Well, what do you think?' he asked.

'I'm not convinced.' Lisa indicated the file. 'He was convicted of murder and robbery. But if it hadn't been for the weapon and some of the stolen goods being found in his lockup garage, I doubt whether they'd have even charged him in the first place. There's no other evidence, no witnesses.'

'I agree with Lisa,' Clara added. 'It's sketchy, and the fact that French couldn't account for how the stuff got there must have been what swayed the jury. What do you think, Mike?'

'Several things disturb me. I have serious doubts as to whether French was fit enough to appear in court. The neurosurgeon who treated him at Netherdale gave evidence to the fact that he believed French to be suffering from traumatic amnesia. That clearly failed to impress the judge — or the jury. But if the doctor was correct, then I'm not surprised French couldn't explain that damning evidence.'

He looked at his colleagues. 'Can either of you remember precisely what happened on 19 August last year?'

They both admitted that they couldn't recall any events.

'What did happen, Mike?' Clara asked eventually.

'I've no idea, and that's my point. We haven't got amnesia, but if French had, he might not have known whether he was innocent or guilty, which would make that trial a farce. Apart from that, I'm intrigued by the identity of the mysterious informant who tipped off the Cumbrian officers. How would they know that stolen goods from Silloth and other burglaries were in a lockup garage on the Westlea estate? And that proceeds of other burglaries committed, *allegedly*, by both

Craig French and Bobby Walker could be found at Walker's workshop in Helmsdale? There is only one way they could have that knowledge, but that seems to have been overlooked.'

'You think the person who informed them was also involved?'

'It's the only explanation that fits what facts we've got. That's one point, but there are a couple of other things that are puzzling me. I'm not sure what French's level of intelligence is, but the gruesome way he disfigured the victims seems incredibly stupid. OK, he might have thought carving a letter F on their foreheads wouldn't mean anything as he was so far away from his own territory. But it's an unnecessary risk to take. Unless he's a complete nutcase of course, which seems to contradict Lisa's opinion of him. And, even if we accept that French is dim-witted enough to store that damning evidence in his garage, why would he leave his victims' blood on the knife blade?'

There was another aspect of the information that gave Nash cause to ponder. But in the meantime, they had to find Craig French.

He decided to pay a call on one person who might be able to help and headed downstairs to speak to Jack Binns. 'Jack, I need your unrivalled knowledge of the residents on the Westlea estate.'

Sergeant Binns looked at Nash suspiciously, wondering if the remark was intended as sarcasm. 'Any particular customer you have in mind?'

'Mrs Brenda French, mother of our absconding prisoner Craig French.'

'My word, Mike, you don't half believe in living dangerously if you're thinking of going near Brenda. Mind you,' Binns continued, 'having said that, I can think of far worse on the Westlea — and elsewhere in Helmsdale, for that matter. Brenda's got a wicked temper and a tongue on her as sharp as a butcher's knife. If you're thinking of asking her where Craig is, I'd wear a stab vest, cricket pads, a box and a batting helmet.'

'I take it she doesn't believe he committed those murders.'

'She certainly doesn't. She's convinced he was framed, and she's been mouthing off about the person who did the dirty on him. So if you come across someone on the Westlea who's minus their testicles, then you'll know that Brenda's found out who stitched him up.'

Nash eyed the uniformed sergeant for a moment. 'Can I take it from your last remark that you also have doubts surrounding Craig French's conviction?'

'Let me put it this way. I was surprised when he was arrested, and even more so when it turned out there was stolen property in his lockup.'

'Yes, that last bit worried me too, so I went through the inventory of the items Cumbria Police linked to the burglaries. I found it very interesting reading.'

'In what way?'

'There was nothing of great value found in the garage. They wouldn't fetch much at an antique shop. It was almost as if someone chose lesser items deliberately, in order to frame French.'

'Why would anyone do that? French strikes me as being a harmless sort of a lad, a bit naive perhaps, but certainly not evil — unless he was talked into it by Bobby Walker.'

'Perhaps we should call up Walker's file as well.'

Binns nodded. 'Leave it with me. However, your main problem is convincing his mother you're not there to clap him in jail for the next millennium. Like I said, the best way to approach Brenda would be by phone — or, if you insist on visiting, stand well back and use a megaphone.'

'Right, I get the picture. Despite that, I'll call on her tomorrow.'

* * *

Next morning, Nash rapped on the door of the address on file for Craig French. The smartly dressed woman who opened it was difficult to recognize from Binns' portrayal.

'Mrs French?' Nash asked.

She looked at him, unsmiling. 'You're that copper, Nash, aren't you? First off, I haven't seen him. Second off, he isn't here. Your lot have already searched this place from top to bottom, trampling all over my carpets with their muddy boots. So, third off, you can't come inside unless you've a warrant. Also, would you mind shifting that cop wagon from outside my door — it's giving the area a bad name. Now, is there anything else, because I'm busy?'

She began closing the door, but paused as Nash said, 'Yes, as a matter of fact, there is something else.'

'What?' she demanded, a world of suspicion in her voice.

'I need your help to solve a problem. I read Craig's file. I hadn't seen it before because the case was handled by another force. Having looked through the evidence, I have to say I'm far from convinced that Craig's guilty. I really need some facts to prove whether I'm right or wrong, and that means asking someone who knows him to answer a simple question.'

The door opened a little wider. Brenda still eyed the detective with suspicion, but with less hostility than previously.

'What question?'

'I think it would be better not to discuss this on your doorstep.'

The door opened fully and Nash stepped into the hallway. 'Craig's lack of defence made his conviction a formality, but if he *was* suffering from amnesia it would explain why he couldn't account for the goods in his lockup or the money hidden here. If I could find out where that money came from, and discover how and why those stolen goods got into his lockup, I might be able to do something about it.' Then, with no hint of expression in his face or voice, he added, 'This is complicated by the fact that Craig isn't available to ask outright.'

There was a long silence as Brenda considered what Nash had said. 'I'll ask round, and if I get anything useful, I'll ring you.'

Nash gave her his card and thanked her, adding, 'The cop car stays, but I'm sorry for disturbing you when you're so busy.'

Brenda watched him turn to leave, with something almost approaching a smile on her face.

Nash pondered the conversation as he returned to the station. When he walked across the reception area, Jack Binns looked him over. 'I can't see any major injuries,' Binns remarked. 'So I assume Brenda French wasn't at home when you called.'

'Yes, she was, and we had a nice friendly chat,' Nash replied. 'She might be phoning to speak to me, Jack, and if she does, I'd like you to put the call straight through, even if I'm busy.'

His expression one of awe, Binns watched Nash sprint up the stairs.

* * *

Nash was cooking dinner, as Alondra set the table and poured wine for them. The house phone rang and she automatically picked it up. She wandered through to the kitchen and passed him the phone. 'It's DC Pearce for you. He was a bit surprised when I answered. I think he was dying to ask who I am, but was too embarrassed.' Alondra had forgotten that the caller could hear every word she said.

When Nash answered, Pearce told him, 'I wasn't embarrassed, just astonished. That sounded like Alondra. It wasn't, was it?'

'It most certainly was, Viv. You see what revelations you miss on your days off? Now, why are you calling? I hope there isn't a problem. Are Lianne and little Brian OK?'

'We're all fine, Mike. In fact it was Lianne who asked me to call you. We heard about this escaped convict on the news. Lianne's on her last night shift before we go away, otherwise she would have rung. I thought the best idea would be for me to bring her to Helmsdale first thing tomorrow morning, as long as you're going to be in your office.'

'I will be, but why does she want to talk to me?'

'Lianne nursed Craig French through his coma and the aftercare following his head injury. When she told me about

31

it she got very angry. I could give you a gist of what she said, but I think it would be better coming from her.'

'That makes sense, and we could do with any background we can get.'

'We'll have to bring Brian along, though, so you'd better warn everyone to be prepared for a noisy little troublemaker.'

Nash smiled. 'That's OK, Viv. I'll just warn them he takes after his father.'

\* \* \*

Next morning, contrary to his father's warning, Brian behaved impeccably during the visit. After they had admired the baby, the detectives listened to Lianne's reasons for wishing to speak to them.

'I nursed Craig French after his fall. He was in a coma, so bad that the surgeons were doubtful he would recover, even considering it might be necessary to turn off his life support if it continued. After he started to come round, it was obvious that he was in a very bad way, although the police officer who had come to arrest him didn't believe that. He thought he was shamming. How anyone can fake a broken arm, a broken leg, a fractured skull, and several broken ribs is beyond me.' She shook her head in disgust. 'The officer even tried to bully the doctors into agreeing to have Craig transferred to a hospital in Cumbria, but our surgeons resisted. Eventually, the police moved him, but by then I'd spent a lot of time caring for him.'

Lianne paused, her anger threatening to get the better of her, but then continued, 'Because of my personal involvement in his treatment, I took a close interest in the trial. I admit that the evidence against him appeared to be watertight, but he didn't seem capable of such cold-blooded murders. When the prosecutors suggested that he had faked his amnesia, I got really annoyed. To be honest, I didn't think he was fit enough to stand trial, not mentally, anyway.'

'How can you be sure he wasn't pretending at the trial?' Clara asked.

'All the symptoms were there, things he could only have known about if he'd researched the after-effects of cranial injuries in detail. And why would he do that, and, more importantly, when?'

'What were the original symptoms?' Nash wanted to know.

'Everything symptomatic of a head injury was there. He was deaf for quite a while, an obvious by-product, his speech was garbled, and he couldn't remember his own name. Mrs French visited her son every day while he was in Netherdale General, and for the first few weeks after he woke up, he didn't recognize her. He'd ask who she was. Then he'd ask me again. That happened most days. He was the same with all the nurses, and Mrs French got very distressed when he didn't know her.'

'But the fact that he was suffering from amnesia doesn't mean he was innocent,' Nash pointed out.

'I know, Mike. But if his memory was still impaired at the time of his trial, how would he know if he had a cast-iron alibi for the night the crime was committed? He certainly wouldn't have been able to tell his solicitor if he had. I just felt I had to tell you — make sure the facts were known. Anyway, I've done my good deed for the day, now I'm going home for my beauty sleep while Viv finishes the packing and looks after this one.' With that, she passed the baby to Viv, took him by the arm, and led him from the room, much to the amusement of the team.

After mulling over what Lianne had told them, Nash said, 'I think it would be a good idea to speak to the officers at Felling Prison and try to discover whether French's memory has returned. If it has, he could be heading this way, but if not he could be wandering around lost, anywhere between Land's End and John o' Groats. I'll give them a ring.'

A while later, he emerged from his office. 'I spoke with the governor. He said that French spent a lot of time exercising in his cell before he got permission to use the gym, going through a rigorous exercise regime in order to get fit. He admits French was very confused for a long time, but gradually seemed to be regaining his faculties, and a few months ago, his attitude altered dramatically. The governor didn't know why, but he told me French appeared to be much more confident and self-assured. He hadn't caused any problems and kept to himself, even after his improvement. So much so, that he was downgraded to a category B prisoner.'

Nash glanced down at the notes he'd made in his pocketbook and then continued, 'Afterwards, I spoke to the prison doctor and managed to get him to waive his patient confidentiality. He said that French had told him his memory had almost fully returned and although he couldn't explain the evidence found in his garage, he *did* know the source of the money found in his loft. And it certainly wasn't from a robbery. He also told the medic that he'd never set foot in Cumbria in his life.'

'Where does that leave us?'

'In the middle of nowhere, I guess. Either French is a superb liar and con artist in addition to being a vicious killer, or he's hiding something, protecting someone perhaps. Alternatively, there's an outside chance that he might be innocent.'

# CHAPTER FIVE

Although Craig French was no genius, he was definitely smarter than either his ex-girlfriend or the police officers who had arrested him believed him to be. Having been successful in making his bid for freedom, he found the going hard, and knew he would be extremely lucky to avoid being recaptured before he reached the river Helm and the dale.

He had been told by his mother about the rumours that were circulating of Tiff's forthcoming departure from England. Craig was determined to try to stop her, and that could only happen if he was out of jail. Her betrayal and desertion in his hour of need sickened him. His feelings had changed. As he felt at present, Tiff could rot in hell and he wouldn't care. But he was desperate to prevent her taking the son he'd never seen overseas.

He couldn't care if he never saw Tiff again, but at least she could have had the decency to allow him to meet Noel before putting thousands of miles between them. If she tried to deny him that, Craig wasn't prepared to dwell on the consequences. There was another compelling reason to have one final confrontation with the girl he'd once adored. He needed to know once and for all why she'd grassed him up.

Craig had taken temporary shelter in a disused barn on a farm. From his place of concealment he watched a woman, who he assumed to be the farmer's wife, carry a basketful of washing to the garage at the opposite side of the farmyard. He was just able to see her load it into a tumble drier. If he could get access and any of the garments happened to be approximately the right size, he could exchange them for his highly identifiable prison uniform.

Luck came Craig's way when the woman got into her car and drove away, leaving the garage open. Hoping that the house was deserted, he made his way round the perimeter of the yard and darted inside. His luck was in: the tumble drier's cycle was over, and inside were a sweatshirt and a pair of jeans that were a good enough fit. In addition, there was a jacket hanging from a hook on the wall. When he put this on, Craig found some crumpled twenty-pound notes in one of the pockets. Things were finally going his way. He straightened them out to discover there were six notes. That was hardly a fortune for the man who'd been accused of stealing jewellery and items worth millions of pounds, but the irony of that failed to amuse him. As he turned to leave he spotted a baseball cap on a shelf and added that to his disguise.

Having bundled up his prison uniform, he carried it for a mile or so along the lane before finding a small copse which was overgrown with brambles and briars. Using every ounce of his strength, he hurled the incriminating bundle as far as possible, and heaved a sigh of relief as he watched it disappear.

He set off, sticking to the hedgerows and praying for a lift. Minutes later, he was lucky once again, as he was given a ride by a passing truck driver, taking him on the first leg of his journey. They stopped at a garage en route, giving Craig chance to buy a couple of sandwiches and a bottle of water.

Craig found a barn to sleep in that night and next morning continued on his journey, thumbing a lift, and sheltering wherever he could along the way. He took an indirect route, conscious that the police would expect him to head straight for home. A Polish truck driver gave him a lift, and Craig reached Netherdale in the early afternoon. So far, he'd only encountered strangers, but by now he guessed that his photo would be appearing on TV and in the evening papers. Not only that, he would have to avoid his home town. There were considerable numbers of people in Helmsdale who would recognize him, especially on the Westlea estate. He was tired and hungry, but knew he still had a long way to go before he reached the refuge he'd selected. It was a place where he could lie low until the police activity slackened off.

The place of concealment was extremely remote, known to only a few people, and only one person was aware of Craig's connection to it. That was Tiff Walker, and she would be unlikely to link Craig to the cabin in the woods — even if she hadn't erased their history in that place from her memory. The retreat in the depths of Thornscarr Forest had been their love nest, the place where they'd first slept together.

Craig had discovered the cabin when he had been acting as beater for a shoot on the Harland Estate. He had been at the end of the line as they made their way through the undergrowth. At one point, he had taken a wide detour to avoid an impenetrable barrier of brambles and had emerged into a clearing. He discovered later that the area had been the centre of logging activity, and once the ground had been stripped back, the owner had ordered the erection of the cabin. This had taken place many years earlier, and the reason for the building of the cabin was much the same as the use Craig and Tiff had made of it.

Knowing they were in effect trespassing seemed to add an extra degree of excitement to his passionate encounters with the girl he believed to be the love of his life. All these thoughts and emotions crossed Craig's mind as he hiked up the dale towards Thornscarr.

He was encumbered by the supplies he had bought in a village store, enabling him to provide for a period of isolation. He had chosen tinned foods, along with a tin opener, for the main part, items that would keep without going off, and restricted his fluid purchases to a couple of bottles of water. There was a stream close to the cabin where he could top up his drinking supplies safely.

It soon became clear that he wouldn't be able to reach his intended destination before nightfall, and walking through the forest in total darkness was something he didn't relish. He was close to Wintersett village when the sun dipped below the horizon, signalling the end of the day. Alternative accommodation had now become Craig's priority. After a while, he spotted a barn, some distance from the farm to which he guessed it belonged. It looked to be a likely prospect, but as he approached, Craig recognized sounds from within the building. He was puzzled that they should be emanating from somewhere so far from the house.

The barn door was bolted. He slid the bolts back, grasped the long iron handle, and pushed the door open. It moved sideways, the swiftness catching him by surprise. As it rolled back, something small and dark shot past him, travelling too fast for him to intercept it. Craig watched helplessly as the creature vanished into the undergrowth. Once it was out of sight, he turned to see what else the building contained.

Although the barn was in near darkness, the early evening provided sufficient light for him to see what was inside. He looked in sick horror as he realized what he was witnessing. Craig muttered several strong expletives before sliding the door closed again. He turned and strode away, his pace little short of a run, his mind filled with anger at the distressing scene he had observed. Had he not been fully occupied with his main priority of avoiding recapture, Craig would have acted on what he had seen. Hopefully, at some stage the opportunity might present itself, but that seemed a remote possibility.

A few hours later, with nothing more comfortable than some bales of silage to rest on, Craig tried to catch some much-needed sleep. The memory of what was inside that barn didn't help, and when he did finally drift off, his rest was punctuated by the awful cruelty he'd witnessed.

* * *

38

Nash had become so accustomed to the country lanes on the route from work to home that the journey had become almost second nature. Despite this, his attention was on the road, but he had no time to do more than swerve violently and hit the brakes as a dog shot out from the hedge.

Nash felt his heart lurch as he heard the sickening thump of something hitting the passenger door. He got out and hurried round, fearing the worst. The dog was lying alongside the car. It appeared lifeless.

He bent down, laid his hand on the dog's ribcage and felt it stir slightly under his palm. Without hesitation he scooped the dog up and, as gently as possible, laid it on the travel rug in the rear compartment of the Range Rover. Although he didn't have much hope for the dog's chances of survival, he knew he had to make the effort. Leaving it out here in the middle of nowhere wasn't an option.

He turned the car and headed back towards town. With the benefit of hands-free on his mobile, he was able to raise Helmsdale Police Station. 'Jack, I'm glad I've caught you. Do me a favour. Please phone the vet's surgery and tell them I'm bringing in an emergency patient. I've just hit a dog, and I don't know what state the poor little thing's in.'

'Oh dear! OK, I'll warn them to have someone ready for you. What breed is it? They're sure to ask.'

'Looks like a Labrador. It's only a puppy and no more than a bag of bones. It has no collar on, so I think it's a stray.'

'I'll get onto it.'

Nash spoke briefly to Alondra and, without explaining why, told her he would be late, then put his foot down and reached the veterinary surgery as fast as he dared. He pulled into the surgery car park on a small industrial estate on the outskirts of town, and was out of the car almost before it stopped moving. As he opened the boot, he saw the dog was still unconscious, but the more pronounced movement of the ribcage gave him cause for some hope.

\* \* \*

Surgery at the vet's had finished, and although she was not on duty, Faith Parsons was still hard at work. A recent comment made by one of her colleagues had struck a chord with her own recent experiences. This caused her to conduct a search through the veterinary practice records. What she found was disturbing, to put it mildly. Between them, Faith and her fellow practitioners had been called on to treat a much greater than normal number of ailing puppies over the preceding months.

What concerned Faith was the nature of the complaints that had caused the owners to bring their pets to the surgery. To her mind, there was a suspicious and deeply unpleasant root cause for this. Before she could attempt to take action by following up what was only a theory, Faith knew she would have to consult her colleagues. She needed the consent of the senior partners before pressing ahead and involving others. As she studied her findings, she heard a vehicle braking heavily in the car park, and headed for the door.

'Are you the man who ran over a dog?' she demanded.

Nash looked up. The woman standing in the surgery doorway would have been good-looking were it not for the scowl on her face. Nash guessed her to be in her early thirties. He also noticed that she seemed angry with him.

'Er . . . yes,' he replied meekly.

'I suppose you were speeding? What chance does a dog have when you hit the poor animal? At least you had the decency to stop.' As she spoke, the woman crossed the car park, her stride more of a march than a walk. Nash watched her, fearful that she might be about to attack him. Instead, she looked down at the dog. In an instant, her whole demeanour changed. 'Oh, poor girl. What a handsome dog.'

She looked up at Nash accusingly. 'Well, are you going to lift her out, or allow her to die in there?'

Nash hadn't even noticed if it was a dog or a bitch. He scooped the animal up, feeling it stir in his arms. As he shifted his burden slightly, he felt a moist tongue lick the back of his hand. He followed the vet across the car park and inside. She pointed to a door on the right. 'Take her into the examination room,' she ordered.

After he laid the dog on the table, Nash watched as the vet gave the dog a thorough examination.

'Right,' she said, after a while, 'her heart sounds OK. Her eyes look all right, and I can't feel any sign of broken limbs, but I think we need an X-ray to make sure. Through there,' she pointed to the door in the corner. She opened it and looked back. 'Come on, man, I haven't got all night.'

The X-ray revealed no breaks, and by the time the procedure was over, the dog had lifted her head and was looking round in an amiable, if somewhat bemused, way. Without thinking, Nash reached over and stroked the top of the dog's head. The vet picked up a scanning tool and ran it across the back of the dog's neck. She frowned. 'No microchip. That confirms what I feared. Where were you when you attempted to murder this lovely creature?'

'Halfway between Wintersett and Helmsdale.'

'That's a favourite dumping ground, so I'm told. And the poor thing has been half-starved, which argues neglect.'

'If someone dumped her, they would have to do it from a car. Perhaps that's why the dog dashed into the road. If she heard the sound of an engine, she might have thought it was her owners coming back to collect her.'

'That may be so, but I'm afraid it's long odds against us getting anyone to come forward and claim her.'

As he spoke, Nash fondled the dog's ears, and was rewarded with another lick. He looked down. The dog was watching him, her brown eyes friendly, her mouth slightly open in what he felt sure was a smile. 'I was considering getting a dog. I suppose, if nobody claims her, I could take her.'

The vet wasn't about to let him get away with it that easily. 'That's as may be, but I doubt whether you're a fit person to own a dog. If you career around the countryside driving like a maniac, it's a wonder you haven't killed more animals.'

Nash had taken enough. 'Right, let's get one thing straight.' He turned and faced the woman. 'I wasn't speeding.

41

I was driving slowly. My job doesn't allow me to exceed the speed limit unless I'm travelling to an incident, and even then it has to be urgent.'

'An incident? I don't understand. What do you do?' She looked confused.

'I'm a police officer, and to set the record straight, the dog shot out from the hedge. I did my best to avoid it, but it was too close.'

'Oh, I see.' She bit her bottom lip and looked away. Her demeanour changed from demanding to friendly as she carried the dog to a cage. 'I'm sorry about that, but there has been a spate of these recently, most of them hit-and-run accidents. What makes me really mad is that many of the victims have been dumped by the roadside. This is a typical example. At least she's not in the same state as a few we've seen lately; they've been in a very bad way. As an act of cold-blooded, callous cruelty, it takes some beating. This lovely dog is less than a year old, little more than a puppy. Sorry to go off on one, but it makes me really angry.' She smiled, trying to change the atmosphere in the room.

Nash nodded. 'Yes, I'd sort of noticed that.'

'Have you owned a dog before?'

'Not recently, but my parents always had dogs when I was growing up, so I'm used to them.'

'Do you have children? I'm only asking because Labradors are great family pets.'

'I have a son. Daniel's away at school at present, so it will be a nice surprise for him if the dog is there when he comes home.'

'Will your wife agree to your taking this dog on?'

'I'm not married. Daniel's mother died several years ago.'

'Oh, I'm sorry.' She nodded sympathetically.

Nash smiled. 'But I do have a partner. I'm sure she'll be in favour of it.'

They went back to the reception area, where the vet extracted a card from one of the filing trays. 'Right, I'll take your details and contact the dog warden. If nobody claims her within a week, everything is already set up for when she's well enough to leave. Then she's all yours if your family agree. Otherwise she'll end up in kennels. I think this might prove to be a lucky accident for both of you. Is there someone else available while you're at work?'

'Not always, but you can contact me via Helmsdale Police Station if no one's at home.' He gave her that number along with his mobile.

'Very well, Mr Nash — sorry, should I call you Officer?'

'Actually, it's Detective Inspector, but I don't mind. Call me what you will.'

'OK, er, Inspector Nash.' She smiled. 'There's just one more detail to decide on. If you are going to adopt this dog, you need to think of a name for her. If you pick one now, she can get used to hearing the sound from the team here.'

Nash blinked. There was more to the business of adopting a dog than he'd realized. He thought of Daniel, and the walk they had taken soon after Alondra's return. Daniel had been entranced by the small bird he had seen gliding effortlessly along the river Helm. 'How about calling her Teal?'

'That's a nice name. Suits her, too. Teal it is, then. I'll phone and let you know how she progresses. And how much is on the account,' she added with a grin.

Nash left and headed home to Smelt Mill Cottage, to find Alondra in the conservatory, busy working on one of her paintings. 'I'll be with you in a sec,' she called out. 'The casserole is in the slow cooker, will you give it a stir, please?'

Nash smiled, happy that his days of cooking for one were all but over, except for when Alondra would have to attend an exhibition, but that was a small price to pay. When she emerged, Nash hugged her, holding her close for much longer than a normal homecoming embrace.

'What caused that?' Alondra asked. 'Not that I object.'

'I was just pleased to walk into the house and have someone waiting for me. And I've got some interesting news for you, something for you to think about.' He led her to the lounge. 'Sit down and listen. You'll never guess why I'm late home.'

He was surprised by her enthusiastic response. 'I always wanted a dog when I was little,' she told him, 'but I never got my wish. I don't need to think about it. I could take the dog with me when I'm out painting. It would be great to have a companion.'

\* \* \*

At nearby Manor Farm, a report was being made. Although the man had worked at the farm for over two years, he was certainly not a farmhand. The work he was involved in had nothing to do with agriculture or stock management. During that time he had never come face to face with his employer. He was not allowed up to the main house, and always contacted his boss using the sophisticated intercom.

The response to his report was not good. 'How do you mean, we must have had an intruder?'

'I went to the barn as usual this morning and when I went inside I couldn't find number fourteen. The cage was open. Someone has to have opened the outside door and taken it. My only other thought is that the dimwit that works with us mustn't have closed the cage properly. I checked carefully, but there was no way of escape from the barn.'

'Why didn't you inform me earlier?'

'We've been searching for it nearly all day. That's how I know it must have been taken.'

'You're absolutely certain it couldn't have found a way out?'

'Go check for yourself if you don't believe me. The other thing I noticed was a set of footprints in the soft ground to one side of the main door. They look like trainer prints. We wear wellies.'

'That means someone has stolen it. Hang on, is that . . . ?'

'The new arrival? Yes, it is.'

'That one cost me a lot of money — and it would have made me a lot more. From now on, I want that barn padlocked. I suppose if someone stole the dog, they're unlikely to report anything they've seen.' The employer paused for a moment before adding, 'I want you to get that idiot you brought onboard to patrol the nearby area regularly. Tell him to watch out for any sign of trouble. If you're right and someone's been snooping around, their life won't be worth living — especially if they've informed the authorities.'

The assistant shuddered at the tone of his employer's voice. He knew little about the person who paid his wages every month, apart from their obsession with privacy. Evidence of this was not only the intercom, but the equally sophisticated CCTV system that provided security for the occupant of the large detached house at Manor Farm. The worker was aware of his employer's name and, because it was so unusual, he guessed it was the same person who owned a chain of jeweller's shops. But beyond that, nothing. He certainly didn't know that the voice he heard when his boss spoke had been disguised by a computer simulator.

# CHAPTER SIX

Without any sightings of the fugitive, speculation as to Craig French's whereabouts began to die down, and media interest, at best ephemeral, waned rapidly. Jack Binns had passed on information from a farmer's wife who reported clothing missing from her laundry. The implication that French had discarded his prison uniform was added to the file, with no guarantee that he was the culprit.

\* \* \*

At first, Craig had been too afraid of recapture to enjoy his new-found and unlikely liberty, but after reaching Thornscarr Forest and taking up residency in the cabin, he started to relax slightly and even began to wonder if he could exist like this on a long-term basis.

During that time, however, he didn't lose sight of his primary objective, the desire to hold Noel, the little boy he had never seen. In addition to the parental urge to connect with his son, he also wanted to confront Tiff. Was it, as his mother had implied, that Tiff had found someone else, and had ditched him in order to hook up with a man who was in far better circumstances? He wasn't sure he believed that, knowing how jaundiced Brenda could be, and her low opinion of Tiff.

The problem was that he couldn't work out why Tiff had acted in such an untypical manner — unless she wanted to be rid of him? His reluctance to believe that she had another love interest brought him to realize that despite the anger and bitterness over the past, he still had feelings for her. But that avenue was one he was unwilling to go down, knowing it to be a one-way street, and a cul-de-sac at that.

Certain aspects of the forest had changed considerably since the previous occasions when he and Tiff had adopted this haven as their private love nest. Craig recalled one special memory, of a long weekend during August when they had camped out in the cabin for four glorious days and nights. They had experimented, cooking over an open fire using logs gathered from the clearing, and discovering the joys of eating in the open air, warming themselves on their makeshift stove. They had experimented in other ways too, the freedom from constraint and the certain knowledge that they would not be disturbed enabling them to take their passion for one another to new levels. It was their youthful ardour during that magical weekend that had resulted in Noel being conceived. Neither of them, or so Craig had believed at the time, could envisage a future in which they would not be together. The little one growing in Tiff's womb was a seal on their love, the creation of a family unit.

How swiftly things had changed, and how dire had his miserable existence become since those halcyon days. The bitterness and rancour that Craig felt at the way the girl he adored had become the orchestrator of his downfall had haunted every waking minute of every day he had spent in his cell in Felling Prison. Until, unable to bear the torment of his confinement any longer, he had managed to escape.

He'd been in the cabin for three days when he realized he had merely swapped one prison cell for another — and, moreover that his new place of detention lacked most of the comforts, albeit limited ones, of his previous incarceration.

There was one way the forest had changed significantly. In response to growing demand, and with the ever-present need for funds, the owners of the land had again employed a logging company to fell a large area of woodland a couple of miles farther from the main road. Although the activities of woodsmen didn't directly impinge on Craig's safety, he deemed it wise to forsake his shelter temporarily during the times when they journeyed to and from the site. Fortunately, the heavy diesel engines of their tractors gave ample warning of their approach, enabling him to take temporary shelter in the dense woodland.

This strategy was necessary at least twice a day, more often on the occasions when the workers had filled a trailer with lumber that would be hauled to the main road on the first leg of its journey to Helmsdale Sawmills.

In the early evening of Craig's fourth day in the cabin, when supplies were beginning to run low and he was contemplating measures to keep body and soul together, he heard the distinctive sound of vehicles approaching. No doubt taking the loggers home for the evening, where they would arrive in time to eat the dinner prepared for them by a loving spouse. Craig dismissed this mental image, concentrating instead on reaching the undergrowth before the tractor, and later, the pickup with its human cargo, reached the cabin.

It was almost dusk when the final vehicle passed by, its bright headlights penetrating the increasing darkness. It was on the periphery of the beam that Craig, his senses heightened by danger, noticed a figure crouching in the shrubs alongside the track. Once the convoy had gone, the man straightened and stepped from his place of concealment and began to walk towards the cabin.

Craig's paranoia led him to wonder if the man's presence was connected to the ongoing search for a missing convict, but then common sense caused him to dismiss that. Few people were aware the cabin existed, and only he and Tiff knew of his connection to it.

Then Craig wondered if it was an estate worker who had been sent to check on the cabin, even to find out if squatters were occupying it, but again he discounted the idea. An estate worker would have a four-wheel-drive vehicle capable of tackling that rough trail. He certainly wouldn't have hiked there. Only men desperate to shun human company adopted such means of transport — men such as escaped convicts, for instance.

As the light began to fail, with no sign of the new incumbent leaving the shelter, Craig became more and more agitated, wondering if he would have to spend the night in the open. The darkness was by now almost absolute, with only the vague light from the rising moon to alleviate the blackness.

Craig considered his options. If the cabin was no longer secure, he needed an alternative strategy, and quickly. It was a while before the idea came to him, prompted, possibly by his surroundings. Craig hadn't many friends, his preference for open-air pursuits being at variance with those of many of his peers. As a teenager the Winfield Estate, Layton Woods, and the Harland Estate had all given him ample opportunity to earn small, tax-free sums of money. During that time, he had discovered several potential refuges hidden in the wooded areas of those estates. It would mean a long hike, with no certainty of being able to reach his destination safely, and the lack of food would also need addressing. Craig was still pondering his few options when things changed dramatically.

* * *

The tramp wasn't lost, at least not in a physical sense. He might have lost his way in life several years ago, but he had entered the forest with a definite objective. His brain, befuddled by a variety of substances he'd imbibed, ingested, or otherwise partaken of, had guided him there. The destination his narcotic-fuelled imagination had conjured up was a place of peace and tranquillity, where he could indulge his anti-social habit without risk of being disturbed by authority.

The means to avail himself of the unquestionably expensive products he craved had come via a fortunate scratch card win. He had picked up the card outside a corner shop, having watched the purchaser drop it as he ran for a bus. Expecting nothing, he had been surprised to find his luck was in. Although by no means a jackpot, the amount was sufficient to enable him to purchase a substantial amount of his favourite addictive substances. It had also allowed him the luxury of a taxi ride to the end of the track leading to the cabin that would become his home until he needed to rejoin civilisation. The cab driver had been sceptical when approached, but when the vagrant had waved a fistful of twenty-pound notes in front of his eyes that reluctance had vanished.

The tramp had seen the cabin once before, as a schoolboy, when he and a group of his fellow students had taken refuge in the small lodge, their hiking expedition interrupted by a thunderstorm. That memory was one of the few that remained, before his mind became clouded over by the addiction that had now all but overwhelmed him. The walk to the cabin from the main road took longer than he remembered, and the duration was further extended by his need to take shelter when the loggers had approached. It was shortly after sundown, the early evening light fading fast, when he eventually arrived at the clearing and entered the cabin.

He was surprised to discover obvious signs of recent occupancy. That concerned him, but only momentarily. Other, more pressing priorities overtook any qualms he might have felt about another inhabitant. Whoever it was had clearly gone, and possession was nine points of the law. His mind eased, he settled down to indulge his craving. To do so, he needed light, but fortunately the previous occupant had left a half-burnt candle, which would provide a small amount of illumination, sufficient for his purpose.

* * *

Craig was still trying to work out how to reach his new destination when he caught sight of a pair of headlights, bouncing up and down as the car was driven slowly along the uneven surface of the logging trail. 'It's like being in Leeds city centre,' he muttered sourly, as he watched the lights approach the cabin. He wondered if this might be an amorous couple keen to sample the delights of each other in the privacy of the cabin. 'If you're hoping to get your leg over, mate, you're in for a big disappointment,' he mumbled. Whatever the purpose of the visitor to the woods, Craig was convinced it had little to do with him. Either way, it was time to move. 'This neck of the woods is getting far too popular for my liking.'

He rejoined the track, hoping to be closer to the main road. The car's engine had been turned off and the light provided by the headlights had now vanished. In the near darkness, he realized he had miscalculated and was between the vehicle and the cabin. The moon, now peeping over the horizon like the top of a 'Kilroy was here' graffito, provided sufficient light to reflect the metal surface of the car roof a few yards ahead of him. He made a slight detour, sidling along the undergrowth until he was close enough to see that the vehicle was unoccupied. He was less than a metre away from the front bumper when he stopped, his gaze transfixed by what he could see before him.

Craig bent over peering closely at the number plate, now fully illuminated by moonlight. Despite the danger that surrounded him he remained there for several seconds. The plate was personalized, and he had no trouble recognizing who the letters represented, and who the owner of the car was. But why should that person have come to so remote a location? His fear returned. He wondered again if this had something to do with him, then dismissed the idea. He couldn't see how the car owner could possibly have associated him with the cabin.

Conscious of his vulnerability, he had nearly reached the main road, glancing at regular intervals over his shoulder, when he heard the car engine start up. He took shelter behind a dense barrier of blackthorn bushes, and watched the car pass, slowly. As soon as it reached the road, the vehicle accelerated swiftly, heading towards Helmsdale at a rate

Craig estimated was well above the legal limit. Having wondered why the driver had gone there, he was now puzzled by the urgency to leave.

It was only when Craig glanced back along the logging trail that he got a clue as to the motive behind the driver's behaviour. The moonlight was all but obliterated, its beams masked by what he thought at first was fog, but then, as the dancing yellow flames grew higher and higher, he realized it was a fire.

The driver had obviously chosen that place to burn something, and by the look of the fire, something extremely large and highly inflammable. It would be much later that Craig realized the full horror of what he had just witnessed. Before long, however, he had more urgent priorities to deal with.

* * *

Craig had only been walking for a few minutes when the moon disappeared and the rain began to fall. At that time of the evening, and on such a little-used country lane, he felt safe enough to walk on the tarmac, which aided his progress considerably. As he strode along, heading to Wintersett village, Craig wished he had his hiking boots.

That thought provoked a memory. It had been when he entered the shoe shop in Helmsdale, to find suitable footwear for his work as a beater, that he'd met the lovely young shop assistant. Within a few minutes of her friendly greeting, accompanied by a warm smile that he could still recall, Craig had fallen for her. He'd protracted the purchase process for as long as he could. By the time he had been compelled, with much reluctance, to make a choice, the floor was littered with open shoe boxes.

Having made his selection, Craig, who had little or no experience with girls, stammered out his wish to see her again, but on a social basis. He had waited in trepidation, his heart racing as he waited for her response, half-hoping, half-dreading her reply. Then Tiff had smiled, and her accompanying words made him dizzy.

'I'd like that — I'd like it a lot.'

His sigh of relief prompted a questioning look, before he'd said, 'I was petrified that you were going to tell me that you weren't interested, or that you already had a boyfriend.'

He didn't know how much he'd paid for the hiking boots, or how he'd got home after leaving the shop. All he could remember was Tiff's reply, in that gentle, attractive tone he already loved.

'I don't have a boyfriend,' she'd told him.

The memory of their meeting caused Craig to increase his pace, his walk now little short of a march in subconscious reaction to that life-changing event. The exercise helped maintain his body heat, combating the effect of the increasingly heavy rain. What he had hoped would be nothing more than a passing shower had become a prolonged downpour. He was unaware that an amber weather warning for the region had been issued, predicting at least three days of intense heavy rain, with risk of flooding in low-lying areas. The phrase, 'I wouldn't turn a dog out in weather like this', came to mind as he squelched along, his misery increased tenfold by the bitterness of his current situation when compared to the memory of happier times. The risk of encountering anyone who might recognize an escaped convict had dwindled to zero, he thought, because nobody would venture outdoors in such atrocious conditions — not unless they were as desperate as him.

# CHAPTER SEVEN

Craig was within striking distance of Wintersett when his worsening state, and the equally deteriorating weather, caused him to contemplate taking desperate measures. Although he didn't think so at the time, luck was definitely with him again when he put his burgeoning plan into action.

He needed shelter, warmth, and a chance to dry out. That meant being indoors. He tried to recall the lie of the land surrounding the village, and remembered there was a row of six cottages, which he believed were holiday lets, located slightly beyond the boundary of the hamlet. If one of those was empty, it might serve his purpose by providing him with protection from the seemingly incessant rain, if only temporarily.

Having reached the small terrace, Craig stared at the cottages, studying them carefully before making his move. The two closest to him were clearly occupied. That much was obvious by the cars parked outside, and by the lights burning in the downstairs rooms. One even had the curtains open, the occupants of the sitting room plainly visible. He could make out the hands on a large wall clock, the dial informing him that it was still not ten o'clock. Moving further along the row, the illumination from the street lamp enabled him to see the vacancy sign hanging in each of the windows — those four properties were empty.

Craig opted for the farthest property from the occupied ones. With luck, the residents wouldn't hear the sound as he broke in. As he made his way to the rear of the property, his biggest problem was lack of illumination. He collected several painful bruises from the stone wall surrounding the building and the fence that ran along the back of the small terrace.

Eventually, soaked through and somewhat battered, he reached a small garden area. He groped his way forward, hoping that there were no unseen obstacles such as a garden bench or a fishpond to cause him further injury. His first piece of luck came when he was within a couple of metres of the back wall of the house, although initially, it seemed less than fortunate.

An outside light came on at the other end of the terrace. Craig crouched and froze, his gaze switching between the building in front of him and the source of the illumination. After a few seconds, the light was extinguished. Craig waited for a few moments to see if there was any further activity. When none came, he decided that it had been nothing more sinister than someone pressing the wrong switch, or a cat activating a PIR light. The light had given him a chance to check what was in front of him. He reached out and located a stone, part of a small rockery. This would be ideal for break- ing one of the glass panels in the old-style door. Craig hoped that the house didn't have double glazing — that might prove to be a bridge too far. He took his cap, held it against the pane nearest the lock, and smacked it with the stone. To Craig, the sound of splintering glass sounded like an explod- ing bomb. He waited, his trepidation intense as he watched for signs that the noise had alerted the other occupants in the row. Eventually, he felt confident that his act of vandalism had gone undetected. He groped inside, praying there was a key in the lock. There was no key, but it was a stable door with an opening top. He found the bolt and swung it open.

Unable to reach the bottom bolt, his next task was to climb through. He heaved his body upwards and forwards, teetering for a precarious few seconds before he stepped down into the room. His wet shoe collided with a slippery surface and he went sprawling full-length onto a cold, hard surface, his legs suffering further bruising from his fall.

After taking several minutes to recover from the various ills he had caused himself, he staggered to his feet and groped his way across the room, stopping only when he encountered a sharp corner of what seemed to be a table. He found the window and drew the curtains without further mishap, and after several attempts, located a light switch. As his vision adjusted to the intense illumination, the reason for his fall became apparent — the tiled kitchen floor was slippery from the rain he'd brought in with him, and his foot had landed on the broken glass. It could have been worse — a few inches to his left, his head would have come into contact with the corner of the table.

Although he was still cold and wet through, at least he was out of the rain. It was time to look round and see if he could find anything to ease his discomfort. His search was highly productive. On the worktop was a complimentary welcome pack, containing teabags, coffee, sugar, long-life milk, and an assortment of biscuits. He opened the door on one side of the room, which led to a utility room. This contained a fridge freezer, a washing machine, and best of all, a tumble drier.

If his break-in remained undiscovered, he would be able to wash and dry his clothing. That would be a huge bonus. He reasoned that if anyone saw him as he was, covered in mud, they might be suspicious. If he looked presentable, he had a better chance of reaching his goal. However, if he was going to strip off, he would need something to wrap round his body in order to keep warm.

Ignoring the lounge, Craig ventured upstairs. Any room on the front of the property would remain out of bounds; using them would be too dangerous. On the upper floor, he found a double bedroom to the rear of the property. Even better, on the end of the bed were two neatly folded bathrobes, ideal for his needs. His next find was even more encouraging. Alongside the bedroom was a bathroom. He opened the airing cupboard and found a stack of towels. The chance of having a long soak in the bath was a luxury he'd long been denied. Equally important, on the wall of the airing cupboard he spotted a switch for an immersion heater, which would supply hot water. He could now place his clothing in the washing machine, use the tumble drier, take a hot bath, retire to bed and next morning he would be warm, dry and rested. But first he would have a hot drink and biscuits to stave off his hunger — beggars can't be choosers.

Two and a half hours later, warm, washed but weary, with his dry clothing stacked on the bedside chair, Craig settled down to sleep. This might prove to be the most restful night he'd spent in the past couple of years. As he was dozing off, the memory of something he had seen in the utility room prompted an idea, which delayed sleep for a few minutes. There was an anorak hanging from one of the hooks, and a backpack alongside that had either been placed there for the use of tenants, or left by a forgetful former occupant.

If it was still raining when he ventured forth, he could use the anorak and be able to visit the village shop in Wintersett without getting soaked. He still had enough money to buy some food supplies. It would be a risky venture, comprising the most danger since he'd made his escape, but Craig was beyond caring. In order to minimize the chance of recognition he could go early. He remembered that the shop sold newspapers, which meant they would be open from six o'clock in the morning or thereabouts. If he went around that time, and luck was on his side, the only person he might encounter would be the shopkeeper. Hopefully, they wouldn't recognize the escaped convict, and equally important, the shop was unlikely to be fitted with CCTV.

The prison regime to which he had become accustomed was such that Craig was awake before first light. As he was dressing, revelling in the luxury of clean dry clothing, he caught sight of his reflection in the dressing-table mirror. It had been over a fortnight since he had shaved. The dark beard he had acquired was sufficiently thick to provide an effective disguise. With luck, he might be able to get to the shop, complete his purchases, and return to his hiding place safely.

He didn't encounter anyone as he headed into the village. This was hardly surprising, given the time of day, and the fact that the rain was heavier than the night before. He was extremely grateful for the protection provided by the anorak, even more so when he discovered that the garment came complete with a built-in hood. This would prove useful to shield him both from the weather and from the gaze of anyone he might meet.

As he was reaching for the door handle to enter the shop, he heard the sound of a car engine. He glanced round, praying that the owner wasn't going to stop to collect a morning paper. He gave a sigh of relief as he saw a Range Rover continue along the road towards Helmsdale.

As a rule, Mike Nash, the driver of the Range Rover, called at the shop for a copy of the morning paper, but on that morning he had delegated the task to Alondra. Asking her to do this, he had explained, 'I've got to be away, darling. I've a meeting with Ruth Edwards in Netherdale first thing, so I've no time to spare.'

'Of course, Mike,' she'd replied. 'It wouldn't have anything to do with the fact that it's raining — what do the English say, "cats and dogs" — would it?'

'Never entered my thinking.'

The stony glare he got told him that he had failed to convince her.

In the shop, the elderly lady behind the counter, peered myopically at the newcomer as he carried his purchases to the counter.

'I'm sorry, young man. I seem to have mislaid my spectacles, would you be kind enough to read the prices to me?'

Craig obliged, paid for his items, and left the shop, marvelling at how trusting the lady was. His relief was unnecessary. Even with her glasses on, her vision was certainly not keen enough to penetrate Craig's disguise.

\* \* \*

The trio of detectives were reviewing their progress.

'Can I have some reports?' Nash asked.

'Yes, I'll start.' Lisa waved a piece of paper. 'You recall I remembered something Craig French said on one of the shoots, about his full-time work?'

Nash and Clara nodded.

'Well, I've managed to track down his former boss. Nice bloke — had to retire on health grounds and close the business. He told me he couldn't believe a word he read in the papers about the murders at the time. Said he thought Craig was a good lad, worked hard, and got on with the others. He'd kept the personnel files in case references were required by anyone in the future. He looked them up and gave me details of those he thought might have been friends with Craig. I know it's a long shot, but it might be worth following up?'

'Good work, Lisa. He seems to agree with your assessment of French. Will you and Clara go and see if anyone's at home? Assuming they still live at the same addresses and aren't at work. If they are, go and find them; they might have some idea where we should be looking for him. I'll be here all day going through what we've got so far, not that it's much. I had a report from HQ that several callers have identified French, some from as far away as West Yorkshire and Newcastle — usual thing, all completely wrong. Apparently an officer in Scarborough went to check a lead and found a homeless man in a doorway. He had his dog with him and threatened to set him on the constable for disturbing his beauty sleep.'

\* \* \*

Later that day, Clara and Lisa reported on their visits to French's former workmates. Although these shed no light on the absconding prisoner's whereabouts, the two men they'd interviewed both expressed their surprise at French's conviction. 'One of them said he thought the charges against French were bullshit, despite the evidence. His actual words were, "There's no way Craig would do anything that bad." He was adamant on the point.'

'That's interesting, in that it backs up the opinions we've already had about French. I think it might be time to talk to someone with an opposing point of view. The Cumbria Police report names French's girlfriend who informed on him, so I think we should interview her.'

'Does she live around here?'

'She does. Her name is Tiffany Walker, lived with her family on the Westlea at the time. Don't forget, her brother was also convicted for some of the earlier burglaries French committed. I checked with the council and they told me the family emigrated, but she stayed behind and now rents a flat on the estate.' Nash passed Clara a sheet of paper. 'Apart from having an idea where French might be hiding out, if French knows it was her who sold him out, she could be in need of police protection. Will you and Lisa go and talk to her first thing tomorrow? Just watch your step in case she's got unwanted company. Call for backup if you need it.'

Nash got to his feet. 'I think I'll take the opportunity to leave early. I had an early start this morning. I want to get to the butcher's before they close. Daniel does his best to eat me out of house and home. And with him being at home with his injured shoulder before the school holidays, I haven't had a chance to replenish the freezer since he returned to school. Now Alondra's also depleting stocks. Lee Giles, the butcher, will be making a fortune and probably swanning off to Crete three times a year.'

'I reckon it's a small price to pay for the benefits you're getting.'

Nash eyed Clara suspiciously. Her face was a mask of innocence before she said, 'Maybe you should consider getting a dog or a cat now that you're playing Happy Families.'

'I'm not familiar with cats,' Nash admitted. 'Daniel keeps pestering me to get a dog, but until recently, it wouldn't have been at all practical.'

'Why not?'

'It would have been downright cruel, leaving the poor thing alone all day. You know as well as I do what anti-social hours we have to work. Now things are different, it's worth reconsidering. And, I have a candidate in mind.'

'I'll await developments then. Go on, get off. I'll cover.'

Nash waved his thanks.

As he was heading for the shop he met Jonas Turner, a spritely pensioner, who lived alone following the death of his wife, and was Nash's gardener.

Nash noticed an absentee. 'Where's Pip?' he asked. Jonas and his Jack Russell terrier were inseparable.

The old man smiled bleakly. 'Poor lad's at vet's. He's etten summat 'e shouldn't, an' bin throwin' up all day.'

'Oh dear, that sounds bad. Is he going to be all right?'

'Lass at vet's reckons so, but she's nobbut a kid. Pretty, though, an' a pair o' legs I'd fancy wrapped round mine,' Jonas added.

Anyone under forty classed as 'nobut a kid' in Jonas's eyes. 'You're an incorrigible old rogue, Jonas. Anyway, I thought you'd lost your heart to my sergeant?'

'Aye, she's a reet grand lass, is Sergeant Miniver.' Jonas had never got used to Clara's surname. 'Anyroad, she's spoken for by yon soldier these days. An' then there's you. I were reet chuffed t' 'ear that young woman o' yours 'ad seen sense an' come back. Proper family man now, wi' young Daniel an' a pretty lass. You just need a dog an' ah'd say you've cracked it.'

'Oddly enough, we were talking about dogs earlier, and I've got the chance of one,' Nash told him. 'The only problem would be what to do with the dog when we're all away.'

Nash was surprised by the old man's response. 'That's easy sorted,' Jonas said immediately. 'If tha gets a dog, me an' Pip would be 'appy to look after it when you're off to France, or when you're working all hours God sends. My Pip doesn't have much company, and I reckon 'e'd be happy if 'e'd another dog t' lake wi'.'

'Thanks, Jonas. I'll give it some thought.'

# CHAPTER EIGHT

The owner of Wintersett Grange, Arnold Hodgson, had purchased the property, a large Georgian building set in seven acres of land, upon his retirement from his job as managing partner of a firm of investment brokers in the City of London. Retirement had been forced upon him, as his declining hearing and eyesight meant that he was less able to cope with the work that had enabled him to amass a large fortune.

'There's no point in having all this money if we're too old and decrepit to enjoy it,' his wife had told him. 'We've nobody to leave it to, so we might as well spend it. If we don't, the Inland Revenue will be the only ones to benefit after we die.'

He had taken her point, entering into her plans with such enthusiasm that, before leaving London, he had bought her a collection of expensive jewellery. 'These are to do your beauty justice, and for you to show off when we go on the luxury cruises we're planning.'

They had just returned from one such, their intention to escape the worst of the British winter, with a tour of the southern hemisphere. Unfortunately, they returned to the rainstorms engulfing the north of England — the centre point of the deluge being the area surrounding Helmsdale and Netherdale. 'I'm beginning to wish we'd stayed in Australia,' she told him as they were retiring for the night.

The only crumb of comfort he was able to offer was by telling her that the weather forecaster suggested the worst of it should be over by the weekend. He didn't add that it was the weekend after next that the weatherman had been referring to. That would have been extremely tactless.

The broker was a heavy sleeper, and having removed his hearing aid before switching the bedside light off, there was no chance of him hearing the slightest sound.

His wife, a long-term sufferer from her husband's snoring, had taken twin defensive measures against this happening, as it did on most nights. She had swallowed a couple of sleeping tablets and put earplugs in place to ensure her rest was undisturbed.

As they settled down, they were unaware the feed to the alarm system had been cut, rendering it silent. Neither of them heard the intruder.

Nor did they hear the stealthy footsteps as he climbed the stairs to the first floor, nor when he opened the bedroom door. The burglar glanced round the room, noting with delight the large jewellery chest, complete with key in the lock, on the dressing table.

The slight draught from the open door disturbed the stockbroker sufficiently for him to turn over and sigh. That small sound was enough for the intruder to take extreme measures against being discovered. He approached the bed with three swift strides. Having dispatched the householder, he turned his attention to the man's wife and sliced her throat. Pausing only to carve his trademark signature on their foreheads, he turned his attention to more serious matters, namely the robbery.

He opened the jewellery chest and admired the sapphire and diamond necklace, accompanied by matching earrings. Discarding the boxes, he discovered a diamond-encrusted bracelet in its gold setting, and an array of ruby-studded brooches, necklaces, and earrings. He turned his attention to the drawers and bedside cabinets where he located watches and rings, before heading downstairs to see what else he could find.

* * *

After having spent many years working in the parks and gardens department of several local councils around the county, Gareth Roberts was enjoying his new role as a jobbing gardener. It was a career forced upon him when council cutbacks had resulted in a call for voluntary redundancies.

Once Gareth and his wife were convinced the package he was offered was satisfactory for their relatively simple lifestyle, he accepted the lump-sum payment, and decided to supplement his monthly pension by putting his skills to use on a freelance basis.

Gareth had some business cards and flyers printed, and distributed these to properties where he thought his talent might be appreciated, simultaneously taking out advertising space in the *Netherdale Gazette*. The tactic paid off, and he was soon in great demand.

He visited Wintersett Grange every week, spending half a day, usually the morning, working on the garden. Gareth liked Arnold, an easy-going gentleman of the old school. He was less impressed by Hodgson's wife, Clarice, who he found to be haughty, distant, and demanding. She gave the impression that she thought Gareth should consider it a privilege to work for them and, by employing him, they were doing him a favour. That, plus the notion that she begrudged the money they paid for his services, did little to endear her to the gardener.

However, it wasn't for Gareth to judge — and, as he worked outside, he was able to keep contact with her to a minimum. Significantly, whereas all his other clients offered him refreshment, he always took his vacuum flask along when he visited the Grange, knowing that neither a mug of tea nor any other beverage would be forthcoming.

If such was normally the case, it was certainly so this spring, but Gareth couldn't blame Clarice for failing to supply him with a drink, as he knew the couple had been away on the cruise they had been planning since their retirement. Gareth had worked assiduously during their absence, determined to leave no opportunity for criticism by Mrs Hodgson. During his period of employment by various councils, Gareth had become involved in several wrangles with personnel from Human Resources departments, thus forming an extremely low opinion of them. When Arnold Hodgson had mentioned in passing that his wife had spent many years involved in that line of work, it had dismayed Gareth — but it certainly hadn't surprised him.

He was due at the Grange, but the inclement weather threatened to cause a cancellation of his visit. However, there was one task — or rather a series of tasks — that weren't reliant on dry weather. The large greenhouse had been disused for a number of years, but now Gareth's employers had decided to become as self-sufficient as possible by growing a variety of vegetables. The tables on either side of the greenhouse were filled with tray upon tray of seedlings, and Gareth decided to attend to these, utilising his time while the weather was unfit.

It was almost lunchtime, and Gareth hadn't seen any sign of either of the Hodgsons. That hardly surprised him, as the rain had been heavy and incessant. The drumming on the glass roof all but drowned out the music on Helm Radio from the old but serviceable transistor set he always carried.

Gareth had listened to the hourly news bulletins, specifically the local items. For the most part, these concentrated on the atrocious weather, which was causing some flooding problems at the lower end of the dale. With no indication of conditions easing, things could only get worse.

At one point, the announcer had mentioned the escaped murderer Craig French was still at large, but there had been no sightings of him since a lorry driver confirmed having given him a lift.

'He's probably holed up somewhere sheltering from this bloody rain,' Gareth muttered. 'No matter what he's done, I pity the poor sod if he's outside in this weather.'

Having re-potted the last of the seedlings, Gareth donned his waterproofs and prepared to set forth. After locking the greenhouse, he went to the rear of the Grange, where he would seek payment for this and his three previous visits.

He reached the back door and was about to ring the bell when he paused, his hand raised in mid-air. One of the glass panels, closest to the handle and keyhole, had been broken. 'That's strange,' Gareth muttered, wondering what had caused the accident. He rang the doorbell and waited — and waited — and waited. When there was no response after several minutes, he tried once more. He could hear via the broken pane the sound of the bell echoing, but again the strident noise provoked no response.

Shuffling as close as he could get to the door, Gareth tried to peer in, cupping his hands round his eyes to block out extraneous light. His first effort was unsuccessful, the raindrops on the door panes proving an effective barrier. He tried a second time, looking though the gap in the broken pane. Now, he was able to discern a line of muddy footprints leading from the back door across the large, farmhouse-style kitchen. His gaze shifted slightly and he saw shards of broken glass reflecting from the dark quarry tiles inside the door.

It was only in that moment, as Gareth reached out, grasped the doorknob, felt it turn easily in his hand, and watched the door swing open, that he began to suspect that something was most definitely amiss. 'Mrs Hodgson?' he called out, raising his voice to little less than a shout. 'Hello, Mrs Hodgson, it's Gareth, the gardener. Is everything OK?'

His voice echoed around the room, but as the last trace died away, it was followed by a long empty silence. He tried a second and then a third time, but with no more success than his earlier attempts. Cautiously, aware that he was entering forbidden territory, he stepped over the broken glass and walked across the kitchen, following the line of muddy footprints towards the inner door.

When he entered the wide hallway, he called out yet again, aware that Arnold was deaf, and that Clarice might be otherwise occupied. All he got by way of reply was the echoing sound of his own voice. He looked round, anxious and wondering what to do next. It was then that he noticed the muddy footprints had continued out of the kitchen. The traces they had left were fainter now, against the background of the grey carpet. They led towards the staircase, and on the edge of the bottom tread was a clump of mud that he knew would have sent Clarice into a frenzy.

Something was dreadfully wrong, but what should he do about it? He hesitated for several seconds before removing his mobile phone from the inner pocket of his coat. He took a deep breath and then pressed the number nine three times.

'Emergency, which service do you require?' The operator's voice was calm, in stark contrast to Gareth's stammering mumble.

'Er . . . police . . . I think . . . er . . . yes, police.'

The next voice Gareth heard was a male one. 'Netherdale Police, how can I help?'

Gareth explained who he was, where he was, what he'd discovered and how he'd found it. The operator gave him assurance and detailed instructions. 'A police patrol car has been despatched. In the meantime, would you please retrace your route to the exterior of the building? Avoid touching any surfaces where possible, and if you have touched something, be sure to tell the officers when they arrive. Will you be OK outside? Do you need to shelter from the rain?'

'Yes, yes.' Gareth was still trying to think straight. 'I have my waterproofs on. I'm at the back of the house, so, I er, I can stand in the old stable block across the yard.'

'It won't be for long. They should be almost halfway there by now.' With a faint trace of humour, the operator added, 'You'll probably hear them well in advance of their arrival.'

\* \* \*

It was a quiet morning at Helmsdale Police Station. Quiet, that is, except for the uniform section under the direction of Sergeant Jack Binns. They had more than enough on their plate dealing with flooding incidents, minor accidents, broken-down vehicles and road diversions. It was nearing lunchtime when the sergeant was heading for the kitchen and stopped at the door to the CID suite. 'Coffee, Mike?'

'Please, Jack.'

He returned and placed a steaming mug on Mike's desk. 'I reckon all our villains have decided to stay at home, where they're warm and comfortable. Viv's lucky he's in Antigua. He'd be bored rigid here, no doubt playing non-stop Sudoku on the computer.'

Nash smiled faintly at Jack's words, but as he heard the rain lashing against the window, said, 'If this weather lasts until the weekend, when Viv's due back, I wouldn't blame him if he stayed there.'

'And where are our lovely ladies this morning? Hiding from the rain?'

'They've gone to interview the ex-girlfriend of our missing prisoner.'

Moments later, the office door opened and Clara and Lisa entered, both carrying umbrellas, their coats dripping with rainwater forming small puddles on the floor.

Jack couldn't resist. 'Still raining, is it?' Ignoring the unladylike responses, he headed back to the kitchen to make them a hot drink, taking their umbrellas with him.

'How did it go?' Nash asked.

'Not quite as planned,' Clara said, as she struggled out of her coat. 'She claimed to have no idea where he could be hiding and refused police protection.' Clara looked at her incident book. 'She said, "If that toe-rag has the balls to turn up here, I'll phone you. That way, you can collect his body. I certainly don't want it known on the estate that I'm hiding behind you lot."'

'Do you think that's wise, given French's capacity for violence?'

Clara shook her head. 'No, neither Lisa nor I do, but the girl was adamant. She thinks he doesn't know where she lives, and said she hopes it won't be long before she gets her visa to take the toddler to live in Australia. She doesn't want the little boy growing up knowing his father is a vicious killer.'

While Clara hung their wet coats up, Lisa continued, 'I don't understand. If French is the baby's father, why did she grass him up? I told her, it states clearly on the police report that she informed the police about the stolen goods in his lockup. She denied it. Said she didn't care what it says in the file, because she didn't grass on him. But then said she'd plenty of reason to.' Lisa shrugged. 'She wouldn't say any more.'

Clara returned. 'I left my card and told her to ring me if she heard from him or changed her mind. I also pointed out that as we haven't caught him yet, and it may be a long time before she leaves the country, anything could happen. But she shrugged it off. One thing I did notice though, despite all the bravado, I think she's scared.'

'So, what should we do about Ms Walker?' Lisa asked.

'I don't see what we can do. We can't force her to accept our help,' Nash said.

'The other problem is she lives at the end of a cul-de-sac with no vehicular access, so we can't even organize for patrol cars to drive past regularly. Her flat is a good hundred yards away from the nearest road,' Clara added.

Nash's phone rang, and he listened for several minutes. Eventually, he responded, 'That's a bit too close to home for comfort. OK, we'll handle things from here. Your lads have more than enough to contend with. As soon as possible, I'll free up the two uniforms at the scene. CSI can mind the shop for a change.'

He put the phone down and shook his head sorrowfully. 'That was control. There's been a double murder at Wintersett Grange. The householder and his wife have been found in bed with their throats cut. It sounds like it's going to be all hands to the pump on this one.'

They were about to leave when Nash paused in reception and spoke to Jack Binns. He updated him and requested an incident tent.

A few minutes later, as they were driving towards Wintersett, Nash explained to Clara and Lisa the reason behind his request. 'I wanted the tent so we can set it up as close to the door as possible. That way we can get into our protective kit without getting soaked through, and reduce the chance of contaminating evidence inside. Some of it might already be compromised, with the gardener and our officers already going in, but we can't do anything about that except prevent it getting worse.'

It was that sort of attention to detail, allied to his natural flair, that made Nash such a good detective, Clara reflected. A short while later that talent would be demonstrated again, but the full consequence of his line of thinking would not emerge for a considerable time.

# CHAPTER NINE

There was no sign of the backup team when they arrived at Wintersett Grange. 'I didn't expect them to be here yet,' Clara told Nash. 'The road this side of Netherdale is closed off. The traffic reports said it's completely flooded to a depth of about a metre.'

'It never rains but it pours,' Nash replied.

Clara groaned at the bad joke, but was soon too occupied to comment. The detectives co-opted one of the uniformed officers to help erect the incident tent. The younger officer looked decidedly unwell and was leaning against the wall of the stable block; the gardener and Lisa appeared to be comforting him.

'You OK?' Nash called to him.

'I'm all right, sir. It's my first, I mean I've never. . .' His eyes widened, he turned, headed for the bushes, and relieved himself of his breakfast.

The senior officer shook his head. 'He'll get used to it, sadly.'

Once their task was complete, Nash spoke to the gardener, listening to his version of events before telling him, 'I don't think we need you to stay here any longer; the officer has your details. I guess you'd rather be at home.'

'I'd rather be anywhere than here,' Gareth agreed.

'I quite understand. If you want to get on your way, I've no objection. I will need you to come into either Helmsdale or Netherdale police stations to make a formal statement, but that's standard procedure.'

As Gareth turned to leave, Nash glanced down and saw that the gardener was wearing wellingtons. 'What size shoe do you take?' he asked.

'Size ten,' — he saw where Nash was looking — 'but ten and a half in wellies. I wear thicker socks.'

'OK, that will help our CSI lads when they're examining the footprints. Could you show me the tread, so we can try to eliminate yours inside?' He turned to Clara. 'Take a photo on your phone of his boot, will you?'

The gardener departed, relieved to be away from the house that had become a nightmare. Although he had left the crime scene, it would be a long time before Gareth was able to put the memory of what had happened to the couple out of his mind.

Nash turned to the senior officer. 'I've arranged for the CSI crew to man the crime scene so that you can be freed up. I'm sure you'd prefer to return to your normal duties, and I know you'll have more than enough to deal with. Speak to Sergeant Binns first and ask if you can get your colleague here a cuppa before you resume.'

The officers nodded their thanks, and as they were leaving, Clara returned from the Range Rover bearing two plastic jumpsuits and latex gloves. 'I've deputed Lisa to keep the incident log and wait for Mexican Pete. When he and CSI arrive, she'll instruct them to wait here after they suit up.'

'He won't be happy.'

'Who?'

'Mexican Pete. No doubt he'll find something to blame me for — the weather for one!' Professor Ramirez, the Spanish pathologist, had acquired his nickname via a rude rugby song, many years ago.

As Nash was speaking, they heard the sound of approaching vehicles. Clara lifted the tent flap, using it as a makeshift umbrella and reported, 'CSI are here, so we'll be able to get on.'

'OK. When we go in, I suggest we take a look around the ground floor before we go upstairs. That should cut down the time element before we hand over to the boffins.'

* * *

The incident tent was in danger of becoming overcrowded as Nash issued instructions. 'There's a stable block across the yard that might be useful to keep your equipment dry, and if you could set up a second tent alongside this one, it will improve access. Any external evidence has probably been washed away. DS Mironova and I will take a look while you lot get sorted. I've no idea when the pathologist will get here.'

Having put the new arrivals in the picture, he and Clara stepped up to the back door, which had been closed by the officers to prevent the rain washing away any evidence. The doorknob was circular; the surface wet and slippery against the latex gloves Nash was wearing. After a short struggle, he opened the door, and they stepped over the broken glass into the kitchen. They walked cautiously across the room, adopting a circular course to avoid the muddy footprints left by the killer, the gardener, and the two officers.

They were now standing in the doorway leading to the large hall of the double-fronted building.

'It's mainly a question of what might be missing. We're not certain this was a burglary, but that would be the most likely explanation. If that's right, then I guess there would be some valuable items in this house. Cash, jewellery, paintings, any portable item could be the prime target. You go that way; I'll go this.'

Clara concentrated on the reception areas, the sitting room and study, noting gaps on the wall containing empty picture hooks. Nash walked through the other side of the property, where the dining room contained a large ornate sideboard, its doors hanging open, and had obviously been searched. On the floor, a large canteen of cutlery stood open — and empty.

He and Mironova made a curious sight as they climbed the staircase. Nash led the way, with Clara close behind, as they walked up one side of the stairwell to avoid the tracks made by the killer, balancing so as not to touch the handrail. Once they reached the first floor and entered the bedroom, their priority was to study the bodies of the murdered couple. The blood from their wounds had, for the most part, been absorbed by the sheets and the duvet.

'Good heavens,' Clara exclaimed, pointing to the distinctive pattern of the scar on the man's forehead. 'That letter F is identical to the wounds we saw in those photos of the Cumbria murders. This is definitely more of Craig French's handiwork. The man is utterly evil.'

'We can't be sure of that, Clara,' Nash objected.

She knew he had doubts about French's conviction, but this seemed like absolute corroboration. 'Come off it, Mike, there's been no other burglary, and certainly no murder, remotely like this, reported for over two years. But now, within weeks of French's escape from prison, which is less than twenty-five miles away, we have two more murders bearing the same MO. The media is going to have a field day when they get hold of this.'

'Let's not jump to conclusions, Clara. We need Mexican Pete to examine these wounds and compare them with the other killings. For all we know, this could be a copycat. There's been plenty of publicity about French since he absconded from jail. The press and TV all gave out details of the Cumbria killings, even warning members of the public about the danger he posed. One or two even went far enough to caution people living in remote areas.'

'There's only one problem with your theory, Mike. Even though the media went into chapter and verse about the murders, there was no mention of the initial carved on the heads.

That detail wasn't released at French's trial, nor has it been made public since.'

It was a good point, Nash conceded, and the evidence certainly pointed towards Craig French as the guilty party. He stared at the bed and the victims again before asking, 'Clara, suppose you were alone at night and something disturbed you. What would you do?'

She looked at Nash, wondering where his thought processes were leading. 'I'd get up and see what was happening. Why do you ask?'

'What if the intruder was too close for you to get out of bed in time? What would be the first thing you'd do?'

'Try and get away. I'd get out of bed.'

'Exactly, but look at the victims here, check out their expressions and then look at the bedclothes.'

Clara did as Nash suggested. 'They look peaceful, as if they're asleep. The woman is almost lying on one side.' Clara looked closer. 'She's got earplugs in. I bet that's because her husband snores.' She gestured across the bed, 'Look, he's on his back, a classic snoring posture.' She glanced at Nash.

'Go on,' he encouraged her.

'They haven't made any effort to get out of bed, or sit up. The duvet is undisturbed, and they show no sign of fear or even anxiety. I think they were killed while they were asleep. If he'd reached the room and hadn't woken the occupants, he could just as easily have removed their valuables and left without needing to kill them. I think the killer wanted to ensure we got the message.'

Nash nodded. 'Good point. I was thinking much the same.' He moved away from the bed and began to examine the rest of the room, concentrating his attention on the dressing table. In the middle, alongside an enamelled vanity set, was the large jewellery chest surrounded by several empty velvet boxes. Nash recognized the name of the world-famous Regent Street jeweller embossed on the inside of a lid.

'Clara, take a look at this.' He pointed to the lining of an oblong box. 'What does that suggest?'

Clara read the name, Garrard & Co Ltd. 'Aren't they the Queen's jewellers?'

'I believe so, but that's beside the point. The merchandise they sell is extremely high quality, as good as you can get, and so it commands a correspondingly high price tag.'

'And your point is?'

'It was the same when the Cumbria murders were committed. The expensive items were never recovered. All the police found in French's garage was a collection of lesser-value goods, plus the murder weapon. If there were some high-class trinkets in here, that's another link to the earlier crime. You wouldn't use a Garrard's box to store cheap jewellery in, would you?'

Clara pointed to the vanity set. 'I'm surprised he left that.'

'What makes you say that?'

'It's beautifully enamelled — it must be worth a bit.'

'How do you know that?'

'Er, I, er, do watch the *Antiques Roadshow*.'

Nash shook his head, and sighed, before continuing to stare at the scene before him. Clara knew not to interrupt his train of thought.

He pondered for a few seconds, staring at the empty box and then asked, 'Did you see a desk or a filing cabinet when you looked round?'

'Yes, in the study. They didn't look to have been disturbed.'

'Do me a favour. Nip back downstairs and look for an insurance policy or valuation document covering jewellery. At the same time, see if Mexican Pete's arrived and ask him to come upstairs and make a start on his grisly task. I think we've learned all we can here. I'll brief him about those wounds, but before I do anything else, I'll phone the ACC and put her in the picture — and tell her who it appears might be responsible. And isn't that going to be fun.' Nash paused, before adding, 'Nearly as much fun as the media conference I'll no doubt be press-ganged into attending.'

Clara was grinning.

'What? What's so funny?'

'You said ACC.'

'And?'

'Ruth Edwards is the Acting Chief Constable, not the Assistant Chief Constable. That's a bit higher up the chain.'

'OK, I got it wrong.'

Clara shook her head and tutted before she headed downstairs and did as instructed. She took pity on Lisa Andrews, suggesting she come inside out of the rain and assuring her there was no need for her to go upstairs, stating, 'The crime scene photos will be enough for anyone.'

The two women had just reached the study when Nash joined them. His attention was drawn to the desk in front of the large picture window. He whistled, a long low sound of appreciation. 'That'll have cost a pretty penny,' he commented.

'What is it, Chippendale or something?' Clara asked as she began opening drawers.

'No, but it's still highly valuable.'

'You've lost me, Mike. It looks like any other pedestal desk to me.'

Nash walked over and pointed to the front edge of the side panel, where the women could see what appeared to be a small rodent scaling the vertical column.

Lisa exclaimed, 'I know what that is. That mouse is the trademark of, Mousey Thompson, a cabinet maker who was based in Kilburn. I have a cheeseboard.' She grinned.

'Quite right, Lisa. Robert Thompson, "the Mouse man", specialized in oak furniture, and his work is the hallmark of excellence. The company still makes everything from large pieces such as this, down to small household items such as Lisa's cheeseboard and even napkin rings. They can even be found in York Minster. I'd guess that this desk would cost several thousand pounds.'

'That lecture on Arts and Crafts furniture craftsmen was delivered by Professor Nash,' Clara responded, as Lisa stifled a giggle.

As Clara was speaking, she opened the bottom drawer of the desk and removed a buff folder marked with the name of a local jeweller. She glanced at the contents. 'I think this is what we're looking for.'

The file contained a lengthy insurance document, attached to which was a valuation certificate bearing the name of the jeweller's, which had branches in a dozen or more towns across the north of England, the nearest being in Netherdale. If Clara had thought the desk seemed an expensive luxury, she revised her opinion when she read the estimated worth of some of the items listed on the assessor's report. The end total was eye-watering enough to make her count the noughts a second time, wondering if the typist had put the comma in the wrong position, or omitted the decimal point.

Her thought process was interrupted by Nash, who asked, 'Clara, did you see any watches in the bedroom?'

She frowned, mentally replaying the scene, before responding. 'No, I don't think so.'

'Neither did I. According to what's on there, we've a Breitling man's watch and a Longines lady's watch to include in the list of stolen items. We're going to need the full details from Forensics ASAP so we can circulate them to all horologists and jewellers. If this is the work of Craig French, he will be absolutely desperate for money, and that means he'll want to turn the stuff from this robbery into hard cash. We must ensure that retailers are on the lookout for the stolen goods.'

# CHAPTER TEN

The following day, Nash was organizing the investigation. If he hadn't forgotten the dog incident, as he thought of it, the accident was certainly not at the forefront of his mind when he received the phone call he'd been hoping for. He didn't recognize the number on the screen of his mobile. 'Hello?' he answered cautiously.

'Mr Nash? It's Faith Parsons, the vet. I rang to tell you that Teal is now fit enough to leave the surgery. I've kept her longer than I said to build her strength. If you still want the dog, you can collect her when it's convenient. There's the account to settle, of course. That's for the initial treatment and tests I did, her board and lodging, and to be on the safe side, I've given her a set of injections, because we don't know if the previous owners bothered to. It's always better to make certain, and Teal is too nice a dog to take risks. If it all works out for you, we can microchip her later.'

'I'm snowed under at the moment.' He paused and thought for a moment. 'Can I collect her this evening? I'll have to sort a few things out first.'

'No problem. We're open until 7 p.m.'

A short while later, he went out into the CID room. 'Hold the fort for half an hour, will you, Clara? I have some shopping to do.'

Clara looked at him enquiringly.

'I'm collecting a puppy from the vet's after evening surgery finishes,' he explained.

'Is that what the shopping's about? You're going ahead with it? That's good, but what does Alondra think of the idea?'

'She's all in favour.'

'What do you need to buy?'

'I'm going to get a collar and lead, a basket, feeding bowls, and some toys.'

'What will you do with the pup while you're at work?'

Nash pointed to his office. 'She'll be fine with me. I'll buy two beds.'

'What will Superintendent Edwards say? Or God, for that matter?'

Nash smiled at Clara's reference to their chief constable, Gloria O'Donnell, known throughout the force as God, only partly due to her initials.

'The super doesn't know yet. And I rang the chief at home yesterday to find out how her husband is, and to keep her in the loop re the murders. I mentioned the possibility of getting this dog. She said that the pup was probably the only female she'd trust me alone with. I assumed that to mean acceptance, if not approval.' Nash grinned.

'How is her husband?'

'He's much better, by the sound of it, and God's considering coming back to work. She also mentioned that Jackie is slow to recover from her injury. Apparently, that bullet wound is still causing her a lot of problems, so it's uncertain when, or if, she'll return. We'll have to wait and see how things develop.'

Clara nodded her agreement before saying, 'We've managed without a superintendent before, so we can manage again. But before you go, can I make a suggestion?'

Nash eyed her suspiciously. 'You usually do, so go on.'

'You might want to add dog food to that shopping list.'

'I thought about that, and decided to get some from the vet. If Teal remains on what they've been feeding her, there should be less chance of tummy upsets.'

'Sounds logical. Have you told Daniel? He must be so excited — I bet he'll love having a dog.'

'That's part of the reason I wanted to keep Teal. I was thinking of making it a surprise for when he comes home for the summer holiday. I think she'll do him the world of good.'

'How is he?'

'He's fine, apart from the illusion that he's the new Ian Botham or Geoff Boycott. Now, I must get this shopping done. Know something? I'm really looking forward to having a dog again.'

'My, we are getting domesticated, aren't we? It'll be slippers and pipe next, sitting with the dog at your feet watching the *Antiques Roadshow*. I suppose it had to happen as you got older.'

She grinned at Nash's response. It was delivered as he went out of the door, and was a sign that had once got a famous show-jumper in trouble.

* * *

That evening, when Nash reached the vet's surgery, there was only one car parked on the tarmac outside. He hurried in, anxious to see the puppy. Faith Parsons was standing by the reception desk. After Nash settled the account, he handed Faith the collar and lead he'd bought, before he carried a sack of dog food to the car.

A few minutes later when he returned, Faith came from the rear of the building, being towed along by a fit, healthy-looking animal. Nash watched the dog with amusement as she tried to fathom out how to get past the gate between the reception desk and the waiting area. He looked up. The vet was watching him watching the dog. Her eyes signalled approval.

'Here's Teal for you, Mr Nash. It would appear that she has had some previous training as she recognizes certain commands. She already responds to the name as I've had the nurses using it all the time she's been here. Don't you, Teal?'

The dog looked up at the familiar sound, her long black tail waving gracefully.

'She looks so much better than when I brought her in.'

'The only problem we've had was getting her to relax in the cage; she certainly wasn't happy. The implication is that perhaps she associates it with mistreatment. However, she settled, and has been eating well and gained weight. You haven't bought a cage, have you?'

'Er, no, I'm hoping she'll be OK in the conservatory. It has a tiled floor,' he added by way of explanation.

'Well, watch her. If you've any problems don't hesitate to get in touch. *Any* problems,' she stressed.

'You've been very kind,' Nash said. 'I only hope she'll be happy with me. Anything more I should know?'

'One question I meant to ask. What will you do with her while you're at work?'

'She'll stay with my partner. Alondra's a landscape artist, so Teal will get plenty of fresh air and exercise. If that isn't convenient, she'll come to my office. Who knows,' Nash laughed, 'we might even make her into a police dog. Alternatively, I've already had the offer of a dog-sitter.'

'You have?'

'Someone you know, Jonas Turner.'

'Ah, yes, the lovely Mr Turner.' She raised her eyebrows and sighed. 'Well, I'm glad you've made arrangements, because dogs hate being left alone. That's where they get their reputation for being destructive.'

Nash nodded. 'Thanks again, and if you're ever out our way and need a coffee, or want to call in and see how Teal's doing, feel free to ring the bell.'

She smiled and handed him the lead. 'Good luck, the pair of you.'

She decided she approved of the detective. They'd got off on the wrong foot, but he'd been patient when she was angry with him. She might just take him up on that offer of calling in. It would be good to see how Teal adapted to her new home. And it might be a good idea, in light of the recent health issues the vet had been dealing with in young dogs. She just hoped Teal wasn't affected.

The telephone began ringing, interrupting her thought process. She sighed, and went to answer it. The day had started early and it looked as if it was going to end late. And she had lots of research to do in preparation for an important meeting.

* * *

Driving home, Nash puzzled over the vet's comment about problems and the way she had stressed it. He shrugged the thought away. He was probably imagining things.

When they reached the house, he watched the dog as she began to familiarize itself with her new surroundings. Although he had reservations as to how Alondra would feel when confronted with the dog, or how Teal would react on finding there was another female pack member in residence, his fears were groundless.

Alondra's delighted smile as she greeted and began stroking the Labrador, whose tail had gone into hyper-drive, was sufficient to make Nash relax. Once Daniel and the dog were introduced and became friends, the family unit would be complete.

As they were eating their evening meal, Alondra said, 'I had a call about the exhibition in Paris. Apparently, it was a great success. The owner of the gallery said they had a better footfall than at any other similar events in recent years. He sold four of my paintings, and there was a lot of interest in three more of them. I'm glad I didn't have to be there, although the weather would have been much better.' She indicated the rain hitting the kitchen window. 'But it was good to stay at home.' Alondra smiled. 'That word has such a warm feel to it. Actually having a home and family is such a treat for me. And now I have a lovely new friend, so when you're not here, or when I'm out sketching or painting, I will have company.'

'Speaking of which, I think we should consider getting you a new car. Big enough to hold your painting materials, and also have room for madam. Check when the lease on your hire car ends, and we can start shopping for a new one.'

Nash glanced at the dog, who waved her tail in salute. 'She is highly intelligent, and very obedient. It seems she only has to be told something once, and I've noticed that she does the right thing even when she hasn't been asked to.'

'Do you think she's had some training?' Alondra asked.

'Difficult to say, the state the poor thing was in when I found her. But the vet seemed to think so, which makes me question why she was abandoned.'

Life, Alondra thought, was so much fun nowadays — which mirrored what Nash was thinking exactly. 'I think we should take her with us when we visit Daniel,' she suggested. 'It's unfair to keep him in the dark until the end of term. He deserves to know about Teal, especially as he did bring us back together.'

Nash agreed to the modification of his plan. It would be exciting to see the expression on his son's face when the Labrador came bounding out of the back of the Range Rover. His only reservation, as he explained to Alondra when they were preparing to go to bed, was about the dog's past. 'I have this fear that an irate owner might turn up on the doorstep demanding their dog back. I have no idea where she came from, or how she arrived at the place where I ran into her. Maybe we'll never know, but I'd hate to lose her after she's settled in here.'

But before he could carry out their plan, all he had to do was find an escaped killer.

* * *

The sanctuary afforded by the holiday cottage had improved Craig's condition immensely. His comfort was disturbed by one constant anxiety, the possibility of having to vacate if a genuine tenant arrived to take up residence. Now, after a week had passed, Craig knew he needed to replenish his dwindling food supplies.

During another early-morning expedition to the village he encountered one pedestrian, a young woman walking her dog. This wasn't apparent at first, but as she got closer, Craig heard her whistling, calling the dog's name as she peered anxiously into the thick hedge. This gave Craig chance to slip past without anything but the briefest scrutiny, as the woman glanced momentarily in his direction.

At that moment, a black Labrador came bursting through a clump of rosebay willowherb, and bounded towards its owner, who promptly lost interest in the bearded man passing by. On reaching the shop, he made his purchases and retreated. Craig heaved a mental sigh of relief. Once again, it seemed, luck had been on his side, and he had escaped unnoticed.

Back at the cottage, he took stock of his situation as he munched the pizza he had removed from the oven. It was far from a normal breakfast, but then, nothing in Craig's life was normal. Although he was at liberty, it was freedom in name only. He'd been a prisoner in Felling, a prisoner in the cabin, and now he was a prisoner in this cottage. He hadn't made any progress towards his goals. He hadn't confronted Tiff, and he hadn't seen his son. He needed a way to get to them. Only by doing that could he discover the truth behind her betrayal. One thing was certain, he couldn't do it by staying holed up in this place. Nor could he walk into Helmsdale, go through the town, onto the Westlea estate, and reach Tiff's flat undetected. Far too many people would recognize him long before he reached his destination. Although some wouldn't have given him away to the police, there was an equal number who would see it as their duty to have him returned to his cell.

This was the same problem he'd faced since soon after his escape. In truth, he hadn't expected to get this far. He'd believed he'd be recaptured within hours. However, Tiff and Noel were as distant as if he'd remained in prison. An idea came to him as he was falling asleep. It was a desperate plan, but then, Craig's situation was a desperate one. In order for his nascent scheme to have any chance of success, he would have to travel a circuitous route.

The only drawback to Craig's accommodation was that the holiday cottage was spartan in the extreme. The sole concession to electronic devices had been made in the kitchen, which boasted an induction hob, a fan-assisted oven, and a microwave. There was no television, radio or even a USB socket. Although Craig was unaware of it, this was a deliberate policy by the landlords, who marketed the cottages using the promise of them being free from the stress of modern-day life — the perfect way to get away from it all, in the undisturbed calm of glorious countryside.

This was a big disadvantage to Craig, as he could not check the progress of the manhunt for an escaped murderer. He didn't even have a copy of the *Netherdale Gazette*, which was an evening paper, and unavailable by the time he made his early-morning visits to the shop. Although this increased his anxiety somewhat, the breaking news would have sent his paranoia into hyper-drive, had he known of it.

# CHAPTER ELEVEN

Nash accepted the unpleasant task of attending the post-mortems on Arnold and Clarice Hodgson. Once they were over, Nash produced the autopsy file on the Cumbrian murders, and asked the pathologist to compare the wounds on the victims.

Ramirez studied the photos before he stated, 'There are similarities, but I'll give it some thought.'

'Thanks, Professor. I'll leave you to it. There's a press conference looming.'

'You'll enjoy that,' Ramirez replied somewhat sarcastically.

Nash headed for the door. As he left the building his mobile rang. It was Clara.

'Are you still at the mortuary?'

'No, I'm just leaving. Why the urgency? Has something happened?'

'No, but you need to know what I've found. I've been reading through the report on the Cumbrian murders again, and there's something we all missed earlier. It leans towards your questioning of the verdict. Have you a copy of it with you?'

'Yes, hang on while I get in the car.' Seconds later, he said, 'OK, I've got it in front of me. What am I looking for?'

'Go to the forensics report at the back, the long scientific analysis. It's a fairly boring screed, which is probably why we all missed the significance of a tiny nugget of information, near the end.'

'OK, I've got it. Let me read it.' He began reading slowly and Clara heard him gasp aloud with surprise.

'Can I assume you've found it, and come to the same conclusion as me?' Clara asked.

'Well done, Clara. That's brilliant. We'll discuss it when I get back.'

Having spoken to Ruth Edwards the previous day, he knew that she had scheduled a media conference for late that afternoon. She had requested Nash's presence, but he was aware that her invitation was more in the nature of a three-line whip. He prepared himself for the ordeal ahead, but even though he knew the press might ask some searching questions, he couldn't have foretold the outcome — and the repercussions of the event.

Nash was able to use a side door, thereby avoiding the scrum that was assembling by the front entrance to the building. He went upstairs and was ushered into the chief constable's office, where Edwards was reading the crime scene report submitted by DS Mironova.

Ruth looked up and greeted him, asking how the post-mortems had gone.

'Like any other post-mortem, ma'am. The professor doesn't think there's any need to wait for toxicology in this case, it all seems straightforward. Said he'd get his report in ASAP.'

'Well, that's good,' she said with a smile, as she gestured towards the paperwork in front of her. 'This is Clara's description of what you found at Wintersett Grange. Has she ever considered becoming a writer? This reads like an extract from an Ian Rankin novel.'

'I'm short-handed enough as it is. Don't encourage her, ma'am.'

She winced. 'Mike, we've worked together often enough for you to call me Ruth when we're alone — just not in front of the troops, or in public.' She then turned to the reason for his presence. 'Are you ready to enter the wolves' lair? I can see the hungry beasts outside. It looks like they're baying for blood.'

'I'm ready as I ever will be. Let's get the rigmarole over with.'

Once the press had assembled in the large meeting room, which was barely big enough to cope with the throng, Ruth and Mike walked to the table and took their seats, with a battery of microphones on the desk in front of them.

Ruth opened proceedings. 'My name is Superintendent Edwards. I have been seconded from IOPC to deputize for Chief Constable O'Donnell, who is currently on compassionate leave. Alongside me today is Detective Inspector Nash. We will be happy to answer any questions, but please bear in mind that we are in the very early stages of our investigation into this tragic event. What I will tell you is that two residents of Wintersett Grange have been murdered, and that the motive for the crime appears to be robbery.'

A journalist representing one of the national newspapers had been sent from London to cover this briefing, and he asked the first question. 'Why is Nash the only officer here? Surely someone with more seniority should be present?'

Ruth gave the journalist a withering look. 'If you had taken the trouble to do some research beforehand, you would have known that the only other senior detective in our small force, Superintendent Fleming, is currently on sick leave, having been shot and seriously wounded when we apprehended a serial killer only a few weeks ago.'

Her tone was far from conciliatory, and it provoked the reporter into asking a follow-up question, one that he soon regretted. 'Do you think it's acceptable that this cold-blooded killer hasn't been recaptured, even though he's been on the loose for almost three weeks, and has now committed another double murder? Would you care to explain that, Superintendent?'

Ruth heard the contempt in the journalist's voice, but merely smiled sweetly before responding.

'First of all, let me put you straight on a couple of points. My title is Acting Chief Constable, so I would be obliged if you use that when addressing me. I know you're from London, which goes some way to explaining your appalling ignorance,' she paused fractionally, but long enough to emphasize her meaning, 'of our area, and the topography. In a rural location such as this, there are many hiding places where someone who is desperate enough can remain concealed. There are large patches of dense woodland, caravan sites, holiday chalets and cottages, remote agricultural buildings, and disused mine workings, all affording excellent shelter. There is also the possibility that someone is shielding French. Checking all those places would take a lifetime.'

'Are you putting your full resources towards finding this murderer?'

'Exactly what do you mean by "full resources"?' If the reporter saw the trap, he ignored it.

'I mean every available detective and uniformed officer.' As the London journalist spoke, Nash saw the reporter from the *Netherdale Gazette* wince, obviously with an inkling of what was to follow.

'I'm afraid your ignorance is showing yet again, compounded this time by your arrant stupidity. There are four detectives available in this force's region. One of those is currently on leave, which gives us three to comb this area. If you want to see why our uniformed colleagues are unable to assist, I suggest you drive around for a while, and if you can make enough progress on roads that aren't flooded, you will understand that those officers have more than enough to deal with combating the after-effects of the recent rainstorms.'

'Can you not increase your manpower by bringing in officers from other forces to assist in the investigation?'

The journalist wasn't prepared to give up easily. The only problem was that the man didn't realize he was in a hole, and therefore continued digging.

'I am indebted to you for the suggestion,' Ruth told him, 'but strangely enough, that idea had already crossed our minds.

However, there are several stumbling blocks to this. These are mainly due to budgetary constraints, which have left not only this force, but many others, hugely understaffed. Even if there were officers available, which isn't so, how would we be expected to pay for them? Our financial resources are stretched to the limit even as things stand. Unlike the newspaper you represent, we do not have a website where we can put a begging bowl out every morning calling for donations.'

The ripple of laughter from his fellow reporters was sufficient to silence the tormentor, who withdrew from the fray to lick his wounds.

Into the silence that followed, one of the other reporters asked, a trifle hesitantly, 'Inspector Nash, is it safe to assume that Craig French committed the crime at Wintersett Grange? Because from what we've been told, it seems to bear the same hallmark as the murders for which he was convicted.'

There was a prolonged silence before Nash responded. 'It is far too early to speculate as to the identity of the killer. We are still assessing the evidence at Wintersett Grange, and it is certainly too soon to make assumptions about Craig French's guilt at this stage. Having only read French's file recently, I find there are elements in the Cumbrian case which are open to question. But that is another matter to be resolved.'

If Ruth's spat with the other journalist hadn't been sufficient to hit the headlines, his reply ensured that the media conference achieved star billing. Everyone had been concentrating on Ruth Edwards until that point, now all eyes turned on Nash, and cameras around the room began flashing, as the pressmen realized this story could get even more interesting.

'Would you care to elaborate on your reasons for saying that, Detective Inspector Nash?' It was one of the TV correspondents who asked.

Nash's reply did little to enlighten the media representatives. 'As Acting Chief Constable Edwards told you, we are in the very early stages of this investigation. In fact, I only attended the post-mortems a few hours ago, and the full autopsy findings are still not available. Therefore I am not prepared to speculate on the outcome without evidence. I prefer to leave such guesswork to you, ladies and gentlemen.'

Although Nash's statement ended the media conference, the speculation provoked by his comments ensured that the 'Craig French affair' remained at the core of all media reports over the ensuing period.

* * *

'Remind me never to rile you,' Nash told Ruth as they returned to her office, leaving the media personnel scrambling in their haste to exit the building — rushing to email or text their copy, or send the recording via their mobiles.

'Did I go too far? I've met that idiot reporter before and wanted to teach him a lesson.' If Ruth was anxious, it didn't show in her expression.

'Certainly not. I thought you handled it very well.'

Ruth closed the office door. 'OK, now that we're out of hearing range of the jackals, would you mind enlightening me as to your reasons for saying what you did about French? I was as surprised as those journalists, so I hope the TV cameras didn't pick that up.'

'I'm starting to believe French didn't murder that couple in Cumbria, even though the evidence found in his lockup garage appears to be overwhelming. If so, it follows that he didn't commit the Wintersett Grange killings.' He explained, 'Clara phoned me as I left the mortuary and drew my attention to something we'd missed in the Cumbria file. She's now beginning to think the same as me.'

Nash outlined their reservations about the conviction, before adding, 'I also find it significant that the goods found in that garage, and in Bobby Walker's place, are of relatively low value. There seems to have been no effort to search for an alternative solution, and in my opinion that is extremely shoddy work by both the police and the CPS. I think that outlines the danger of setting people achievement targets. It tends to give them tunnel vision.'

'So you're suggesting that not only was French's conviction flawed, but that of Walker as well? That might be difficult to prove — and it would be even more difficult to convince the CPS to re-open the case, given the seemingly watertight evidence.'

'I agree, Ruth, and it's nothing more than a feeling I've got that we're missing something important in that evidence. Anyway, I'd better get back to Helmsdale. We're a bit under-staffed at present, you know.'

Ruth laughed at the reference to the way she'd given the journalist a dressing-down, before saying, 'Be sure to tell Clara how pleased I am with what she discovered. It shows she uses her initiative and investigative talents.'

As she watched the detective leave, Ruth pondered what he'd told her. His doubts over French's guilt had come as a shock, but Ruth was aware that Nash had been proved right too often to ignore his thinking. Even if this was another such instance, as things stood, Ruth couldn't see how they could resolve the issue, despite the evidence that had just come to light.

As Nash was walking through the ground floor of the building, Tom Pratt called on him to wait. 'Are you headed for Helmsdale, Mike?'

Nash nodded and Pratt continued, 'Would you mind dropping me off en route? My car's in for servicing and the garage has just phoned to say it's ready for collection.'

Pratt looked at Nash sharply as he heard the detective gasp. He was about to ask what was wrong when he noticed the expression on Nash's face, and remained silent. He waited patiently, knowing from experience that something he'd said had started a train of thought in Nash's mind.

'Why didn't I think of that earlier?' Nash muttered. He smiled ruefully at Tom and told him, 'Yes, of course I'll give you a lift, but I'd like you to do something for me in return.'

He cadged a piece of paper from the desk sergeant, and made a note of what he needed.

Pratt looked at the details and told him, 'No problem, Mike. I'll look into it first thing tomorrow.'

\* \* \*

That evening, the six o'clock bulletins on most TV networks broadcast the news conference as one of their main items. This made compulsive watching for viewers throughout the country, but closer to home, it both enthralled, and bewildered, those who had followed the story.

For others personally involved, the briefing raised disturbing — and unanswered — questions. In the O'Donnell household, the chief constable watched the footage along with her husband Charlie, now recovering from his recent heart surgery. 'I'm going to phone Ruth and Mike and tell them "well done",' Gloria announced.

Charlie smiled, knowing how fond his wife was of the best detective on her force. At times, although Gloria would never admit as much, Mike Nash was like the son she had never had. This certainly wasn't evident from the way she referred to him, as the subsequent telephone conversation proved.

The call didn't begin as planned, because the first voice Gloria heard was that of a woman. To discover a female in Nash's house was in the past by no means uncommon, but for one of his visitors to answer the phone was highly unusual, especially one with a Spanish accent. Gloria almost gasped with disbelief, having met Alondra in very upsetting circumstances some time ago. She disguised her delight, but when Nash came to the phone, she couldn't resist teasing him.

'I assume Miss Torres is your house guest, and as such you are behaving like a perfect host, occupying separate rooms and so on. You don't want to corrupt young Daniel with your louche behaviour.'

'You're wrong, ma'am — three times out of three,' Nash responded. 'In the first place, Alondra is a permanent resident.

Secondly, she is sharing my bed and will continue to do so, and finally, as for Daniel, I'm afraid it's too late — he's already been corrupted. It was Daniel who sought out Alondra when he was on holiday with Clara and David and persuaded her to come back — to come home and share my life.'

'Like father, like son, I suppose,' Gloria retaliated. 'You're going to have to watch him carefully in a year or two. Seriously, I'm absolutely delighted by your news, but I rang to congratulate you and Ruth for wiping the floor with that ignoramus of a journalist. It's the best bit of television I've seen in a long time.'

They talked for a few minutes longer, and when he ended the call, Nash explained the content to Alondra. 'Apparently the press conference was on a lot of the early evening bulletins.'

'I didn't realize it would be on so quickly,' Alondra told him. 'I'll watch it later, and after I've seen it, I can go to bed with a TV star. Now, what would the celebrity like for dinner?'

* * *

Elsewhere, two residents of the Westlea estate who held widely differing opinions about Craig French's innocence, or guilt, watched the broadcast with growing interest, culminating in astonishment at the detective's final comments.

Brenda French could not explain the presence of such damaging items in Craig's lockup garage, the large amount of money secreted in her loft, or the fact that the recent murders had been committed when he was at large. But she was convinced that her child could not have committed such appalling violence. She had reared her son and taught him to respect both the welfare and property of others, and was unable to reconcile what she knew of his nature with those unspeakably horrid deeds. Some might have called her staunch support an example of blind faith, while others would have referred to it as misguided maternal instinct. It was a constant torment to Brenda that Craig's amnesiac state had rendered him incapable of providing some defence against the charge of murder.

The shock provided by the content of the news clip caused Brenda French to pour herself a large gin and tonic, and to follow this action by doing something unique — in her house and probably elsewhere on the estate. She raised the glass in the direction of the TV and drank a toast to the health of a police officer — definitely unheard-of behaviour.

No such prejudice in favour of the fugitive coloured Tiff Walker's thinking as she watched the broadcast. Her strong belief in French's guilt, and her abhorrence for the murders he'd undoubtedly committed, was compounded by the latest example of her former lover's capacity for extreme violence. Her loathing for the man she had once adored was allied to the growing fear that he would turn that propensity for evil on her. Towards the end of the conference, when the detective made his statement, Tiff wondered if the transmission was real or some horrible nightmare. For a senior police officer to imply doubt over Craig's guilt — and to do so in public — was too surreal for Tiff to take in.

What had prompted the detective to say such an outlandish thing? Had he become privy to information that suggested another culprit? She tried to dismiss the idea, but despite her efforts to shrug it off, the doubt kept recurring. Had it been anyone of lesser standing who had made the statement, Tiff would have ignored it, or treated it with contempt, but the words had been uttered by a detective, one Tiff knew to be highly respected — or feared, in local circles.

DS Mironova and DC Andrews watched the bulletin along with their respective partners. Given their inside knowledge of what prompted Nash's final statement, they agreed with his implication and wholeheartedly approved the way Ruth Edwards had slapped down the ignorant, insensitive reporter.

One person who most definitely did not watch the broadcast was the man who was the focus of the media attention, and whose supposed misdeeds were discussed throughout the briefing.

# CHAPTER TWELVE

Next morning, Nash, Clara, and Lisa sat down to reassess the investigation in the French case, given the new evidence before them.

'I want to go through it carefully. Correct me if I'm wrong, OK?'

Clara and Lisa's eyes met.

'Yes, sir.' Clara said.

Nash stared at her. 'DS Mironova, I have a message for you from the acting chief. She said you have initiative and investigative talents. Of course, I disagreed with her, told her it was a fluke; I've never seen it.'

Clara turned to Lisa. 'If that was a compliment, even backhanded, I'll take it.'

Lisa nudged her. 'Well done, Clara,' she whispered.

'Yes, well done, Clara.' Nash nodded. He then looked at the paperwork in front of him. 'OK, let's start at the beginning. When the police raided French's lockup garage, they found items that had been stolen from Cumbria where the murder was committed, plus the knife used to kill the two victims.'

Clara and Lisa both nodded agreement.

'They also found goods from two previous burglaries. At Bobby Walker's work, they found only goods from the first two, implying French was alone in Cumbria. Still with me?'

Again, they nodded.

'The forensic report is very informative. In it, the officer details what they *did* find, and that was a considerable number of microscopic fragments of fibres infused with,' he glanced down at the paperwork, 'amongst other chemical components, disinfectant, benzalkonium chloride and some methyl substance whose name goes on for a week and is totally unpronounceable. And, as Clara pointed out, we probably come in contact with them on almost a daily basis — the basic components of anti-bacterial wipes.'

The women nodded again.

'What they *didn't* find when they tested all the recovered goods was a single fingerprint belonging to either French, Walker — or even the rightful owners. A fact which, for some reason, was ignored by the Cumbrian investigators. Some of the items were cheap jewellery, and other bric-a-brac, yet, despite these objects being stashed away in the safety of the alleged perpetrators' property, there wasn't a single print of any description. Even if the thieves had worn gloves, the prints of the rightful owners would still be in situ.'

'I get that, Mike, but that doesn't prove French's innocence,' Lisa said.

'Fair comment, but the other part, the bit our tame genius Clara discovered yesterday, certainly does. The wet wipes had not only been used on the stolen property, but also on the handle of the murder weapon — but not the blade. Cleaning the handle of the knife and leaving blood on the blade doesn't make sense if Craig French is the killer. However, it makes perfect sense if someone is determined to fit French up for the crime — and equally if they want to frame him and Bobby Walker for the other burglaries. The strategy worked so well that once French was on the run from Felling, and therefore unable to provide an alibi, the murderer felt confident enough to strike again. He left the same trademark on his victims at Wintersett, as if to say, *Hi, it's Craig again, your friendly neighbourhood serial killer, come and admire my handiwork.* The killer would have continued to get away with it, but for one of the smartest bits of detective work I've seen for a long time.' He smiled at Clara.

There was a long silence as the detectives pondered the information that had all but totally destroyed the damning evidence against French.

Into their silence, Nash added, 'I think we have to face the fact that someone doesn't like Craig French very much, and that they detest him sufficiently to frame him for four murders. What worries me is French's safety. If the frame-up technique hasn't achieved its objective, whoever hates him might decide on more direct action. In fact, as nobody has seen neither hide nor hair of French since his escape, it might well have already happened. If, because of his amnesia, French hasn't worked out he was set up, he would be unaware of the identity of that person — he would be an easy target.'

His words sounded almost like a prophecy to Clara, but she didn't comment, which, for her, was unusual.

Nash turned to the section of the file containing the report of French's trial and flicked through the transcript until near the end. 'Listen to this,' he told them. 'It's the verbatim account of the judge's summing up. He sentenced French to life imprisonment with a recommended minimum of twenty years, citing the following, "*You have steadfastly refused to acknowledge your guilt, in spite of the overwhelming evidence against you, nor have you put forward a shred of credible explanation in your defence. If you had shown the slightest remorse for the ruthless slaying of two innocent people who were unlucky enough to get in the way of your overwhelming greed, it might have swayed me to a degree of mercy. Had you admitted your undoubted guilt, assisted the police to locate the other highly valuable items you stole, or given them the details of how and where you disposed of them, that would have been a different matter. If such had been the case I might have been predisposed to impose a more lenient sentence. However, you have failed to do so, and have thereby subjected the family of your victims to the fresh ordeal of hearing again how you ended their loved ones' lives in so brutal a fashion. You must now suffer the full consequences of your actions."'*

There was a long silence after Nash finished reading, before he said, 'There are two possibilities here. If French was suffering from amnesia, he wouldn't know if he was guilty or not. He would also be unable to cooperate with the police in trying to trace the stolen goods, if he had no idea what they were, or who had taken them. On the other hand, if he *did* remember, French would refuse to confess to a crime he knew he hadn't committed. I lean towards the first theory, because he offered no defence, which suggests amnesia.'

'I know we believe French is innocent, but it's still all rather speculative, don't you agree?' Lisa suggested.

'That's true, and if we are right, it seems that French appears to have been dogged by bad luck throughout. With nothing to back up his version of events, it isn't surprising that the police were sceptical.'

Nash provided them with further food for thought. 'Again, this is only speculation. But let's take the inventory of the goods stolen from the Cumbria murder first. In total, the thief or thieves got away with jewellery, watches, silverware, and an original Lowry painting, altogether worth in excess of three million pounds. Almost all of those items have never been recovered. The value of the goods found in French's lockup was less than five thousand pounds. You could argue that French had already disposed of the rest, but if that's the case, what happened to the money? Admittedly, there was a large amount secreted in his mother's loft, but nowhere near enough to account for such high-quality merchandise — unless he has a secret bank account in Switzerland or the Cayman Islands.

'In the Bobby Walker file, I found a similar story. Stuff recovered from Walker's place was worth about eight thousand pounds, whereas the total value of the goods taken during the robberies he's supposed to have helped to commit is in excess of seven million. That suggests someone is doing very nicely out of burgling properties, and getting someone else to take the blame for their handiwork. We need background on Arnold and Clarice Hodgson. Other than their expensive lifestyle, is there a link between them and the Cumbrian couple? Get digging and see what you can find.'

After their discussion ended, Clara remained in Nash's office. 'Don't be too hard on yourself, Mike. You might have missed the evidence in that report, but so did everyone else.'

'That's cold comfort. What we've got to do now is prove our theory is correct — and won't that be fun?'

'Yes, and I'm going to have fun explaining all this to Viv when he gets back.'

* * *

Craig's tenure of the cottage ended abruptly, five days after the grim discoveries at Wintersett Grange. It was early evening, when the first indication that he was about to be uprooted came via the sound of a vehicle pulling to a halt outside. Craig peered cautiously round the curtains in the lounge, and was horrified to see a car parked directly outside the gate. The vehicle engine was switched off, and Craig's worst fears were confirmed when he saw the couple study some paperwork and point directly at the cottage. A woman emerged from the passenger seat, closely followed by a man getting out of the driver's side.

Craig realized he had to move — and move quickly. By the time they were in the process of removing suitcases from the vehicle's boot, Craig had run into the kitchen, pausing only to grab his jacket, the anorak and backpack, snatched a loaf and a packet of biscuits from the table, and made his exit by the back door to the fields at the rear.

He was now left with no choice. He had to activate the plan he had conceived. As he began to walk swiftly away from Wintersett towards open countryside, he was blissfully unaware that the manhunt for him, which he hoped might have been scaled back, had now intensified.

* * *

Nash had just arrived home and greeted Alondra, who was working on a new project, a departure from her usual genre. He glanced at the half-completed portrait and smiled. The model had stopped posing and was pawing agitatedly at Nash's leg, demanding attention. With one arm still around Alondra's waist, Nash bent down and stroked Teal. The Labrador gambolled around her master for a few minutes until she obeyed a gently issued command from the artist and resumed her posture sitting on the dog bed in front of the easel.

'I reckon you should do more of this,' Nash told Alondra. He gestured to the sketch. 'You've caught her likeness really well.'

'I used to do a lot of portraiture when I was at art school, but one of the lecturers saw the potential in my landscape paintings and encouraged me to enter a competition. I won it, and so I concentrated on landscapes.' She gestured towards the easel, adding, 'This is relaxation. With the bad weather, I haven't had a chance to go out in search of new scenes worth painting.'

Nash was about to ask what Alondra wanted for dinner when his mobile rang. He glanced at the screen and pulled a face that made Alondra smile. His opening words explained his dismay. 'Yes, Jack, what can I do for you?'

Nash listened as Binns relayed his message. 'A couple arrived at one of the terrace of holiday cottages owned by Wilson Dream Holidays on the outskirts of Wintersett, about an hour ago, and discovered that a pane in the back door had been smashed. By what they told the control room, it looks as if someone has been dossing there for a while, because there's food and milk in the fridge, plus an open box of tea bags on the worktop. It might be a homeless vagrant keen to escape the lousy weather, but on the other hand, I thought it might have been Britain's Most Wanted. As you're the closest thing to a detective nearby, I thought you might ask for permission to play out and attend the scene. I've asked for a CSI, and I could send one of my lads, if you want?'

Nash grinned at the insult and rose to the challenge. 'I'll see what I can do, Jack, but I should warn you that my undoubted talents might be required to perform an intimate domestic function that goes back to prehistoric times. If that's the case, I might not be released, so I'd have to phone you back.' There was a long silence as Binns pondered Nash's implicit suggestion. When Nash thought that their sergeant had suffered enough, he explained, 'It's my turn to cook dinner, Jack.'

He ended the call and explained to Alondra the reason for going out. 'Hopefully, I won't be gone long.'

'Good, because I'm getting hungry.'

As he drove the short distance to the scene of the incident at the far side of the village, Nash puzzled over something Binns had told him. The name of the landlords of the cottage, Wilson Dream Holidays, was familiar, but he couldn't remember why.

His duties at the crime scene were limited to interviewing the couple, taking their statements, and instructing the officer from Forensics who arrived shortly after him. When Nash spoke to the intended tenants, he noticed how upset the woman was, and this explained the decision they had made while waiting for the police.

'I'm afraid the officer will be quite some time checking the house over,' he told them.

'That doesn't matter,' the husband replied, 'because we've decided against staying here. I've booked us into a hotel in a place called Netherdale. We'll stay there tonight and then return home. My wife can't bear the thought of sleeping here. For all we know it might have been that monster Craig French who was here — and if we'd arrived earlier, we might be laid on the kitchen floor with our throats cut.'

If Nash thought the man was being over-dramatic, it wasn't apparent from his reply, as he told them he quite understood their point of view.

The man continued, 'This has completely ruined our plans. We'd hoped for a relaxing break away from the stress of work, but we've decided to book something for later in the year — probably in Spain.'

'I can't blame you,' Nash agreed, 'so if you want to leave the keys with me, I'll take charge of the cottage and you can get on your way. I'm sorry that your holiday has been ruined.'

As they'd been talking, the forensic officer had started work, concentrating first on the kitchen which had been the intruder's point of entry. Nash was watching the couple's departure when the officer summoned him.

'The place is plastered with prints. They're on the fridge door, the worktops, and the kitchen table. And they're quite distinctive, with a scar across the first finger on the left hand. Judging by the number I've found, I'd say whoever it is has been staying here a while.'

'Will you do me a favour?' Nash asked. 'If I leave the house keys with you, will you lock up, and in the morning, contact the owners to find out when the cottage was last used by a legitimate tenant? That way we might get an idea of how long this person has been in residence.'

The officer looked at him as if he was about to point out that wasn't his job, but instead he said, 'I'll do better than that. I'm going to get one of my colleagues out here to help, then I can take these prints back and get them checked. I assume you're anxious to know if they're French's?'

Nash nodded his thanks and asked him to phone him as soon as he knew the outcome. 'Tonight, if possible, then we can start tomorrow knowing he is definitely in this area.'

He headed home, and had barely finished clearing away from the meal when his mobile rang again.

Alondra looked at him. 'I hope you're not going out again.'

Nash glanced at the screen. 'No, not this time. I was expecting this.' He answered and listened for a moment. 'Great job, thanks for doing that. At least we're getting somewhere . . . He'd done what?'

\* \* \*

It was all very well discovering where French had been hiding, but as Nash told Ruth Edwards when he brought her up to speed next morning, they were still no closer to finding the fugitive.

'This looks like putting a hole in your theory, Mike,' Ruth responded.

'It does — and yet again, perhaps it doesn't. From what the forensic officer told me, it would seem French was trying to keep the place clean. He'd even swept up the broken glass from the door pane. He obviously made use of the facilities available to him, he'd made the bed, and it seemed he washed a bathrobe and the towels he'd used.'

'How do you know that?' Ruth looked sceptical.

'Because they were in the drier, and it was still warm — hardly the act of a vicious killer. I admit the proximity of French to the murder scene looks highly suspicious. But looking at it another way, no matter how desperate he is, wouldn't it be extremely stupid to commit such a crime so close to where he was holed up?'

'I don't think anyone has suggested that French would be eligible to join MENSA.'

'Possibly so, but that doesn't mean he'd be dense enough to . . . er . . . mess on his own doorstep.'

Ruth smiled at Nash's euphemism, but listened carefully as he expanded his theory.

'There's another aspect to this development that might be worthy of consideration.'

'And what might that be?'

'French is an escaped convict. That fact alone has made him newsworthy. However, as a result of what happened at Wintersett Grange, he's now become the subject of almost unprecedented publicity. That means he has to keep out of sight. If he's in hiding, out of contact with everyone, how would he go about disposing of the expensive jewellery stolen from the Grange? There wasn't anything in the cottage, and he certainly can't stroll into the nearest pawnbroker and hock it. They'd set the alarm off and close the shutters before he could get through the door.'

'That's a very good point, but I reckon you'd find it difficult to persuade a lot of people to accept your line of thought.'

Nash agreed, and was wary about the reaction of his colleagues when they heard of this development. However, when he updated DS Mironova and DC Andrews, Clara immediately responded. 'I think you might be right, Mike. I can't believe French would be either daft enough, or desperate enough, to kill someone so close to where he was hiding.'

Lisa added her support. 'I agree with Clara,' she said, 'but where do we go from here?'

'That's a very good question, Lisa, and I'm afraid it's one I can't answer at present.'

'Mark the date on the calendar, Lisa — it's a rare event for Mike not to have all the answers.'

# CHAPTER THIRTEEN

In Netherdale, Vicky, a staff nurse at the general hospital, had been delighted to hear from her brother, Kyle. He was nine years her junior, and his welfare had always been a cause of much concern. This was in part due to her being called on to play the role of surrogate mother to her baby brother, his natural parent being unwilling to forego her active social life to care for the child. In his mother's jaundiced view, Kyle was a painful reminder of her unfaithful husband, who had disappeared down south in search of a job, and never returned.

Kyle wasn't too concerned about his father's desertion, or even his mother's love affairs. But he was disturbed when the new man in her life let it be known, in the strongest possible terms, that he didn't want their love nest cluttered up with the offspring of her previous relationship.

Vicky's pleasure was also tinged with relief. She hadn't heard from him for a long time. When Kyle told her about his girlfriend, Shannon, and mentioned they were about to become homeless as a result of him being made redundant from his job in a packaging factory, she had been sympathetic enough to offer them accommodation. Whether she would have been quite so willing to take them in had she known Kyle's story was a complete work of fiction is another question. The idea that Kyle might have been lying never occurred to her.

Kyle had been totally unprepared for the harsh reality of life on his own. Legally, his mother was supposed to provide him with support and a roof over his head until he was eighteen, but with her mind totally obsessed by her new love interest, such technicalities were easily forgotten.

A succession of dead-end, cash-in-hand jobs left Kyle homeless, and desperate, on the streets. His situation caused him to embark on a new life, one that called for him to cross the line of legality. If nobody was prepared to provide for him, he would simply take what he could.

Somewhere along his path of unrighteousness, Kyle had met up with Shannon, known on the streets as Shazza. Their stories were not dissimilar. Raped by her stepfather at the age of thirteen, she had become pregnant two years later, following a one-hour stand with a fellow student.

The emotional stress following her abortion caused her to forego the act of sex for a long time. Eventually, having been introduced to the benefits of birth control pills, she had been able to earn money by selling the body she no longer respected. During that low period in her life Shazza had secured one conviction for soliciting, but she had been fortunate to escape with only that single blemish on her record.

Then she had met Kyle. To begin with it was simply a case of lust at first sight. But as they got to know one another better, they each recognized a kindred spirit, and a genuine affection soon stemmed from their common bond.

In the seven years since he'd left the straight and narrow, Kyle had been fortunate to avoid detection and arrest, the amounts purloined had been small. Then, one day, he announced, 'We've got to shift. Things will get rough if we stick around here.'

'But I don't want to move.'

'You should have thought of that before you dreamed up the idea for me to break into Heroin Harry's place while he was busy screwing you. It didn't take Harry long to work out who lifted his cash. I heard he's put word out on the street — for us!' Kyle drew a finger across his throat to emphasize his message. The latest offence had moved him into the major league.

Shazza shivered. She knew Heroin Harry's evil reputation — had known it even before she seduced him. But desperation for money had called for extreme measures. Much as she liked Leeds, she enjoyed living and breathing even more. Options, it seemed, were limited. Get out of town or get buried there. 'Where are we going to move to?'

'That's a bloody good question. Somewhere Harry won't think to look for us, that's for sure. We'll have to come up with an answer quick.' It was then he'd thought of his sister.

Shazza had agreed, albeit reluctantly. She was uncertain how welcoming this woman might be, and to add to her misgivings, she had absolutely no idea where Netherdale was, let alone what the town was like.

* * *

The couple had been staying with Vicky for a few weeks, and the arrangement had worked satisfactorily. They had managed on the stolen money. This enabled them to maintain the fiction of previous employment, by claiming that the sizeable sum came from severance pay. But they knew they had to come up with an alternative source of income.

'We'll need more money,' Kyle told Shazza, stating the obvious.

'I can always go back on the game,' she offered, somewhat reluctantly.

'No way!' Kyle was indignant. 'I don't want some sweaty bastard mauling you, just because he's got some money, and isn't getting his end away at home.'

Shazza was touched by the strength of his feelings. She had never inspired such devotion before, and was determined to reward it. She rolled over in the bed they shared and began to caress him. It was a long time before they returned to the topic of money.

When they first arrived in Netherdale, the arrangement was that Vicky would fund the shopping, if Shazza and Kyle did the cooking, kept the flat clean, and washed and ironed clothing for all of them.

It was on one of their visits to the local Good Buys supermarket that Kyle noticed a minibus parked on a road in an area nicknamed *bungalow land*, because all the houses were single-storey. He read the logo on the side of the minibus, but it meant nothing to him.

When he noticed the same minibus pulling into the pick-up point at the supermarket, he saw a group of elderly passengers queuing to board the request-a-ride bus. Kyle stopped to watch, and as he did so, he saw a Good Buys employee clad in a hi-vis jacket pushing a chain of trolleys towards the docking station.

One idea followed another as Kyle pondered the scheme he had just thought up. The question was how to activate it. Before then, however, a little research was called for. It took him several weeks to engineer his plan before he explained the details to Shazza.

'We've never done anything that bad,' Shazza's comment was more of a question than a statement. Her next words confirmed her unease. 'It's one thing nicking stuff from a house when there's nobody in, but you're talking about attacking someone. I don't like it, Kyle.'

He attempted to soothe her fears. 'I'm not saying we should bash them over the head. This is our only way to get money. And before you say anything, no, you're not going back on the game. I told you before, no chance!'

Shazza refused to consider Kyle's scheme. But when their last remnant of cash had almost gone, she agreed to listen again to his idea, but subject to severe modifications.

'I've already picked a target — been watching them for a few weeks,' he told her.

'What are we after?'

'It must be cash — and only cash. It's not like we're still in Leeds. Stuff we nicked there was easy to flog in any of a dozen pubs, no questions asked. No way can we risk that round here. For one thing we'd be too easy to ID. Besides, we don't know which pubs are safe — or who we'd be dealing with.'

'What did you mean about watching our target?'

'I know their routine, and made sure they live alone.'

\* \* \*

Muriel Croft had found life difficult following the death of her husband. That wasn't surprising, as they'd been together for over fifty years. The heart attack had happened two years earlier, and despite the passage of time, Muriel was still not accustomed to living alone. Admittedly, she was visited every other weekend by her daughter, but as she lived and worked over fifty miles away, more frequent contact was far from easy.

Apart from the emotional stress, Muriel had more practical matters to deal with. Although she and Ronnie had shared household chores, particularly as they got older, jobs such as shopping, collecting their pensions, and paying household bills had always been his concern.

Muriel wasn't helped when the Netherdale branch of her bank, along with several hundred others belonging to the same company, closed down. She had to make alternative arrangements, and elected to use her local post office as a pick-up point for her pension, paid on a four-weekly basis. This was more than enough to fund her shopping bills.

Muriel decided to go to the post office on the last Tuesday of every month. She reserved her shopping expeditions for a Friday. The other advantage to this arrangement was that there would be several other passengers travelling the same route — and with the same destination and intention in mind. These would be pensioners, who, like Muriel, lived alone and were similarly in need of company, and someone to talk to, if only for the duration of the journey. Several of her fellow travellers enjoyed Muriel's lively company, and she took consolation from their concern for her welfare.

It was Tuesday, and even though the weather had turned and it was raining heavily, she still made her usual foray into the outside world. Muriel had only been back in the house for half an hour, when the doorbell rang. She was more than a little surprised, as she received very few callers, even of the nuisance type. She occasionally speculated as to whether salesmen of solar panels or double glazing had declared the district a no-go area, because of the age of the majority of the residents. However, on this occasion, her first glance at the caller standing on her doorstep seemed to challenge Muriel's theory.

The young woman was in her early twenties, Muriel guessed. She was wearing a bright yellow fluorescent jacket with the hood pulled low against the downpour, and carrying a clipboard. The caller smiled briefly before glancing down at the clipboard. 'Are you the resident of this house, Mrs . . . er . . . ?' She turned over sheet of paper and looked up again. 'I'm sorry. I don't appear to have your name.'

'It's Mrs Croft. Yes, I am the resident. Why do you want to know?'

'Do you have a current television licence, Mrs Croft? Our records don't show one listed at this address, and yet when our detector van was covering this area, we picked up a signal suggesting that a television set was being used here.'

Muriel was irritated by the slipshod bureaucracy that had caused this error. 'Yes, I do have a current licence. Perhaps it doesn't show on your records because I am over seventy-five years old, and I qualify for a free one.'

'I think you're right, Mrs Croft. Free TV licences don't always show up on our records.' She smiled reassuringly. 'So that I can put our paperwork in order, would you let me have a quick look at the licence? Then I'll make a note of the number and ensure you don't get troubled again.'

'Give me a minute and I'll get it.' As she headed inside, she failed to see the caller turn and gesture with the clip-board. Muriel had only taken a couple of paces towards the sitting room when she heard a scuffling noise behind her.

Before she could react, something soft dropped over her head and she was suddenly in darkness. She felt someone's arms around her, pinioning her into helpless immobility. She tried to squirm and wriggle her way free, but the grasp was too strong. She heard the woman's voice again. 'I've got it, let's get out of here.'

Muriel's captor plonked her on the sofa and released their grip. As she fought to remove whatever had trapped and blindfolded her, she heard the door slam, the sound followed by another that she recognized. The intruders had exited, locking the door behind them so she would be unable to follow, unable to see and recognize them.

Free at last, she stared at the pillowcase, tossed it aside, and looked round. She was alone. Alone and penniless, she realized with dismay, as she noticed her handbag containing over five hundred pounds was missing. Muriel then saw something else that puzzled her slightly. There, on the doormat was her key ring. The people who had robbed her had returned it, through the letterbox.

# CHAPTER FOURTEEN

DC Lisa Andrews had taken some files over to Netherdale headquarters, and was on her way out of the building when Tom Pratt detained her.

'I've just had the control room on the phone. A woman has been attacked and robbed in her home.' Tom handed Lisa a note. 'Her name is Muriel Croft, seventy-six years old. A couple of uniforms are on site, plus a paramedic, there to check the old lady out. By what she told our lads the villains got away with her handbag and purse containing over five hundred pounds.'

Lisa whistled with surprise. 'That's a lot for her to be carrying around, isn't it?'

'Yes, apparently she's just collected her monthly pension.'

'Is she badly hurt?'

'I don't think so. It sounds more like shock to me.'

'OK, I'm on my way.' Lisa started to move away, then turned. 'Do me a favour, will you, Tom? Let my boss know where I've gone and why.'

'Which boss, Mike Nash or her upstairs?'

'Just Mike, I think. No need to get Superintendent Edwards involved at this early stage. Could you ask someone from CSI to attend as well? It might be a long shot, but perhaps the thieves left some trace behind.'

'One thing that could help you, Lisa,' Pratt's voice was slightly hesitant as he continued, 'I know it isn't my brief any longer, but you might want to look into whether the villains got lucky, or if they had some inside info.'

Pratt had risen to the rank of Detective Superintendent prior to retirement on health grounds. Obviously, Lisa thought, he hadn't lost any of his skill.

'You think they might have known that she would be carrying a large amount of cash, and that's why they targeted her?'

'It seemed like a reasonable question to ask.'

'I think you may be right, Tom — and thanks.'

As Lisa headed to the car park, in their bedroom at Vicky's flat, Kyle watched as Shazza opened the handbag and looked inside the purse. She stared in awe at the wad of notes. 'Fuck me,' she whispered in astonishment.

Kyle took the purse and placed it on the dressing table. He pushed Shazza gently back onto the bed. 'That's just what I had in mind,' he told her.

Shazza smiled gently, obviously happy with his idea, but then whispered, 'Before you do, Kyle, I want you to promise me something.'

'What's that?'

Kyle didn't think anything Shazza said or did would surprise him, but he was wrong. Her request shocked him rigid, but eventually, he agreed to her demand.

* * *

The meeting between the partners of the veterinary practice in Helmsdale and their counterparts in Netherdale and Bishopton was an unusual event, but the reason that brought them together was a compelling one. It was Faith Parsons' senior partner who summed up the findings. As he glanced at the grim expressions on the faces of the attendees, he knew they were as determined as he was to stamp out what they suspected was happening within their region.

'We are all indebted to Ms Parsons for her diligence and single-minded resolution in identifying and then highlighting this problem. And I think it would be sensible to ask her to continue the investigation, and also involve the RSPCA and the local police. If we are in agreement, I suggest we work together by sending files on all current suspect cases to her, particularly the four with such an unhappy ending, and advise her of any new instances. Hopefully, that will provide sufficient evidence to take the matter forward.'

There was overwhelming approval of his suggestion, but once the meeting broke up, Faith's boss issued her with a word of caution. 'This is no sinecure we've given you, Faith, but hopefully it won't turn into a poisoned chalice either. One thing you must be wary of. If you identify the people behind this despicable trade, remember they are desperate, and might become aggressive or even violent. Don't attempt to confront them yourself unless you have sufficient backup to provide adequate protection.'

Faith was determined to obtain as much evidence as possible to back up her findings. She thought of another puppy, the stray that had been brought into the surgery and later adopted by the police officer, Inspector Nash. It might be worth giving him a call to check up on the well-being of his Labrador and to see if there was anything that was causing him concern.

Driven by her determination to get to the bottom of the problem, Faith brought up the owner's details and dialled his home number. A woman answered, and Faith asked, 'Is that Mr Nash's house? Can I speak to him, please?'

'It is, but he's not here at the moment. Can I help?'

Faith explained who she was and heard the woman's voice crackle with anxiety as she asked, 'Is this about Teal? Has someone come forward to claim her?'

Having reassured her, Faith asked, 'Is Teal OK? I know it's only been a few days, but has she shown any evidence of illness, such as a stomach disorder?'

'The only stomach disorder she has is trying to eat anything within reach, edible or not.'

Faith laughed. 'That's typical Labrador behaviour. Apart from her appetite, is she fit and well?'

'She's fine. She's currently trying to beat me to death with her tail, which I think sums up her state of health. Why do you ask? Is this a normal follow-up call, or is there a special reason for it, something that should concern us? I'm asking because we're planning on taking her to Harrogate at the weekend, where we're going to introduce her to our . . . er . . . Mike's son, who is at school there. Well, I hope we are. Mike is so busy at the moment.'

'I'm glad Teal's OK. I called because there have been a lot of puppies brought into the surgery recently suffering from a variety of ailments, and I wanted to be sure your dog wasn't another of them.'

'Is it a virus, something that we should be aware of?'

'Not specifically,' Faith tried to reassure her again. 'It's more likely to be that they haven't been given the proper injections. Alternatively, it might be due to genetic deficiencies. Unfortunately, either of those could point to some illegal activity, and the sheer number of cases is what triggered my suspicions.'

'Do you want me to mention this to Mike? It sounds like something that would interest him — in a professional way, I mean. But like I said, he is very busy.'

'I can well believe it, if the news headlines are anything to go by. If necessary, I'll call again, if that's OK?'

'Of course, and I will tell Mike about our conversation in case you need him to become involved. *Adiós.*'

'Oh, yes, thank you. Er, goodbye.'

* * *

Next morning, when she started her shift, Lisa was reading through her report on the theft from Mrs Croft. Her principal concern was to ensure she had included all pertinent facts. Spelling, grammar, and syntax were secondary considerations. She found it strange that only the handbag had been taken when there were items of silverware, and other things of interest to a thief. The fact that they sat her down, and returned her keys, seemed to suggest they cared about her welfare.

As the old lady described how she'd been overpowered, she had pointed to the pillowcase lying in a crumpled heap on the sofa. Once Mrs Croft had told her everything she remembered, Lisa had summoned the forensic officer, who was busy wiping down all the surfaces that the villains might have touched.

'I thought I'd clean up the dust from the fingerprint powder,' he explained, 'and save Mrs C from having to do it.'

'That's very considerate of you,' Lisa replied. 'But I've had an idea.' She pointed to the pillowcase and suggested, 'If you take that for analysis, it might yield some DNA. If it does, we'll either be able to match it with someone in our database, or, if this is their debut offence, when we catch them, we can add this to their list of heinous crimes. I'm sure Mrs Croft won't mind giving us a sample for elimination purposes.' She smiled at the old lady.

'Anything I can do to help,' she said.

The man nodded. 'It's definitely worth a shot. I'm only sorry I didn't think of it.'

'You were probably too busy being her charlady,' Lisa joked.

'It's not only you women who can multi-task,' the officer retorted.

She was about to email the report to Nash, when her phone rang. She was surprised when Jack Binns gave her the caller's name. What Mrs Croft revealed shocked her even more.

'DC Andrews? It's Muriel Croft here. I've found it.'

'Sorry, found what?'

'My handbag. It was on the doorstep this morning. Somebody put it there, rang the doorbell, and ran away. By the time I opened the door, they were out of sight.'

'You mean whoever stole your handbag has returned it? Why would they do that?'

'I've no idea, but I'm ever so grateful they did. All the cash has gone, of course, but that's not important. There were several items inside the bag that were irreplaceable. They weren't worth much in monetary terms, but they were of immense value to me. Photos of my late husband, plus his key ring and stuff like that. There's no way I could replace them, or the memories they hold. The only thing I haven't found is my bus pass, but that's easily replaced. I thought I'd better tell you in case you wanted the bag checked out.'

'I'll ask someone to pop round and give it a once over, but they're a bit busy at the moment. In the meantime, would you put it in a safe place? Also, when you handle it, be sure to avoid touching it without first covering your hands with a handkerchief, or a towel.'

'I've already done that.' Mrs Croft's final comment left Lisa in admiration of the old lady's resilience and her wicked sense of humour. 'Perhaps you could ask that nice man who came before. The lounge and dining room need vacuuming, and I have some ironing he could do, if he can spare the time.'

Lisa was still chuckling after she added the gist of their conversation to her report and emailed it.

# CHAPTER FIFTEEN

At Thornscarr Forest, the foreman of the logging crew surveyed the flooded track through the windscreen of his pickup. His employer had issued clear instructions that work should recommence as soon as possible. 'We've already lost over a week's valuable time to the weather. I want us to restart ASAP. The quicker we get back on site, the sooner we'll get paid. If we don't start earning, before long I'll have to lay men off.'

The foreman had driven to Thornscarr with that threat ringing in his ears. As he looked at the lake caused by the heavy rain, covering the trail to the logging site, he wondered whether he should phone the bad news through to his boss before, or after, visiting the Job Centre. The surface water was bad enough on the metalled main road, but at the start of the track the ground formed a natural hollow. With the depth of the water, even his 4x4 vehicle would have problems.

He thought it better to take precautions, so before phoning his boss, he photographed the scene from his vehicle. He would have got out of the pickup to take shots from a different angle, but was wary about getting his trousers wet.

He sent the photos via SMS and followed this with a short but acrimonious phone call. 'We're not going to be able to start work for a while,' he announced.

'Why not? The rain has stopped and the forecast is good.'

'That's as maybe, but we can't access the site. The trail is flooded.'

'Can't you use four-wheel drive?'

'Take a look at the photos I've sent you. The main road is bad enough. That we could cope with, but we can't use the trail into the forest.' The foreman grinned, and then added, 'Unless you can hire a yacht or a submarine.'

'You're joking! What do I tell the Harland Estate manager? He's already jumping up and down demanding to know when he's going to get paid for the lumber.'

'You could try telling him that if he'd spent a few quid getting the drainage ditches cleaned out, we wouldn't be in this mess. They were choked up before the rain started. Now they look as if a colony of beavers has been working overtime creating dams. Hang on — I'm sure I spotted a couple of dolphins swimming past.'

By the time the foreman's sarcastic tirade had ended, his boss had seen the photos. 'OK, OK, I get your point, no need to rub it in. I suppose it might help if I ask the estate to clean out those ditches.'

The foreman couldn't resist one final dig. 'It might be useful here, but there would probably be a tsunami round Bishopton.'

Two days later, contractors working on behalf of Harland Estate had unblocked the drainage ditches, and the floods had begun to recede. The logging crew foreman made a second inspection visit and reported that he and his team would recommence activities. He had ended his call by adding a sarcastic rider, 'That is, weather permitting, of course.' However, his boss failed to rise to the bait.

The crew arrived early the following morning, keen to make up for the time and money lost to the extended wet weather. Their progress up the track was slower than normal to avoid the heavy five-seater pickup getting bogged down in the muddy, marshy ground. This enabled one of the men to see the blackened shell of what had been the cabin. He told the foreman to stop, before pointing out what had attracted his attention. The fire had destroyed most of the outer wall. Although parts of the interior were still standing, sections of the roof had collapsed, giving the wreckage the appearance of a tiny, lopsided pagoda. As they speculated about the cause of the blaze, one of the team suggested it would have been much worse but for the incessant rain.

'That cabin was intact when we left, so the fire must have started later. If it hadn't been pouring down since, there would have been nothing left — and it might have spread much further.'

They were still pondering the cause of the blaze when their leader said, 'There's no way a fire could have started spontaneously. I think one of us should take a closer look.'

His colleagues glanced at one another before one of them said, 'If you're so bothered about it, I reckon you should be the one to go.'

The foreman climbed out of the cab and fought his way through the undergrowth, getting soaked from the foliage en route. He reached the edge of the clearing and signalled for the others to join him. When they arrived, similarly damp, he pointed to one corner of the building. 'What do you think that is?' he asked, directing their attention. Although the form was blackened almost beyond recognition, the size and shape were familiar enough to cause one of them to shudder with horror.

'It looks,' he said, in a whisper that seemed as loud as a shout to his colleagues, 'it looks like a body.'

Despite their trepidation, they moved forward in unison, as if guided by a puppeteer. Another three paces altered their angle of vision sufficiently for them to take in the macabre significance of the scene. 'We'd better go back to the main road,' the foreman said. 'We need a signal to phone the police.'

His colleagues had absolutely no trouble in agreeing with that idea.

* * *

Having kissed Alondra goodbye, Mike Nash was pulling his ringing mobile from his pocket, while trying to prevent Teal from making an escape bid through the open door. He glanced at the screen and grimaced, an expression of comical dismay that made Alondra smile.

It was soon apparent that the caller was Sergeant Binns, and that the subject of the conversation was no laughing matter. 'Did you say it was a group of loggers who found the body? Where is it?'

Nash listened and then groaned. 'Thornscarr Forest? I know that path. It was under water until a few days ago. Accessing the site will be a nightmare. Have you sent any uniforms to check it over? If so, I'd recall them. Anything without four-wheel drive won't stand a chance. I'll set off now. Viv Pearce is due back this morning, would you ask him to collect Clara and Lisa and get them to join me? Tell them to bring their wellies. I'm not suggesting this will turn out to be a crime scene, but it sounds suspicious. Ask them to come in one car and I'll meet them at the roadside. If you could also contact Mexican Pete and Forensics, and advise them of the conditions they'll encounter, that would be really helpful.'

He turned back inside and told Alondra, 'I think I'm going to need a change of clothing.'

'I'm not surprised. I drove past Thornscarr last week. The main road was waterlogged, let alone the woodland trail.'

'I've got a task for you,' Nash gestured towards Teal, who was hovering hopefully nearby. 'Do you think you can smuggle my wellies out and put them in the back of my car without madam seeing? She might get excited, thinking she's going for a—' He stopped suddenly, aware that he had been about to utter one of the dog's favourite words.

Alondra smiled. 'I'll do the best I can.'

When Nash arrived at the end of the track, he saw a tractor and trailer parked by the entrance. One of the men climbed out of the cab, a mobile clutched to his ear. As he approached, the detective heard him say, 'You'll have to take that up with the police. I believe one of them has just arrived. I followed their instructions.' He listened and then added, 'No, he's not a Plod, he's in plain clothes. OK, I'll put you onto him.'

By this time, Nash had taken his warrant card out and showed it to the site foreman. He handed Nash the mobile and asked, 'Sorry about this.' He grimaced. 'Would you please explain to my boss why my team hasn't started work?'

The foreman listened as Nash told his boss that the crew would be unable to resume activities until the scene had been assessed and cleared. 'The alternative is I can seal the track off, and have your men sent to Netherdale police station while we take their statements. That will be a long process, as we'll have to interview them individually to ensure their accounts tally.'

Nash handed the mobile back to the foreman and nodded. 'He accepted it, grudgingly. Now, would you explain what you saw in detail? All I have so far are the bare facts. It might be as well if the rest of your team listen. That way nothing gets missed.'

He listened to the foreman's account, supplemented by the other loggers, and then asked, 'Could you give me a more detailed description of the cabin? What condition was it in before the fire?'

When they had finished, Nash asked, 'Could you do me another favour? If the pathologist and our scientific officers arrive before I get back, ask them to wait here for me. My team will travel in my Range Rover, but I'll need another rough terrain vehicle available to help transfer CSI with their equipment.'

The foreman looked surprised. 'That's not a problem; I'll bring them.' He indicated his pickup. 'If necessary, we can also use the tractor. You don't think it was an accident, then?'

'It sounds like what is euphemistically referred to as a suspicious death.'

The foreman was about to ask Nash how he'd arrived at that conclusion when another car pulled to a halt. A tall Antiguan man got out of the driver's door, and the foreman eyed, with appreciation, the young women passengers who also emerged. If these were detectives, he thought, it might be worth considering a career in the police force.

Having phoned Jack Binns to inform him that transport had been arranged for the boffins, the detectives headed up the track, driving slowly and with four-wheel drive constantly engaged.

'I wasn't aware this is a "come dressed as you like to work" day,' Clara said.

'Knowing where we were coming, did you think I'd wear my suit and tie?' Nash responded.

'I wish someone had told me earlier,' Viv said, as he smoothed the arm of what the team realized was a new suit. 'It was a gift from my grandfather.'

'Oh, stop complaining, Viv. You've had three weeks off while we've had to deal with a mountain of work. Not that you do much, anyway.' Clara grinned at Lisa.

They stood by the car and surveyed the clearing, the focus of their attention being the burnt-out shell of the cabin. 'I reckon we've about another half-hour before the body snatchers arrive, so I vote we take a closer look at the crime scene.'

Clara, Lisa, and Viv stared at Nash in surprise. 'What makes you think this is a crime scene?' Clara asked.

'I'd prefer you to come to your own conclusions.'

Clara groaned. 'Have you started watching TV quiz shows, Mike? Because I'd rather you didn't try them out on us.'

They donned their plastic suiting, and walked slowly across to the cabin, their progress hampered both by the undergrowth and the restrictive effect of their apparel.

Close to, the devastating effect of the fire was apparent, and as they stared at it, Clara murmured, 'How strange that the outside walls are almost burnt away and the inside ones are less badly damaged.'

She glanced at Nash as she was speaking and saw his smile of approval. 'That's what you were referring to, wasn't it?'

'Partly, but perhaps you should also use your other senses, not simply your eyesight.'

There was a pause. Then, as they sniffed the air, Viv exclaimed, 'Petrol!'

'And that means this fire originated on the outside of the cabin, hence the damage being more to the fabric of the building. If that's so, the only remaining question to address is, did he fall, or was he pushed?'

'What?'

'I mean was it suicide, or was the occupant murdered?'

'It's going to be difficult to find out after such a bad blaze,' Lisa commented.

'It depends what we find in and around the cabin — and equally importantly, what we don't find.'

As the fire had burnt through several of the floor-boards, entering the building was by no means possible. In addition, the collapsed sections of the roof hindered their efforts.

As they looked across the interior, Clara pointed towards a couple of items. 'They could be syringes.'

Nash nodded absently, his attention elsewhere. 'Yes, and that tends to suggest the dead man was either a drug addict, or in receipt of regular medical attention. Neither of which provides a motive for his murder, and until we find out more about him, there's little to work on.'

'Are you certain it was murder? You said it could have been suicide.'

'That was before we came so close. Now I'm fairly certain it was murder.'

'How?'

'Because of what we didn't find. Let's go, we can't do anything more for this poor fellow. It's up to the boffins now.'

Clara stopped suddenly. 'Cans!' she exclaimed.

'You got it,' Nash replied.

Lisa frowned. 'Sorry to appear dense, but I don't understand.'

Clara answered. 'There are no petrol containers, inside or outside. That's what Mr Clever Clogs here noticed and tormented us with.'

127

'And that means,' Nash added, ignoring the insult, 'the person who set the fire took those containers with them. That suggests it was murder. But it also means, unfortunately, that there is nothing for CSI to work on to discover trace evidence.'

They had almost reached the Range Rover when Lisa told them, 'Stop, don't say anything, or make a sudden movement.' Her voice was only a whisper as she added, 'Turn very slowly to your right and look across the clearing.'

They all did as instructed, and were rewarded by the sight of a quartet of fallow deer, who were eying them with undisguised curiosity.

'They're beautiful,' Clara said, without thinking.

Although her remark was highly complimentary, the deer turned tail and departed rapidly, bolting into the dense woodland and were soon lost to sight.

'Did they hear me?' she asked, somewhat dismayed.

'Of course they did. Alan reckons their hearing and sense of smell is phenomenal. He once told me he'd dropped a glove in the woods near our place, and a roe deer, over five hundred metres away, took off like a rocket.'

'Don't worry about it, Clara. They'd have disappeared soon anyway when our pathologist and more men in white suits arrive.'

'Yes, and Mexican Pete's enough to scare anyone, or anything, away,' she retorted.

'Well, you two will be quite safe here. Viv can look after you while I go and fetch him.'

# CHAPTER SIXTEEN

Professor Ramirez, their long-serving pathologist, was waiting at the end of the lane. Nash's mobile rang, but the pathologist didn't notice. Ramirez blinked in astonishment as Nash approached him and said, '*Hola, querida, que tal?*'

Ramirez waited as Nash concluded his conversation. 'That was a highly affectionate greeting,' he said gently.

Nash smiled. 'Much as I admire you, Don Pedro, my respect does not extend to calling you "darling".'

'You have no idea how relieved I am to hear that. From the fact that you were speaking in Spanish, and with quite a good accent, am I right in assuming you may have been speaking to a young woman I met briefly a couple of years ago?'

'You are correct, and I am delighted to say that she has returned to England — for good.'

'In that case, please accept my congratulations.' He patted him on the shoulder and then smiled at him, a rare occurrence. 'Now, I suppose we'd better get to work.'

Nash ushered him to the Range Rover and explained, 'From what we've determined so far, we believe this to be a murder scene.'

Ramirez sighed. 'That doesn't surprise me. Your presence alone suggested as much. It's clear that the improvement in your love life has done nothing to curb your ghoulish instinct. What led you to that conclusion?'

Nash explained the absence of a container for the accelerant, which they believed to be petrol, from the smell that remained in the air. 'Given the amount of rain that's fallen, my guess is that it must have penetrated the soil in areas where it couldn't be washed away. If it was sheltered by foliage, or under the floor of the building for instance, and the downpour started after the fire was set, that scent would linger for a very long time.'

'That sounds like a remarkably good piece of deductive reasoning. I think you've got the makings of a detective, Don Miguel.' With this subtle dig, Ramirez moved away to confer with the CSI team, who had made their way to the site in the foreman's pickup.

As Nash watched, he noticed one of the officers was studying the earth where it had been churned up by the wheels of the vehicles. The officer signalled to Nash and told him, 'We'll have to take impressions of your car tyres, plus those made by the others, and look for any that don't match. There would have been plenty of soft ground here, even before the fire, and there's a good chance we'll be able to pick up the trail left by the killer.'

Nash looked at the scene again. 'Then I think the four of us should get out of your way and check over the rest of the clearing, avoiding the proximity of the cabin.'

They spent half an hour on this task, and when they returned, neither Viv, Lisa nor Clara had anything to report. Nash however, called over the lead forensic officer he had met at the holiday cottage.

'You're keeping me busy, Inspector Nash. Got something for me?'

'I've been to the toilet,' he announced.

The man blinked, but before he could say anything, Clara interjected. 'I'm not sure we need to know about your personal habits, Mike.'

Nash grinned. 'I said I'd been to the toilet. I didn't say I'd used it. There's a small building behind the cabin that serves as a latrine. Someone has obviously been using it recently, which might give us a clue as to the victim's identity.'

'I'm not at all sure I want to know the answer, but why do you think that?'

Nash's smile widened at the implication. 'Someone has torn up several pages from a newspaper to use as makeshift toilet paper. My immediate thought was that there might be fingerprints or DNA.'

'I'll have a look.'

Less than ten minutes later, the officer came striding towards them, and signalled to Nash he needed to speak to him. 'That was worth doing. I've found prints on those pages. They have what looks to be an identical scar to the one on French's prints I found at the cottage. But I should have a definite ID for you tomorrow. I take it you will be working over the weekend?'

'With a caseload like we've got at the moment, there's no option.'

Both Nash and the scientific officer were unaware that the foreman of the logging crew was within earshot.

* * *

Early next morning, news came through confirming that the fingerprints on the paper at the cabin belonged to Craig French, and they could call off the manhunt.

'That will ease the media pressure no end,' Ruth Edwards stated.

Nash stared at the acting chief constable, his surprise apparent. 'I'm sorry, Ruth, but I think you're jumping to several conclusions there.'

'Why do you say that?'

Nash began to enumerate them. 'For one thing, we have only those fingerprints in the privy to indicate that French was ever at the cabin. Secondly, where is the high-end jewellery he stole from Wintersett Grange — if that robbery was his work? He wouldn't have stashed it in the woods with all the loggers about. There was nothing found at the holiday cottage, neither was there anything inside the hut — apart from the corpse, empty beer bottles, some tins of food and a couple of syringes. And as far as we know, French isn't a user. Finally, based on what I saw at the scene, I believe that fire took place before the rain started. Maybe not long before, otherwise that logging crew would have noticed. My guess would be that French *had* been hiding in the cabin, but then deserted it. He would be wary of being seen and recognized by the logging crew. Perhaps French then broke into the holiday cottage because he needed to find a new bolthole.'

'It may be the other way round. What if French went to that cabin after he left the holiday cottage? I'm not disagreeing with you, Mike, you've visited both the scenes, I haven't.' She shrugged her shoulders. 'Any ideas as to how we proceed?'

'I think we'd be better releasing a statement that will tell the media very little, apart from the fact that we're treating the death of an unidentified person as suspicious. Once Mexican Pete has done his work with DNA from the body, we'll know one way or the other. I'm off to see him now.'

Having assured her he would keep her informed, he drove to the mortuary.

Ramirez looked up from the autopsy table to where Nash was standing. 'There is one thing I can tell you already, this man was alive when the fire started — he has smoke in his lungs. There's also an injury to the back of his head. It could explain why he made no attempt to escape the flames. Whether intentional, or caused by a falling beam during the fire, it will be difficult to determine. The position he was in suggests he may have been asleep, facing the wall of the cabin when the blaze started. Alternatively, as syringes were at the scene, he may have been in a drug-induced state. We'll have to wait for toxicology.' He put down his scalpel.

'You're quite correct, it wasn't suicide. But if this proves to be Craig French, you can rule him out as a suspect in the Wintersett Grange murders.'

Nash frowned, puzzled by the remark. 'Why is that, Professor?'

'Judging by the rate of decomposition of the less-bar-becued parts of the body,' — a fleeting smile crossed the pathologist's face as he saw Nash wince — 'this man had been dead for several days by the time those people at the Grange were killed.'

* * *

Back in Helmsdale, Lisa Andrews had reminded Clara about her plans for tomorrow. Several days ago she had been begging for her assistance, telling her, 'If the weather improves, we're still going to Leeds on Sunday. Even though we're so busy, Mike said I could take it as my day off. Alan has some tickets for a one-day cricket match at Headingley. They were a gift to Alan's business partner, Harry Rourke. Harry has little interest in cricket, so he donated them. There are four tickets, so we're taking Barry and Shirley Dickinson with us. You remember Barry, don't you?'

'He's the head gamekeeper on Winfield Estate, isn't he?'

'That's right, and they're great friends of ours. Barry and Shirley were about the only two people apart from Mike and me who didn't believe Alan was a murderer back in the day.'

'I recall it now. I missed all the excitement because I was down with the flu.'

'The problem we have is finding someone to look after Nell. She doesn't like being left alone all day. We had Sir Maurice's assistant Falstaff lined up for the job, but they have to travel to London to deal with something that's just cropped up.'

Clara had met Nell, the Labrador, a few times. Alan Marshall's beloved pet had been with him for many years. 'Why is it everyone around here has become black Lab owners? By all means, bring Nell over. David will enjoy making a fuss of her and giving her a walk.'

* * *

Craig had trekked for a day to reach his new shelter on the Winfield Estate. He'd noted the vast difference between his current surroundings and his previous hideaway. Thornscarr Forest had been vastly untended, and had obviously been that way for a long number of years, before the loggers had arrived. In stark contrast, the Winfield Estate bore the hallmarks of careful husbandry. Fallen trees had been hauled into a large clearing, created specifically to store them. There, close to a woodman's hut, the branches had been lopped off and carted away, before the trunks were stacked to dry out. A substantial proportion of the estate was covered by conifer plantations. The timber from these was less suitable for firewood, but was in greater demand for building or woodworking. Other stacks contained a variety of deciduous woods with more diverse usage.

The neatness of Craig's surroundings might have seemed irrelevant to many people, but in his desire to avoid recapture it was highly important. All the required forestry work had been completed, so there was little likelihood of anyone needing to enter the woodman's hut that was to become his new asylum. There was another bonus, in that the recent heavy rains had saturated all the nearby timber stacks, some of them still under several inches of water, and therefore there was no chance of anyone coming to the clearing to collect them in the near future.

The rudimentary structure was limited in respect of facilities, but there was a chemical toilet plus a couple of old, battered, but still functional armchairs. Another find that pleased the fugitive was a long, oblong piece of stout canvas, the cover from a tractor-pulled trailer. The eyelets down all four sides of the tarpaulin, plus the rope threaded through them, would enable him to put the canvas to use.

Before beginning the project, he'd tested the strength of the upright poles supporting the shed roof. Having satisfied himself that these were durable enough, Craig had begun untying the lengths of rope and then knotted them together to form two long sections. He'd attached one to either end of the canvas, creating a rudimentary hammock.

Although the makeshift bed might enable Craig to get some rest, his most urgent need remained unsatisfied. He knew he would have to abandon his sanctuary to find something to assuage his hunger. That would expose him to the risk of being recognized, and thereby concentrate the manhunt in his locality. But the need now far outweighed the potential danger.

During the construction of the hammock, simple tasks such as untying and retying knots had become extremely challenging, and he could tell that his level of concentration was not as it should be. Although the project was straightforward, it had taken him far longer than anticipated. When it was finally completed, the effort had left him exhausted. Had he been in a fit state to interpret them, these were further indications of his rapidly debilitating condition.

He had been penned up in the woodman's hut for five days. Other than the bread and biscuits taken from the cottage, Craig hadn't eaten for two days. Even prior to that, his diet had been less than sumptuous. The effect of his prolonged abstinence from anything more sustaining than drinks of water from a nearby stream was beginning to have a serious effect. His hunger was now intense, to the point that he was beginning to suffer prolonged, and painful, cramps as his stomach rebelled against this starvation.

When he stepped cautiously out of the hut, Craig was relieved to see the grey skies had been replaced by bright blue, the monotony broken by occasional scudding white clouds. The brisk, cool breeze driving those clouds was strong enough to penetrate even the denser parts of the woodland.

For Craig, in his weakened state, this sudden exposure to fresh, cold air brought another problem. More than once, as he tried to reach the cottage that was his objective, a journey of less than two miles, he had to pause and rest. On each occasion, he leaned against a tree until the dizzy spell passed. Had he been in a crowded town or city, with vehicles passing virtually every second, this would have represented peril of one kind. Out here, in a lonely, remote area of forest, another, equally acute, danger threatened. Unless he could reach some form of habitation before he was overcome, then it might be weeks, months, or even years, before his lifeless body was discovered.

Craig's misery was deep enough to make him consider surrendering to the police and accepting defeat.

Had he been party to the conversation between Lisa and Clara, it would have saved him some time and effort. He was trying to reach Barry Dickinson's cottage, in the hope that the gamekeeper might help him.

The shortest route involved crossing Layton Woods, then re-entering the Winfield Estate. When Craig emerged from the junction between the tracts of land, he knew he would be close to the rear of the Westlea, near to where Tiff was living.

There was one snag, but Craig knew it was a risk he would have to take. If Barry was unwilling to assist, he might turn him over to the police, in which case all his efforts would have proved futile.

He was using well-defined paths, ensuring he made as good a progress as his weakened condition allowed. Normally, he would have completed the walk within twenty-five minutes or so, but had been forced to rest several times to recoup what remained of his failing strength. By the time he reached the house occupied by Barry and Shirley Dickinson, another hour had passed. Not only that, but Craig was now on his last legs.

He paused, wondering whether he should continue. The tremor in his lower limbs was the deciding factor. As he approached the cottage, weaving slightly like a drunken man, he noticed Dickinson's Land Rover parked alongside

Shirley's smaller saloon car. At least someone was at home. Uncertain whether or not he would be greeted with hostility, he knocked on the door.

There was no answer. He tried again, but without success. As he turned away, his dejection now complete, Craig stared at the outbuilding opposite the house. Seeing it, brought back a memory that in turn spawned an idea.

Twenty minutes later, Craig was seated at the Dickinson's kitchen table, munching on a cheese-and-ham sandwich. He had already devoured a large bowl of breakfast cereal, and been warmed with the aid of two steaming mugs of tea. He was beginning to feel slightly better. It had been a stroke of luck that had enabled him to gain this much-needed sustenance. He had recalled the one previous occasion when he'd entered the outbuilding, that time at Barry Dickinson's instruction.

His memory of that traumatic day had paid off when he found the door key, and was able to access the house. Having finished eating, conscious that his next meal might be a long time coming, Craig made two more sandwiches which he wrapped in foil. He added a chocolate bar he'd filched from one of the cupboards, washed up, and tidied everything he'd used away. Then he searched the kitchen. After a couple of minutes, he found what he was seeking, and sat back down at the table to compose a short note of thanks and apology.

Having locked the door, and returned the key to the outbuilding, Craig braced himself for the final leg of the journey. He'd seen the time on the kitchen clock and reckoned it would be the middle of the afternoon before he reached Tiff's place — and was finally able to confront her.

## CHAPTER SEVENTEEN

Nash had just finished his evening meal when his mobile chirped. He glanced at it before answering. 'Lisa, is there a problem? I thought you'd be in the pub celebrating a Joe Root century or Ben Coad taking six wickets.'

He listened in surprise as she told him, 'We got back a few minutes ago. We're at Barry and Shirley's place. We were going to have dinner with them, but someone has been in their house. They haven't stolen anything, but Shirley reckons, from looking in the fridge, some food is missing. The thing is, they left a note apologizing for the theft. It's signed, "Craig".'

'I suggest you get in touch with Forensics and ask them to send a couple of CSI guys out. Is there much damage to the door?'

'None whatsoever, so at first we were a bit baffled as to how he got in.'

'Don't tell me he used the French window?'

Nash grinned as he heard Lisa groan. 'No, Mike. Eventually, Barry remembered that French knew they keep a back door key in the outhouse. He must have used that. So that seems to confirm it was French.'

'Does anyone else know he keeps a key there?'

'Just a minute, I'll ask.' There was a pause before she told him, 'Barry says some of the other beaters might know of it.'

'In that case, it could have been anyone. How do we know Craig French wrote that note? Anyone could have signed it. Besides, we have an, as yet, unidentified body. I don't see there's much we can do, Lisa. I don't think I'd get authority for a search party to go tramping through Sir Maurice's estate. Apart from it being a futile exercise, the overtime would probably use up our budget for the next two years. Keep me posted if there are any sensational developments. I'll wait until Monday morning for your ball-by-ball account of the match.'

He smiled at Lisa's response. It was quite rude and definitely insubordinate.

* * *

On Monday morning, Nash was about to brief the team when Lisa Andrews joined them, saying, 'I've just taken a call from the guy in Forensics. It turns out French's prints were on the note and in the kitchen at the Dickinsons' place. He can't be dead.'

Nash nodded. 'Professor Ramirez is waiting on DNA results from the body at the cabin, but he said it's unlikely to be French. So in that case, he remains our prime suspect for these latest killings — at least officially speaking.'

Lisa explained to the others what they had found when they returned from the cricket match, while Nash went to answer his phone.

'Yes, Tom, what news have you got?'

Nash was silent, merely making a couple of notes on his pad, before saying, 'Thanks, that's extremely informative. Will you follow it up for me? I think you know what I need.'

He put the phone down and looked at his colleagues. 'That was Tom Pratt. I asked him to do a bit of research for me a week ago. I've now got more to add to our doubts

139

about the Cumbrian murders, sparked by Clara's eagle-eyed reading of that forensic report. Plus'— he nodded at Pearce — 'your Lianne's misgivings. Viv, how far do you reckon it is to Silloth from here?'

'It will be over a hundred miles or so.'

'Yes, that's what I thought. I was wondering how Craig French got there and back, something the Cumbrian police neglected to ask.'

'He must have driven,' Lisa said. 'Or he could have gone by train or bus,' she added.

'Doubtful,' Viv said. 'I don't think there's a direct route, it would have taken hours. Besides, he wasn't just carrying jewellery, he had pictures and silverware. It had to be by road.'

Clara looked at Nash's face — saw the twitch at the corner of his mouth. 'I suppose he could have rented a car,' she said. 'Or hired a taxi and asked the driver to wait outside, while he popped in and committed a murder. He might even have asked him to help fill the boot with his swag. Or it could have just been a bloody long walk with a rucksack on his back! Come on, Mike, stop playing about. Tell us what Tom said.'

'Tom's call more or less sealed it for me. Unless he'd rented a car — which is very unlikely — Craig French couldn't have travelled to and from Cumbria by car because, at the time those murders were committed, he didn't have a vehicle. He *had* owned a car, but he'd advised DVLA a month before the date of the murders that he'd sold it. Tom has confirmation from DVLA of the new ownership, and there is no record of French acquiring a replacement. Therefore, he wouldn't have needed the lockup garage where the property was found.'

'He could have kept it for storage, or to use as a workshop,' Viv pointed out.

'Seems doubtful, there was nothing to indicate that. Forensics reported the place was empty and appeared to have been cleaned out, other than the stolen property.'

Half an hour later, Tom Pratt phoned back, telling Nash he had checked with the council and discovered that French had surrendered the key to the lockup at the same time as he sold the car.

Nash called Pearce into his office. 'Viv, I've got an important task for you.' He handed him the information Tom Pratt had given him, and outlined what he needed. 'Phone the man whose name is listed there and check those details. If he confirms they're correct, I want you to visit him. It's a long shot, but he might just have what we need. If so, I want you to take photos that ensure every detail is recorded. A lot might depend on the information you get.'

\* \* \*

Lisa Andrews was so busy that she had all but forgotten the mugging of Mrs Croft, until she received a phone call from the forensic officer who had attended the scene. His opening words brought the case instantly back to mind and were just reward for her clear thinking. 'You were dead right, there was DNA on that pillowcase. We've been able to match it with someone on file, a woman who was convicted of soliciting in Sheffield five years ago.'

'Blimey, that's a fair distance away.'

'People do move around a bit more these days.'

Lisa could tell the officer was laughing.

'I've emailed the file. The rest is up to you.'

Lisa thanked him and turned to her computer. After reading the sparse information, she went through to Nash's office. 'I think it might be worth putting this girl's details in the *Gazette*,' she told him. 'My guess is that the couple who robbed the old lady are amateurs, and wouldn't think not to dirty their own doorstep. So if this girl lives locally, someone might recognize her and come forward. I know the photo is a few years old, but with luck she won't have changed her name, and her appearance will be much the same because she's only twenty-four.'

'That's a good idea, Lisa. I'll let you run with it. If we're successful and make an arrest, it will be down to your hard work and skill.'

Moments later, Nash was making a note for a commendation on her file when his phone rang with a call from the vet.

'Ms Parsons, how can I help? Alondra mentioned that you'd rung, something to do with sick puppies, wasn't it?'

He listened, his face taking on a grave expression as she revealed what she suspected, backing it by quoting some details of what she'd discovered thus far.

'So you believe that the ailments these puppies suffered from, including the ones that died, were as a result of puppy farming and trafficking, correct?'

'That's it, Mr Nash, and we're concerned that there might be even more that we don't know about. My biggest worry is that this might prove to be the tip of a very large iceberg, because if they're engaged in this vile trade to make money, they'll be operating on a nationwide scale.'

'That presents an immediate difficulty, as we can't be sure where the perpetrators are based. For all we know, this might be the result of the activities of one of their branches. The other problem is that I know very little about how these things operate. I'm also uncertain what we can do to help. Have you or your colleagues spoken to the owners to discover if there is a common thread, such as the name of the person who sold them their puppy?'

'They all seem to have been bought from different people at different addresses. It's highly frustrating.'

'Have you spoken to any of these dealers?'

'No, I don't have the authority to do so. I've been liaising with the RSPCA, but, unless there are animals in situ at any of those addresses, they're also powerless.'

'That might be so, but we're in a stronger position, providing we have something to work with. I suggest you contact some of the people who bought suspect puppies, and ask them if they'd be prepared to make an official complaint. If we have that, we can call on the dealers and ask some awkward questions. I'll get one of my team to contact you as liaison.'

Faith agreed with this idea. When he'd ended the call, Nash thought for a moment before going through to the outer office. 'Lisa, I've an extra job for you.' He outlined what the vet had told him and the course of action he had suggested. 'I'd like you to work with Ms Parsons and deal with the owners. Once you have the necessary information, I need you to interview the dealers. Take a uniform with you if you do. We need to stop this at source.'

Nash could tell by Lisa's horrified expression that he'd made the right choice.

\* \* \*

Craig French made his way towards the Westlea estate, heading for the flats where his mother had told him Tiff now lived. He avoided main roads, sticking to the open ground alongside the disused railway line. He was able to call on his knowledge of the area. He was relieved when he reached the flats without being noticed and knocked on Tiff's door. There was no reply, so he decided to wait at the back of the building. A clump of trees provided shelter and cover from prying eyes. It also enabled him to see past the corner of the building to the walkway that formed the approach.

\* \* \*

Tiff emerged from Good Buys. As she was coming through the entrance, she noticed the placards alongside the news stand. All the papers carried the same headline. '*Helmsdale Killer Still On The Run.*' Tiff grimaced. She'd hoped that Craig would have been recaptured by now. One crumb of comfort was that she guessed he'd be a long way from Helmsdale, from the Westlea and from her. The hatred she felt for her baby's father had gone into hyper-drive following news of the further appalling crimes he'd committed since his escape.

Now, thanks to him, she was about to uproot herself and her son, deserting the country of their birth, to settle in a strange land with a different culture. Her sister had written in glowing terms of life Down Under, but even with her recommendation and sponsorship, Tiff wouldn't have dreamed of leaving Helmsdale had she and Craig still been together.

'Damn you, Craig, you ruined everything, simply because you couldn't keep your hands off Bobby's wife, or your dick in your pants,' she muttered to herself.

The rage she felt caused her to increase her pace. She no longer cared about a confrontation, so she took the direct route, walking via Good Buys car park and along the street parallel to the market place. This would entail passing the front of Brenda's house, but she was beyond caring.

The ordeal of the expedition had unnerved Tiff to some extent, and when she passed Craig's mother's house, with the police patrol car parked outside, she vented her feelings with a single-fingered and unmistakeably vulgar gesture. Inside his pushchair, Noel giggled, which Tiff interpreted to be a sign of approval.

# CHAPTER EIGHTEEN

On reaching home, Tiff put the brake on the buggy and opened the front door. Entering the flat with several carrier bags and a pushchair containing an infant was a tricky procedure. She left the child for a few seconds as she took the shopping inside. She returned, took the brake off, and wheeled the pushchair over the threshold. As she tried to close the door behind her with her outstretched leg, she found it was blocked. Something was obstructing the swing of the door, preventing it from closing. She muttered something impolite, and turned to see what the problem was. A split second later, hands were on her shoulders pushing her backwards, before the door slammed violently shut.

Tiff was still in shock as she saw the intruder, his back towards her, locking the door, sliding the bolts across and securing the chain. She knew who it was.

She darted to the kitchen, snatched a kitchen knife from the drawer, and raced back into the hall to confront the menace.

In the seconds she'd been gone, Craig had moved out of her line of sight. Tiff felt her arms being grasped, then twisted, forcing her to drop the weapon. He pushed her against the wall, holding her arms above her head, his body pressed against hers. She writhed and twisted, tried to lash out with her foot, but to no avail, as he retained his grip. All the while she was mouthing obscenities, using every weapon in her desperate defence of herself and her son.

Up close against her face, Craig's was a mask of anger and bitterness. But elsewhere, his body told a different story.

After what seemed an age, he released his grip and turned away. Tiff darted to the end of the hall and picked up the knife from where it had fallen. She was about to thrust the weapon at him, but stopped dead as she saw him lift her son from the pushchair, and cradle him against his shoulder.

'Put him down,' she spat the demand out. 'You're not fit to touch him, you loathsome piece of shit.' Noel had begun to cry. In the arms of a stranger he was showing his disapproval.

Craig began jigging the child up and down. 'And I suppose you are fit? Ever heard of that song, "Stand By Your Man"? No, probably not. Standing by someone doesn't mean fitting them up for a crime they didn't commit, and then grassing on them, so they get a life sentence inside a hell-hole. I don't even know why I'm talking to you. It wasn't you I came to see, it was this little man. My son, in case you'd forgotten. The son I've never met. The son I would never see if you'd buggered off to Australia while I was locked away.' He shook his head in disgust. 'And I had the stupid idea that you loved me. What a bloody fool I was to believe that load of shite.'

Tiff held out her arms. 'Please, pass him back. I didn't grass you up.' Tiff's tone was sullen, her mind preoccupied with how to get out of this mess, how to get Noel away from Craig without hurting the boy. If she had her mobile, she could call the cops and have him carted off to jail, but the phone was in her handbag, which was slung across the handle of the pushchair, inches from Craig's hand.

He noticed her glance at the buggy, opened the handbag and took the phone out, shifting Noel to his other arm as he did so. He pocketed the mobile and passed the boy back to his mother. 'He needs changing,' he told her curtly. 'You'd better do it. You're more used to dealing in shit than me. And while you're doing it, you can explain why you lied. I know you grassed me up. I was told. Now I want the truth. Why did you plant that gear your brother stole in the lockup, and why dump on me to the cops?'

Without thinking of the possible danger, Tiff turned away and took Noel through into the lounge. She knelt on the carpet alongside the boy, and began to take his little dungarees off. 'Make yourself useful for once in your life. Pass me that bag of nappies and the other bag next to them.'

Craig did so, and Tiff began the changing process, making gentle cooing noises to the little one, who had now ceased crying. After a few moments, she passed the dirty nappy, neatly folded in a nappy sack, to her ex-lover. 'Take that and put it into the kitchen bin,' she ordered him.

When Craig returned to the lounge, he leaned against the wall watching Tiff, who was seated on the sofa, cradling the wriggling child. 'Well,' he demanded, 'are you going to talk?'

Although still terrified, Tiff had calmed down a little, her priority now being to protect Noel from this monster. 'I don't see there's anything to discuss,' she replied. 'What will you do if I decide not to talk to you? Knife me, like you did all those other people?'

'I didn't kill that couple in Cumbria. I've never been to that place Silloth, or anywhere near there. I know that now, but when they tried to arrest me, the fall caused me to lose my memory. It only started to come back when I was in jail.'

'Don't try to explain. Nobody believes in fairy tales. And what about Wintersett Grange — are you going to claim you were nowhere near there?'

'Wintersett Grange? What's that got to do with anything? The place has been empty for donkey's years.'

Tiff stared at him, noticing the baffled expression on his face. 'Have you really got amnesia, or have you killed so many people you've forgotten one or two? Wintersett Grange was bought by a retired couple nearly two years ago. After you escaped from prison, they were killed during a burglary, which the press reckon was committed by escaped murderer Craig French.'

The shock of this news, added to his already debilitated condition, was too much for him to take in. Tiff watched in astonishment as he collapsed, sliding down the wall in a dead faint.

She waited, uncertain what to do. She needed to ring the police, but her phone was in his pocket and she daren't try to get it. After a few moments, she saw him begin to stir, then sit up, his eyes still glazed. He shook his head to clear his benumbed brain and looked at her. 'Is that true?'

His question seemed to highlight his confusion. Instead of speaking, she got up, hefted Noel onto her hip, and told Craig, 'Wait there.' She went into the kitchen and picked up a copy of the *Netherdale Gazette* with a suitably lurid headline, returned to the lounge, and thrust it into Craig's hand, before resuming her position on the sofa.

Tiff watched as he scanned the article and saw his face whiten with renewed shock. The hands holding the paper trembled as he read the reporter's quote from police sources, highlighting the similarity between these killings and the ones he had already been convicted for. Eventually, he looked up, and Tiff was shocked again when she saw tears streaming down his face.

This final action convinced Tiff that something was dreadfully wrong. Whatever had happened in Cumbria, the news of the Wintersett Grange murders had come as a total shock to Craig — and if he hadn't murdered those people, how come the press reckoned it had been the same killer in both cases?

He turned his tearstained face towards her. 'I didn't know there was anyone living in that house. The last time I went past the Grange there was a sale board on the gates. If you don't believe me, there's no point carrying on.' He plucked her mobile from his pocket and gave her it.

'Ring the police and get it over with. You'll be able to brag that you sold me out a second time. I loved you, Tiff. Loved you so much, but all I got in return was betrayal. I don't care what happens to me now. Without you, my life isn't worth living, so I might as well go back inside, and you can go ahead with whatever you have planned.'

Craig's declaration, coupled with his earlier astonishment cast further doubts in Tiff's mind. She hesitated for several seconds before replying. Setting aside the later atrocity, she returned to the subject of the crime he'd been convicted for. 'I didn't grass you up. And I certainly didn't plant that stuff in your lockup. Where you got those ideas from beats me.'

'Really.' His tone was witheringly sarcastic. 'I was told by the police that it was a woman who informed them I'd committed those murders. The cops even told me who had ratted on me — they mentioned you by name. So come on, Tiff, out with it! Why the hell did you do that? I thought we had something going, but you ruined it.'

Tiff was getting angry. 'I didn't fit you up! I didn't put that stuff in the lockup. I wouldn't have done that to you even if you'd slept with a dozen women. How would I have got my hands on stolen property from Cumbria?' She glared at him. 'I didn't speak to the police, so how they got my name is a mystery. I might have done if I'd known you were committing those robberies, if only to get back at you for what you did to Bobby. But then, I didn't know he was also involved. What you did to Bobby was loathsome. Getting him into trouble and then betraying him — and me into the bargain.'

Craig had been pacing the floor. Now he stood stock still. He stared at her for a few seconds, his expression one of bewilderment. 'Bobby? Your brother Bobby? What's he got to do with it? Apart from the fact that he was found guilty of those other burglaries they charged me with. I wasn't that close to him. I rarely met him, apart from when he came to visit you. I don't know why he didn't tell the police I wasn't involved.'

'Well, I do. I suppose you'll tell me next that you weren't shagging Bobby's wife. One thing that hasn't changed while you've been inside is your ability to talk bullshit.'

Craig blinked with surprise. 'Is that what all this has been about? Somebody told you I was shagging Bobby's wife? That's bloody rubbish, Tiff. I hardly knew the woman. At a guess I'd say I met her twice, three times at most — no more than that. I don't think I'd recognize her if she walked in the door right now. Somebody's been lying to you, Tiff. And you swallowed the bloody lot, hook, line, and sinker.'

Tiff looked at him, her smile one of triumph, her tone withering. 'Not just somebody, Craig, I got the information from two sources, both reliable, and both without an axe to grind. My milkman also delivers to Bobby's address, and he told me he'd seen your hideous, bright green metallic sports car parked outside their house at five o'clock in the morning. I might have taken that with a pinch of salt had I not been told by someone else.'

'Go on. Who was it this time?'

'John, the guy who owns the paper shop, said he'd seen your car there an hour later when he was delivering papers, and when I checked the date, I found that it was when Bobby was working in Birmingham.'

Having delivered this *coup de grâce*, Tiff sat back on the sofa, with Noel nestled against her shoulder. She watched in silence as Craig resumed pacing round the room, puzzling over what he'd just learned. It was several minutes, during which the atmosphere became strained, before he spoke. 'That time when Bobby was in Birmingham, it was just before I was arrested, wasn't it?'

'It was the week before, as you know perfectly well, or have you shagged so many women you can't remember?'

It was obvious that Tiff was still convinced the evidence was irrefutable. Craig's next sentence caused the first doubt to creep in. 'I didn't have the car then.'

'How do you mean, you didn't have the car? Where was it?'

'I'd sold it. I decided to buy something more suitable. I thought that when the little one came along we'd be better off with a family saloon rather than a sports car.'

'So who was driving it?'

'How the hell do I know? It must have been sold on.'

Tiff looked suspicious. 'You didn't tell me you'd got rid of it.'

'No, I wanted to surprise you. As it turned out, I was the one who got the surprise. A right bloody shock it was too, and one I'd rather not get again.'

'Suppose I believe you about the car, can you explain about that huge sum of money you hid in your mother's house? If it didn't come from the burglaries, where did you get your hands on such a wad of cash? Did the fairies deposit the money in your loft bank account? Wait — don't tell me, let me guess. You won it on the National Lottery. Please don't try and spin a yarn like that, because nobody in their right mind would believe you.'

'I didn't win it on the lottery. I won it on a racehorse.'

Tiff stared at him, her disbelief apparent, before she responded, her sarcasm undiminished. 'Of course, why didn't I guess that? You're obviously a famous racing tipster in disguise.'

He knew that nothing short of the whole story would convince her, so he asked, 'Have you ever heard of Sir Lionel Birch?'

The question and Craig's earlier comment left Tiff totally confused. She wondered if the head injury had caused permanent damage. Eventually, she remembered the name he'd quoted. 'Isn't he some kind of banker or business tycoon?'

'That's right, and he's also one of the richest men in the country.'

'What's he got to do with all this?'

'He's the man who gave me the money — or a chunk of it. The rest came from Coral's, Ladbroke's, William Hill, and a few other bookmakers.'

By now, Tiff was convinced that she was talking to a deranged man, his mental capacities irretrievably damaged by the trauma he'd suffered.

Seeing her disbelief, Craig tried to explain. 'Sir Lionel was a guest on the Winfield Estate shoot. He lives abroad most of the year, and only returns for part of the shooting season, and to watch his horses run. He was the owner of Slowcoach. Do you remember? The horse that almost got the trainer warned off. It was only when they tested it that they discovered the animal produces cortisol naturally.'

'I read about that, but what has it to do with you?'

'When I was beating on the shoot, Sir Lionel was a back gun. That's the guy who moves with the beaters. His job is to fire at any pheasants that fly the wrong way. It doesn't matter if he hits them or not, his job is to drive them towards where the guns are standing. As we were going through a densely wooded section, I spotted a gin trap set by poachers. Sir Lionel was about to step on it when I stopped him. I might have saved his life, but I certainly saved his leg. He was so grateful that he came to find me a few days later, and offered me ten thousand pounds. He told me I could do what I wanted with the money, but he advised me to take half of it, and put it on his horse in a race that was coming up at Wetherby. He promised that if it lost, he'd come back and give me the five thousand I'd used as a stake. He also said I should spread the bet between bookmakers, that way the odds wouldn't shorten too much. Slowcoach won by over fifteen lengths at a starting price of 6/1, so I collected thirty thousand pounds in winnings. That, together with my stake money, the other five thousand he'd given me, plus the cash from the sale of the car, accounts for the forty-five thousand.'

'If there was an innocent explanation for the money, why did you try to run when the police went to your house?'

'At that point, the alleged doping was making headlines, and I thought they'd traced my bets and were under the impression that I'd nobbled the horse, or knew something about it. You have to produce ID and sign a receipt when you're collecting a huge amount of winnings.'

The story was too fantastical not to be true. Tiff knew Craig well enough to be certain he could never have dreamed all that up. 'Why didn't you tell anyone? Surely if you'd asked him, this Sir Lionel would have backed up your story?'

'I couldn't tell anyone because I didn't remember.' He waved his arms in the air in frustration. 'By the time I *did* remember what had happened, I'd already served over a year of my sentence. The amnesia was so bad I couldn't remember my own name at first, didn't recognize my mother, couldn't hear what people were saying to me. The memory started to come back slowly, but it was very patchy. I'd even forgotten about us. I only remembered about you and me being lovers when I saw a book in the prison library called *Uncle Tom's Cabin*. Apparently, this little man was born around the time I was being shown my home in a cell at Preston Prison, but if I'd been told, it would have meant nothing. It was only when my mother visited me a good while later that she told me about Noel. But even then, it was as if all that had happened to someone else.'

Although Tiff accepted much of what Craig had told her, she still had reservations. 'What about the other evidence, though?'

'I have no idea how that happened. But one thing I am certain of, I didn't own that car when it was seen outside your brother's place. I'd even surrendered the tenancy on the lockup garage because I thought with the money I'd won we could find somewhere more suitable to live, and perhaps more convenient, once I'd got another job.'

Tiff bit her bottom lip, deep in thought. 'So you're saying that someone went to a lot of trouble to frame you. But if you were being set up, how did they do it? Why lie to me? What was in it for them?'

Craig sat on the sofa, his head in his hands, as he tried to work out what had happened. Eventually, he looked up, his expression a sombre mixture of surprise and acceptance. 'I think I'm beginning to work it out. Let's say, for a minute, that I believe you didn't grass me up, or place that stolen gear in my lockup.'

Craig began to enumerate every point on his fingers. 'The police told me it was you. They went as far as giving your name, taunting me, telling me even you didn't believe in me. I hadn't mentioned you, because at that time I couldn't remember you, so how did they know it? Unless someone lied to them, like they did to you. If the informant was a woman, someone who knew about the lockup, I'd be bound to think it was you. Someone not only went to a lot of trouble to frame me, they also wanted me to believe that the girl I loved and trusted, the girl who was carrying our child, had betrayed me for no reason. That didn't matter, because of my amnesia. Even if you'd confronted me, and given me a chance to challenge it, I could hardly deny it if I had no memory. I suppose a lot of people thought I must be guilty because I didn't put up a defence.'

Craig paused and then told Tiff what she thought was the cruellest part of everything he'd suffered. 'The truth was, I couldn't offer any defence, because even *I* was uncertain as to whether I'd done it or not.'

Craig stared at Tiff for a long time and as she returned his gaze questioningly, he continued, 'Couple those two huge lies with the fact that someone else had access to my car. They parked it in front of Bobby's house, so that the milkman, and the guy delivering papers, were sure to remember it, and that made the story more convincing.'

'Are you saying these people conspired to make me believe you were having it off with Bobby's wife? Don't you think that sounds farfetched?'

'I don't understand why they did it. But I never went near Bobby's wife. And one thing I know for certain is, when they saw my car parked outside Bobby's house, they were wrong. I can prove I no longer had the car. All I have to do is get the sales receipt. It's still in my room at Mum's, I'll bet.' He paused, then added, 'Oh, God, I've just thought of something else.'

'What?'

'When I gave notice on the lockup, I'd cleared it and handed the key back to the council.'

# CHAPTER NINETEEN

Along with the other facts Craig had given her, the tiny detail about the lockup was sufficient to convince Tiff he was telling the truth. Any last remaining doubt was dismissed by the image she retained of Craig's shocked, horrified, and unmistakeably genuine reaction to the news of the Wintersett Grange murders. There was no way even the most consummately superb actor could have faked that — and Craig was certainly not capable of hiding his feelings to such an extent.

Tiff began to cry, softly at first then more copiously as she saw Craig's expression of doubt. 'I'm sorry,' she hiccupped through her tears, 'sorry I didn't trust you. I should have known better — known you weren't capable of such horrible things.'

It was as hard for Craig to accept that Tiff wasn't the one responsible for betraying him, as it had been for her to accept his innocence. He knew he had to demonstrate he believed in her. 'Someone went to a lot of trouble to convince you. I don't know who, or why, someone hates me that much, but when I catch up with them I'll ensure they regret it — and this time I might be guilty of murder, for taking the girl I love from me.'

Tiff grabbed his arm. 'No, Craig, please, you mustn't do anything like that. Now that I know the truth, or part of it, can't we start again? If we do that, and if we face things together and show them, whoever they are, that their scheming hasn't worked, that will be the best way to get revenge.'

'That's going to be difficult, if I'm locked away and you're at the other side of the world.'

'I don't . . . I haven't actually decided to go. My sister offered, and I was so miserable I was prepared to accept, but now I'd rather stay here and fight this with you.'

'I don't know, Tiff, maybe it would be better if you went. I don't think I'll ever be able to convince the police that I'm innocent, and you'll be better off out of it.'

'No, Craig, I'm not having that. I want to stand along-side you and help. Even if you go back to prison, you'll have my support. The thing is, the longer you stay out, the better your chance of finding a way to tell your side of the story. You need a breathing space, and that means finding some-where safe to stay. Somewhere the police won't look for you and where you'll be warm and well fed.'

Craig shrugged his shoulders in despair. 'Where can I go? The obvious place would be my mother's, but that's the first place they'll look. In fact, they've probably already searched there.'

'They have. And there's a patrol car parked by her gate.'

She took a deep breath. Although she didn't realize it, what she was about to say would be a life-changing decision, for her, for Craig and for Noel.

'You could stay here if you want.' She made the offer without any inflexion in her voice that signified emotion or enthusiasm.

'Won't they think this is an obvious place to look?'

Tiff gave a twisted smile. 'They've already been. And if they've spoken to your mother, they'll know the way I've been bad-mouthing you since you were arrested. I told them there was no way I wanted anything to do with you, so I don't think they'll come back. They might suspect me if your body was found in the back garden with a dozen stab wounds, but they certainly wouldn't believe I'd allow you to stay here.'

'It's a great offer, Tiff, but what if they *did* find me here? You'd be in trouble, and that would mean Noel would be taken into care. And it would mean saying goodbye to any plans to go to Australia. If you've been in trouble, they won't let you in.'

'If we have to, I think we can get round the problem with Noel. We could fix it so that your mother was given alternative custody. If they knew that, they'd hardly be likely to take him away for some complete stranger to have control of him. Besides, if you stay here, you'll get to spend some time with him. I owe you that, having missed so much already.'

He looked at his son, who had given up hope of more maternal cuddles and was asleep. Craig was still undecided when Tiff tightened her grip on his arm slightly. 'Apart from that, I'd like you to stay,' she told him.

This time there was plenty of emotion in her voice. Craig looked into her eyes and said, 'What about Australia?'

'If you don't want us to go, then we won't. I only agreed because I was angry about the way I thought you'd let me down, and I wanted to be away from all the bad memories.'

Craig saw the tears trickling down her cheeks. He wiped them away gently. 'Hey, Tiff, please don't cry. We'll sort something out.' Even as he said it, Craig wondered if there was a realistic chance that they could find a solution.

He put his arms around her, a gesture of comfort, no more. After a moment, Tiff pulled away slightly. 'If you are going to hide out here, there is something I insist you do immediately.'

He frowned, puzzled by her statement. 'What's that?'

'You must take a long hot shower. While you're doing that, I'll stick your clothes into the washing machine.'

'Do I stink?' Craig had become accustomed to going unwashed.

'It is a bit noticeable now that you've warmed up.'

'I haven't anything else to wear.'

'You can borrow my dressing gown for tonight. I'll put your stuff into the tumble drier, and it'll be ready for you by morning. While you're showering, I'll make you something to eat. You must be starving.'

\* \* \*

Once Craig had finished in the bathroom, and eaten the meal Tiff had prepared, it was late evening. If the food and shower hadn't erased the perilous predicament he faced, it had pushed it to the back of his mind, at least for the time being. He was even able to sit in comfort on the sofa, having helped to bath his son, and cuddled him until the infant fell asleep. This, in turn, caused Craig to doze off.

Tiff watched in amusement as father and son snored gently in harmony. After a few moments, she reached for her mobile. The image of Craig, his long beard giving him the appearance of a trainee Santa Claus, clad in a bright pink floral dressing gown, cuddling Noel, who was attired in equally vivid dinosaur pyjamas, was too good to miss.

After watching them for a few more minutes, and with a degree of reluctance, Tiff woke Craig and lifted Noel from his arms. 'I'm not sure what hours you keep in Felling Prison,' she told him, 'but it's way past this one's bedtime.'

Craig yawned. 'Sorry,' he mumbled, 'I'm a bit flaked out. Have you a spare blanket?'

'What for?'

'For me: to doss down on the sofa.'

Tiff looked at Craig for a while, remembering that moment after he burst in the flat, and his reaction when she tried to attack him. His face might have been filled with anger and bitterness, but as his body pressed against hers, she'd felt his arousal.

'You can sleep on the sofa if you want, but the bed's more comfortable.'

Craig looked at her, hope and disbelief mingled. Tiff grasped Noel in one arm, while holding her other hand out to the boy's father. 'Come on, Craig. This might be the only chance we have to be together before they haul you back inside. Let's make the most of it. Not that we'll get much sleep.'

He began to smile, but Tiff told him, 'Don't get your hopes up, I didn't mean that the way you thought. Noel's teething, so he wakes up every two hours and needs comforting. Actually, seeing you're here, you can take your turn looking after him.'

If anything, Craig's smile widened. He hugged Tiff and whispered, 'That's OK by me. I was beginning to think I'd never have the chance.'

\* \* \*

In Smelt Mill Cottage, the phone beside Nash's bed rang. He realized that the configuration of the furniture would have to be changed. The position of the handset had never been important when he was alone. As Alondra picked up the receiver, Nash shook off the last remnants of sleep, in time to hear her say, 'Yes, of course he's here, Sergeant, where else would he be at this time of night? Hang on, I'll get him for you.'

She was smiling as she passed the phone across, and mouthed, 'Sergeant Binns.'

There was no humour in the message Binns had for him. 'Message from control. It looks as if French has struck again, but this time he was disturbed before he could get away with the loot. Sadly, despite the house-owner making a treble nine call, our guys didn't arrive in time to save her from being killed.'

'Did they catch the intruder?'

'No, but it must have been close. Apparently, the victim had installed an alarm with vibrate mode fitted, and that woke her. She made the call, but didn't have a chance to escape.'

'Where was this?'

160

'Kirk Bolton Hall. Clara's already en route. I rang her first because she's on the duty roster, but she asked me to phone you and disturb your sleep.'

'Thanks, Jack, I'll be on my way as soon as I can. Have you alerted Mexican Pete?'

'I have, and luckily, unlike some around here, I don't speak Spanish, so I didn't understand what he was saying.'

'*Adiós*, Jack.'

As Nash was dressing, he explained the reason for the callout. It was then that he remembered her smile. 'What were you laughing about when you passed me the phone?'

'Oh, I nearly told Sergeant Binns that I would rouse you, but I thought he might take that the wrong way. My English is not perfect.'

Nash grinned. 'Very sensible — knowing Jack's dirty mind.'

'This murder you're going to investigate, is it that man French again?'

'Possibly, but maybe not.' He saw Alondra's puzzled frown and added, 'The MO sounds identical.'

'MO, what is MO?'

Nash smiled, as he struggled into his trousers. '*Modus operandi*. It means everything is done the same way. But I'm not convinced that French has killed anybody.'

Alondra snuggled back on the bed and murmured, 'One thing I do know, Mike, if anyone is capable of getting to the truth, it is you.'

'Thanks for the vote of confidence.' He leaned over and kissed her cheek. 'At least when I get back, I won't be returning to an empty house or a cold bed.'

Downstairs, Teal came to greet him, but soon sensed that it wasn't time for a walk, or to be fed. Nash stroked the dog's head and told her, 'I'm leaving you on guard duty, so keep your eyes and ears open, and protect your mistress, OK?'

\* \* \*

The crime scene looked depressingly familiar, Nash thought, as he donned his protective clothing and entered the house. He noted the trail of muddy footprints crossing the kitchen and was about to examine the evidence strewn across the floor when Clara summoned him. On visiting the bedroom, he noted the victim had obviously been interrupted in the process of making a phone call, as the receiver was next to her hand. 'Did the operator say if the call was terminated abruptly?'

Clara nodded. 'Yes, that was the first thing I asked, and they said the woman gave the address, mentioned her alarm going off, but then she stopped speaking, screamed and uttered one word that sounded like "you", before the line went dead.'

'That sounds as if she recognized the intruder. I don't think we can do much more in here. This is obviously the same killer as at Wintersett Grange. The injuries are identical, even down to the trademark letter F, don't you agree?'

'I do.'

'Let's go back the kitchen and look at what's there.'

The items they saw suggested that the treble nine call, and the sound of the approaching patrol cars' sirens, had panicked the killer. This seemed obvious because of the smashed wooden box on the tiled floor. The array of jewel-encrusted bracelets, necklaces, and earrings suggested that the burglar had dropped his spoils in his panic to escape.

As they surveyed the evidence, Clara filled him in with what she knew about the victim. 'Her name is Alison Stokes. She bought this house approximately nine months ago.'

'Is she married, or in a relationship?'

'She's single, but I believe she had a lady-friend who visited here occasionally.'

'By lady-friend, I assume you mean, er . . . ?' Nash struggled to find the politically correct term.

Clara nodded. 'I checked the victim's mobile phone, and judging by the texts, I'd say they were extremely "er". The woman's name is Hilary Bennett, and she's due to visit

Ms Stokes this weekend. All I've managed to discover is that she's about forty to fifty years old, and drives a Volvo.'

'That's not too helpful. Almost every other car round here is a Volvo.' Nash eyed his subordinate and then suggested, 'That is either astonishingly good detective work, or you had the benefit of someone with local knowledge.'

Clara smiled. 'One of the patrol officers lives in Kirk Bolton, and his wife runs the village shop. Those places are a rich source of gossip. He even mentioned your change of domestic circumstances.'

Nash seemed unfazed by being the subject of local tittle-tattle. He listened as Clara continued, 'There is one more piece of information I culled from the paperwork on the desk in the study. Apparently, the alarm the intruder triggered was fitted by our friend Jimmy Johnson only a few days ago. The invoice and receipt were on top of the pile. Sadly, though, the alarm wasn't sufficient to save Alison's life.'

'No, but it might still be worth paying Jimmy a visit. He might have more to tell us. Will you pop in and talk to him?'

Clara agreed, always happy to chat to Johnson. He had once been instrumental in saving Clara's life, and on a later occasion, the system he'd installed at Smelt Mill Cottage had provided a vital clue to help Nash solve another mystery.

'One more thing,' Nash said. 'Try and contact the friend, Ms Bennett. We don't want her turning up on the doorstep for a romantic weekend and finding a crime scene. We also need to interview her, and find out what she can tell us about the victim. If there's no family, we'll ask her to conduct a formal identification.'

Having briefed CSI, and withstood a barrage of sarcastic comments from the pathologist, Nash and Clara decided there was nothing further they could do on site. 'I'll bring Viv up to speed when he arrives. And I'll brief Superintendent Edwards first thing — no point having the entire force awake. Can you drop in on Jimmy before coming to the station in the morning?' Nash asked.

Clara agreed and left.

After handing the crime scene over to Viv, Nash was about to depart when he remembered something. He turned to one of the forensic team and asked if they would ensure that the size of the footprints on the kitchen floor was recorded.

The officer with several years' experience in the force nodded. 'Certainly, sir. I would never have thought of that.'

Nash shook his head. 'Sorry, I wasn't thinking straight — too many murders, and too many late nights.'

He returned home, to be greeted enthusiastically by Teal, and then drowsily by Alondra. He found sleep difficult to come by, the memory of the horror he'd just witnessed still too fresh in his mind. What sickened him most was the senseless brutality of the crime, and the motive for the murder. The sordid greed had proved futile when the killer had escaped empty-handed.

# CHAPTER TWENTY

Although it was too early for the Kirk Bolton murder to have reached the media, breaking news the following morning was equally dramatic. The streamer flashing across TV screens during the bulletins matched the headlines in many of the papers. Under the banner '*Lumberjacks' Grim Find*', the story recounted the discovery of charred human remains. Alongside this account was an assertion that was equally startling in its impact, and was newsworthy enough to merit another headline, '*Cabin Corpse: Could Killer Be Craig French?*'

Reading that section, it became apparent that the foreman of the logging crew had overheard the forensic officer's reference to the fingerprints found in the privy. Alternatively, one of the force had spoken out of turn. Although totally unconfirmed, the hearsay was enough for the media to descend on the titbit like a pack of ravening wolves.

Nash heard the story on the radio as he was driving to Helmsdale. Before leaving home, he'd briefed Ruth Edwards on the Kirk Bolton murder. The acting chief constable had responded by shelving her plans for the morning, saying she intended to hold a crisis meeting with her team of detectives instead.

'One more thing,' Nash said before ending the call, 'obviously it was too late to do anything last night, but we need to arrange an interview with the victim's girlfriend. Clara's going to try and contact her this morning. All we know about her so far is that her name is Hilary Bennett and that she drives a Volvo. Thankfully, we have her mobile number. We don't want her to hear about this on a news bulletin. It's going to be bad enough in any case, without learning what's happened third-hand.'

When he arrived at the station, Nash found Lisa and Viv's cars were already there. As he pulled into the car park he was followed by Clara, who accompanied him into the building, their progress slow as she told him of her talk with Jimmy Johnson, the security specialist.

'He couldn't add anything to what we already know, except that his work at the house wasn't finished. Ms Stokes had ordered CCTV, but sadly Jimmy hadn't all the equipment in stock. It was due to be fitted as soon as it arrived.'

'That's a shame — if it had been operational, we might have been able to identify the killer.'

Pausing only to forewarn Jack Binns of Superintendent Edwards' imminent arrival, they went up to the CID suite where Lisa greeted them with the news, 'Mexican Pete's been on the phone already. He wants you to ring him back the minute you get here. He said it was extremely urgent.'

Nash raised his eyebrows. 'Urgent? It's probably only to schedule the post-mortem on last night's victim.'

However, when Nash returned the call, he discovered that the subject Ramirez wanted to discuss was far from routine. Nash was still pondering the information from the pathologist when Superintendent Edwards arrived.

Whatever Ruth's expectations were, the outcome of the meeting was far different.

She opened with a definitive statement of the current situation. 'The problem seems straightforward. If Craig French committed the murders at Wintersett Grange and Kirk Bolton Hall, whose is the body found in the cabin?

Alternatively, if that corpse does turn out to be French, we're faced with the dilemma that someone else committed these murders, and likewise, the killings for which French was convicted. I'm not sure which of the two I favour, so I'd welcome any constructive ideas.'

'I don't think it's quite that easy,' Nash responded, 'because there is a third option. I've just taken a phone call from Mexican Pete. There's a DNA match. The body in the cabin definitely isn't French. It's a homeless, habitual drug addict, who has multiple convictions for a range of drug offences, shoplifting and petty theft.'

'Well, that seems to confirm my first option, that Craig French is the murderer. He could have also killed this drug addict, although the motive isn't clear.'

'Not necessarily, ma'am. If French *didn't* commit the Cumbria murders, then he is equally innocent of the more recent crimes. I question how French would know there was expensive jewellery in that Silloth house. Equally, how did he know that Wintersett Grange was occupied? When he was imprisoned, the Grange was empty, had been for several years. Not only that, but after he supposedly committed the robbery in Cumbria, what did he do with all the expensive jewellery? Where are the paintings? If he sold everything, where's all the money?'

'I suppose there must be a logical explanation, if we look hard enough.'

'There is the point I believe everyone connected to the original inquiry overlooked. We also overlooked it, but luckily Clara discovered the vital piece of evidence.'

'What, the wet wipe thing?'

'Yes. What everyone missed, including me, is the significance of that action.' Nash provided further ammunition. 'I told you I checked the file on Bobby Walker's burglary convictions and discovered that the items recovered from his house bore the same chemical traces — and a similar lack of fingerprints. I also find it significant, that in both instances it was a woman who informed the police where the stolen goods were located. In French's case, she claimed to be his ex-girlfriend, but when the woman told police about Bobby Walker, she didn't give a name. When Clara and Lisa visited the ex-girlfriend, she denied having been the person who grassed on French.

'I firmly believe that Craig French was framed for robbery and murder, and Bobby Walker framed for burglary. I also find it pertinent that no similar offences took place during the time French was incarcerated, but almost as soon as he escaped, the killing spree began again. I believe the real murderer was free to resume his activities, confident that with French on the run, he would be saddled with the blame. The natural assumption would be that French had returned to his old ways. I think that is what we were intended to believe.'

Nash paused, but only for breath, it seemed. 'There is another point to consider. How did French get those items into his lockup garage, when he had surrendered the key to the building a month before they were stolen? And what still puzzles me, apart from the identity of the killer, is how that killer could be sure that French wouldn't be arrested before one of the more recent burglaries took place.'

As Nash finished speaking, he glanced down at his jotter. He barely heard Ruth say, 'Well, that's certainly put the cat amongst the pigeons, Mike. I think I need time and caffeine to digest all that. Would you make coffee for all of us, Clara? On second thoughts,' she added hastily, 'perhaps it would be better if Viv makes it.'

Clara was too preoccupied to notice the implicit slur on her coffee-making ability. She was watching Nash, having seen the distant expression on his face, and wondering what line of thought he was following now. What had provoked it, and where it would lead?

Ruth also noticed Nash's abstraction and knew him well enough not to interrupt. It was only when Pearce returned with coffee and biscuits that Nash looked up and said, 'I have an idea.'

'Is that all?' Clara asked, sarcastically. 'You went so broody I thought you were about to lay an egg.'

Although he smiled faintly, Nash ignored her interjection. 'What if the killer knew French had been using the cabin, and believed him to be the occupant when he torched it? If the fire was set at night, he wouldn't be able to see the person inside clearly enough to make a positive identification. If he believed French was dead, and his body would remain undiscovered for weeks, possibly months, he would think he'd got the perfect scapegoat. The killer would probably have been unaware that there was logging activity taking place nearby. Had it not been for the heavy rain, the lumberjacks would have discovered the body sooner, and the killer might have been unable to blame French for his handiwork — and three more people would be alive.'

There was a long silence as they pondered Nash's theory. Eventually, Mironova responded. 'That implies the killer knew French well enough to work out where he was, which suggests someone close to him. Perhaps French even made contact after escaping from prison, pleading for help, or a place to hide. Alternatively, he could have told the killer where he was heading.'

'We can't be certain, but I'm determined to find out, because I believe that Craig French is both an extremely unlucky, and very fortunate, young man.'

'Make your mind up. Which is it?' Ruth asked.

'Both, I think. He was unfortunate to have been convicted in the first instance. But then he was lucky that he wasn't the occupant of the cabin when the arson attack took place.'

Ruth Edwards shook her head and sighed. 'I admit that everything you've suggested is feasible, but without firm evidence to back it, this is nothing more than a theory, and it begs the question, where do we go from here?'

'I know where I'm going,' Nash replied instantly. 'I need to visit Brenda French. Clara, you're with me, get your coat. I think she needs to be told that it wasn't her only child who got burnt to death.'

'Before we go, Mike, I managed to get hold of the latest victim's girlfriend, Hilary Bennett, earlier this morning, before she left for work. She works as a "commodities broker", whatever that means. At present she's in London, but she's driving straight here. I've arranged for her to meet us at the Golden Bear in Netherdale later today. I thought it would be less upsetting than at the station.'

'That's very thoughtful.'

They were about to leave when Nash asked, 'Did you authorize the search of Brenda French's house, ma'am? She told me the police had been round, but I didn't apply for a search warrant.'

Edwards smiled wryly. 'I did. Standard procedure — and that was when everyone was convinced that her son was a latter-day Jack the Ripper.'

'I think it would have proved French's stupidity had he been found there, knowing that would be the first place we'd look.' Nash then issued instructions to his colleagues. 'Viv, would you open a file on this new murder? Then go back to Kirk Bolton Hall and liaise with Forensics. We need to know when they'll be finished so we can inform the victim's partner she can have access. Lisa, I'd like you to follow up on that puppy farming case. Talk to Faith Parsons, the vet, again.'

'And what about me, boss?' Ruth asked, mockingly.

Nash grinned and waved as he left. 'The coffee mugs need washing.'

* * *

Earlier that morning, Tiff and Craig had been discussing the best way to tackle their appalling dilemma. Now that Tiff was certain Craig hadn't committed any murders, robberies, or been unfaithful to her, she was determined to prevent him suffering further anguish. Last night had shown the depth of his feelings for her, and she knew they had something worth fighting for.

To try to clear Craig's name, they would need any help they could get. First, they would have to ensure he remained out of the police's clutches. Equally important was the recruitment of a strong ally and in Tiff's mind, only one person fitted that bill.

'We should tell your mother where you are and what we've found out,' she suggested.

'Is that wise? She hates you — she might turn nasty.'

'The only reason Brenda hates me is because she thinks I betrayed you. Once I've put her straight on that, and told her I believe you're innocent, things will be easier.'

'How will you do it? You can't phone her. Mum's phone might be tapped. Police are looking for me everywhere, so it stands to reason they'd be listening in.'

'They're not looking for you here, and that's another reason for me to talk to Brenda. If I tell her what's going on, I'll suggest we have a massive slanging match in public, then she can go spouting off about me. That might get back to the police. If she lets everyone how much I detest you, it should put them off the scent.'

'OK, but how will you contact her?'

'If you look after Noel, I'll nip round now.'

Ten minutes later, Tiff set off to Brenda French's house. She waited on the doorstep, pretending to lock the door until she heard Craig slide the bolt, then peered round the corner of the flats to see if anyone was around. She was within a hundred yards of her objective, when a car passed her and stopped. Range Rovers are not unknown on the Westlea, but they are uncommon enough to attract curiosity. As Tiff stared at the vehicle, the occupants stepped out. She recognized the man who emerged from the driver's seat. She'd seen his photo in the papers often, and recently she'd watched him on television. It had been his doubts, expressed during the media conference, that had been the first indication that someone believed Craig to be innocent. Despite that, Tiff dare not risk encountering him. She turned abruptly and retraced her steps.

On reaching the flat she gave the pre-arranged signal. She waited for what seemed an age until Craig opened the door, hiding behind the wooden framework until she was inside.

'Was Mum out?' Craig asked.

'No, but she had visitors. One was that copper — Nash, I think his name is. He's the one who thinks you might be innocent, but I daren't risk him finding out you're here.'

* * *

It was a while before Nash's knock was answered and he was surprised to see a man standing in the doorway. 'This is a very bad time,' he told the detectives. 'Mrs French has just had some terrible news.'

'I know that,' Nash replied, and showed his warrant card. 'Who are you?'

The man introduced himself as Brenda's neighbour. 'We came round as soon as we saw the TV bulletin about Craig. My wife's with Brenda now.' He stepped aside and invited them in.

On entering the sitting room he saw Brenda on the sofa, holding a handkerchief across her face in a vain attempt to stem the tears that were coursing down her face. He turned to the neighbour. 'I'm sorry, but I need to speak to Mrs French, alone.'

The man looked at his wife, who shook her head.

'No, I'm not leaving. Can't you see I'm comforting my friend?'

'That's as may be, but as I said, I need to speak to her — alone. My colleague will attend to Mrs French.'

The woman glared at Nash, as she stood to leave. 'Don't you worry, Brenda. I'll come back round when this . . . this . . . person has gone.' With that she turned, grabbed her husband by the arm, and stormed out of the house.

Nash turned his attention to the distraught woman, as Clara sat beside her and put her arm gently round Brenda's shoulders.

Nash crouched in front of them. 'The TV got it wrong,' he said, speaking slowly and distinctly. 'The body in that cabin isn't Craig.'

His words made no impression, so he tried speaking even slower and louder, 'Brenda, listen to me. It's DI Nash, and you don't need to cry.' He looked at Clara for support.

'Mrs French, Brenda.' Clara shook her gently. 'Stop crying and listen to what he has to say.'

Nash tried again. 'I had news from our pathologist this morning, and that's why I came straight round. DNA tests prove beyond doubt that the dead man is a known drug addict and petty thief. It's *definitely* not Craig.'

Brenda lowered the handkerchief and stared at Nash, her expression changing as she saw the smile on his face. Her first words surprised him. 'You came here immediately you knew? Really? That was considerate. Thank you, Mr Nash. Thank you, thank you, thank you.'

'Clara, perhaps you should make Brenda a cup of tea while I have a word.' He indicated the kitchen with a nod of his head, then broached the secondary reason for his visit. 'Don't worry,' he reassured her, 'it's nothing to fret about. I need your help, that's all.'

He sat down opposite Craig's mother, looked into her eyes, bloodshot and red-rimmed from crying, and smiled again. 'The confusion came about because we know Craig *had* been there. A fingerprint matching his was found, and that led to many of us jumping to the wrong conclusion. However, there is no way the DNA could be wrong, which is good news for you. That was the main reason for our visit, but we also need as much background as possible about Craig. We want to prove he didn't commit the crimes he's been accused of. Not only do we believe Craig to be innocent, we are also convinced that someone went to extreme lengths to frame him for all five murders.'

'You mean four murders, don't you?'

Nash sighed. 'I'm sure you'll hear this on the news soon. There was another murder last night.'

Mrs French looked shocked. 'Another one?'

Nash nodded. 'Do you have any idea who hates Craig so much that they set out to ruin his life?'

There was a long silence as Brenda pondered Nash's question. 'I've no idea, Mr Nash. I can't think of anyone who would want to hurt him, but then, I couldn't believe him guilty of anything so evil.' She paused and looked at the detective, searching for clues as to how his mind was working, and then asked, 'Do you have children?'

'I have a son. He's eleven years old.'

'I'm sure you've brought him up to respect right and wrong, just as I raised Craig to respect other people and their property. We might not be well off, but we've never resorted to stealing, or violence. Just because we live on a council estate, maybe everyone here gets tarred with the same brush.'

Nash sensed that Brenda was in danger of becoming depressed by her son's predicament and changed the subject slightly. 'What about this woman who informed on him?'

'Tiff Walker? She's a little bitch. I thought she was a really nice girl, and I was glad she and Craig were together because they seemed so right for one another. But I was wrong about her. Why she did that, I've no idea. The only good thing I know about her now is that she's given me a grandson — or it would be, if she ever allowed me to see the poor little mite.'

'Are you certain she was the one who informed on him? Because we have our doubts on that score, too. It seemed curious from reading the file that she rang the Cumbria police, rather than our local force. And she also made a point of giving her name — almost as if she was trying to ensure that Craig knew it was her.'

'Oh, she denied it, all right. When I confronted her, it led to some harsh words. After Craig was arrested and his memory started to return, he said the police told him it was Tiff who'd grassed him up. I told her a few home truths, and I've never spoken to the little cow since.'

'When I read the police report, it seemed as if she was trying to hurt him — twisting the knife in the wound, you could say.' Nash stopped speaking and Brenda watched, wondering what the detective was thinking.

'You mentioned your grandson. How old is he?'

'Noel is eighteen months old. Craig was already in prison when he was born, so he's never seen so much as a photo of his little boy.'

'Did Craig know she was pregnant? Before the accident, I mean? Was he looking forward to becoming a father?'

'I'll say so. In fact they were both very excited by the idea. Craig's only concern was trying to get a job so he could support a family. He hadn't been lucky work-wise after he got made redundant, so money was very tight.'

'Was that why he sold his car?' Nash's question seemed little more than a throwaway comment.

'Yes, he wanted to surprise Tiff with some nice baby stuff, a pram, and a cot, you know. He had some money left over from the sale of the car when he'd settled the HP. But it was nowhere near the amount they found in the loft.' She shook her head. 'I don't know where that came from.'

The cup of tea was passed to her as Nash got to his feet. 'Thank you for your time; you've been extremely helpful. I'm glad to be the bearer of good news. Too often we have to tell people the last thing they want to hear, so it's nice to do something different.'

Mrs French nodded, and smiled at Clara. 'You've both been very kind.'

'There is one more thing, if you *should* happen to hear from Craig, I'd be keen to know the answer to one question.'

He saw her guarded expression and held up his hand. 'I'm not trying to trap him. It would be handy if Craig had a cast-iron alibi for the time these new murders were committed, but I guess that won't be feasible as he's in hiding. Failing that, I wish I knew where that money came from, even if it's something illegal — that wouldn't matter. If you come up with anything, you've already got my card and mobile number. One more thing — the last part of this conversation never took place, OK?'

# CHAPTER TWENTY-ONE

Tiff had only been back in the flat for half an hour when her mobile buzzed, signalling an incoming text. 'It's from your mother.' She showed it to Craig.

'Need to talk about C,' it read. He frowned. 'I thought you weren't speaking. Do you reckon it's to do with that copper you saw at her place?'

'It must be. She hasn't said a word to me in months, although she's been bad-mouthing me all over the place. Now this, all of a sudden.'

'Do you think it's safe to go? It might be a trap. That copper could be waiting.'

'If he'd wanted to trap me, he wouldn't have driven up in a Range Rover. They're about as common as rocking-horse droppings round here. In any case, the way Brenda thinks about me, there's no way she'll suspect you're hiding here. Still, let's play safe, shall we?'

She reclaimed her mobile and typed a text that read simply 'Are you alone?'

Seconds later, the reply came in. 'I am now. Coppers here earlier. Came to tell me C isn't dead.'

'What does that mean? Why would Mum think I'm dead?'

'I've no idea, but there's one way to find out.'

Tiff sent a text telling Brenda she was on her way and then picked up her coat. Craig stopped her. 'Hang on. You'd better take Noel with you. We should have thought of that before. If anyone sees you without him, they'd wonder where he is, and who's looking after him. Hopefully, you weren't spotted last time.'

It made sense, and Tiff's departure was delayed while they togged up the little boy. After he locked the door behind them, Craig wandered through the flat. He was restless, his fear of discovery returning in full measure without Tiff and Noel there. To distract his mind, he switched on the TV to catch the news bulletin. What he saw and heard shocked him to the core. It was a long while before he was able to make sense of what the report implied.

* * *

On hearing Tiff's knock, Brenda tried to remain calm, and hoped she'd be able to keep her feelings under control. The antipathy she felt towards the girl she believed had let Craig down mustn't intrude, because that might impede the attempt to obtain vital information.

She was surprised when she opened the door to find Tiff smiling at her, albeit with a trace of nervousness.

'Come in,' Brenda greeted her curtly, including her grandson in the invitation.

'Let's get one thing straight,' Tiff said, once the door closed. 'I love Craig and I didn't betray him. And I also know he didn't commit those four murders.'

Brenda blinked with surprise. 'Then why did the police tell Craig it was you? Where did they get your name, if you didn't contact them?'

'Because they were lied to, just as I was lied to. I didn't know about the stuff in the lockup. Even though I believed he was screwing Bobby's wife, I wouldn't have grassed. But I know now, that wasn't true either.'

Brenda listened as Tiff revealed what she knew, and after a while came to the obvious conclusion. 'You've spoken to him, haven't you? And recently, that's why you weren't worried by that news report suggesting he was dead.'

It was Tiff's turn to be surprised, and the shock increased when Brenda told her about the body found in the cabin.

'Craig did stay there for a while,' she replied at last. 'But he moved on before the fire. He's safe and well.'

Brenda eyed her, suspiciously. 'You've not just spoken. You've seen him!'

Tiff glanced round, half expecting to see uniformed police officers lurking in the corners, then whispered. 'He's at my place. He sends his love, and says he's sorry for the trouble he's caused.'

Brenda sank down on the sofa with relief. Then she asked, with no inflexion in her voice, 'Staying at your place, does that mean . . . ?'

Tiff blushed, and then lifted her head defiantly. 'It means we're together again, and this time, no lies or deceit will keep us apart. So heaven help anyone who gets in our way.'

Brenda leapt up and hugged Tiff, before scooping up her grandson, who was making a determined effort to upend the coffee table. 'Good one, Tiff,' she responded. 'But there's one big problem — we need to prove Craig is innocent.'

'I know, and it was bad enough when there were two murders, but now they think he committed two more.'

'There have been five murders in total,' Brenda corrected her. Seeing Tiff's shocked expression she explained. 'The latest one hasn't been on the news yet. It happened last night. Inspector Nash told me about it. He said it was identical to the others. He came to reassure me that Craig hadn't been killed in that cabin fire, and also to say he wanted information to clear Craig's name. He's convinced he's innocent, Tiff. Nash is a really nice bloke — for a copper.'

As Brenda explained more about the detective's visit, neither she nor Tiff were aware that although she'd adjusted the tally of murders from four to five, even that total was inaccurate.

* * *

When Tiff returned to the flat, she was surprised to see Craig's sombre expression. No sooner had he locked the door than he asked, 'Did you tell anybody about the cabin? Did you say that might be where I was hiding out?'

'No, of course I. . .' Tiff's voice tailed off as her memory cleared and she remembered her visitor. 'Hang on. There *was* someone who asked me. Is it important? Your mum told me about a body they thought might be yours, but I knew it couldn't be, so I didn't take it all in.'

'I've just seen it on the news. It's really weird hearing people talking about you as if you're dead, but if people think I'm a goner, they won't be hunting me. Now tell me who it was you mentioned the cabin to?'

Tiff told him, and saw Craig's face whiten with shock. It was a moment before he recovered sufficiently to speak. 'I wasn't inside the cabin when it was set on fire — but I'm bloody sure I was intended to be. I was meant to die in that fire.'

'How can you be sure of that? Isn't it possible that it was an accident?'

'No bloody way was it an accident. You want proof? Listen to this.' Craig told her what he'd seen in Thornscarr Forest, and her shocked expression was sufficient for him to know she believed him.

The only question she asked was one he couldn't answer at that point. 'I accept everything you said, but why? What motive would they have for doing that to you?'

'I've no idea. Just as I haven't a clue who committed those four murders. All I am certain of, is I didn't kill anyone.'

'It's five murders, not four.' Tiff repeated what Brenda had learned from Nash and saw Craig's expression change to one of frustration.

179

He threw his hands up in despair. 'And again, I have no alibi. I don't think they'd accept your word I was here all night.'

News of the Kirk Bolton Hall murder didn't reach the media until later that day, but it was the lead story on the main bulletins. A reporter, standing in front of the wrought-iron gates of the Hall with the Georgian building's facade in the background, told the anchor in the studio of some confusion.

Tiff heard the newsman say, 'Despite earlier reports that a body found in Thornscarr was suspected to be Craig French, it would appear the killer has struck again.' He went on to report the victim's desperate appeal for help — help that didn't arrive in time to save her life. When the reporter mentioned the time the police received the treble nine call, Tiff stared at the screen in disbelief.

She walked over to the table, picked up her mobile, and checked the screen. She turned to Craig and smiled. 'Look at this.'

Craig saw her excited expression, and glanced at the image on the screen. 'I didn't know you'd taken that. What's so special about it?'

Tiff pointed to the corner of the screen. 'Check that out. We should phone your mum. She told me she has Inspector Nash's business card. I think he needs to see this ASAP.'

* * *

Alondra knew immediately Mike walked into the cottage that his day had not been a good one. She waited until they had dined before she asked him what was wrong.

'It started off OK,' he told her, 'but it went downhill later. I went to visit Craig French's mother. She'd seen the report about the body in Thornscarr Forest and assumed that it was true. It was nice to be able to reassure her that the media had got it wrong.'

He saw Alondra's puzzled frown and explained, 'Someone must have overheard the conversation about

180

fingerprints at the cabin, and put two and two together. Unfortunately, their arithmetic wasn't correct, because it wasn't French who died there. Telling his mother was the good part, but this afternoon Clara and I had to interview the girlfriend of the latest victim. Dealing with bereaved family members and close friends is one of the most distressing parts of our job. And it never gets any easier, no matter how often you've done it. The woman was calm enough, given the circumstances. In fact, I was surprised how easily she took the news, but maybe she was just bottling up her emotions. She's staying in a hotel in Netherdale until we've arranged for her to make formal identification, and then she'll return to London.'

Nash frowned, and Alondra asked what was puzzling him.

'It's nothing important, but although the woman said she was from London, I thought there was a trace of a Yorkshire accent when she spoke.' He shrugged. 'Maybe it was just my imagination.'

Alondra commiserated with him, holding back from telling him her news. She'd only just finished speaking when his mobile buzzed, signalling an incoming text.

He examined it, his brow furrowed by a puzzled frown. 'That's odd,' he said, speaking as much to himself as to her. 'It's from Craig French's mother. She has some information, and is warning me to expect a text from someone else. It will contain a photo I must check carefully. What that's about I have no idea.'

Ten minutes later, the enigma was solved as he examined the second text. He looked at Alondra and she was relieved to see his delighted smile.

'This is just what I needed,' he told her. 'Sorry for disturbing our evening, but I have to deal with this immediately. Quite a few people are going to have their cages rattled tomorrow.'

He saw Alondra's look of mild disappointment, and asked if he'd upset her. 'No, don't worry about it, Mike. I have something to tell you, but it can wait until you've finished. Nothing is wrong,' she added reassuringly.

As Nash was waiting for Ruth Edwards to answer her phone, he wondered what it was that Alondra was keen to share with him. It was later, as they were getting into bed that he remembered and asked what her news was.

Alondra smiled and told him, 'I submitted photos of three landscapes for consideration by a big art gallery in New York, and this afternoon I had an email from them. They're featuring a collection of contemporary European work, and I've been asked to send all three paintings for people to view and purchase. This is a highly prestigious event. So it's an honour to have been selected.'

'That's marvellous news. Well done, darling.'

Alondra grinned. 'They've told me to have the works ready to send once they've obtained a valuation.'

She saw Mike's puzzled frown and explained, 'To cover the paintings while they're in transit and on display in the gallery, they must be insured against damage or theft. It's common practice. It was the same with my Paris exhibition. To obtain the right level of cover they need to have them valued.'

There was a short silence before Nash said, 'Of course, I should have guessed it ages ago.' He reached across and hugged her, holding her for a long moment as he kissed her. 'Thank you, darling.'

'Thank me for what?'

'Something has been puzzling me all along about those murders, and I think you've just provided me with the missing piece of the jigsaw.'

'Oh, and there I was thinking you were getting amorous.'

Nash pulled her towards him until their bodies were touching and smiled.

# CHAPTER TWENTY-TWO

The argument between Kyle and Shazza began when he told her they had all but run through the money they had stolen from Muriel Croft. As he mentioned the idea of repeating the offence once they had selected a new target, Shazza steeled herself to tell him the decision she had made — a decision that could damage their relationship, and might even end it.

'I'm not doing anything like that — ever again. I don't care whether we've got any money or not. I'm not going to put anyone else through what we did to that poor lady.'

'Oh yeah?' Kyle sneered. 'So how are we going to afford to live — or have you won the lottery and forgotten to tell me, because there's no way I'm letting you go back on the game.'

'I don't do the lottery. And I don't care whether we've got money or not. I feel safe here. I want to try and manage.'

'And what about me?'

'I want you to try as well. We've both had a lousy start in life. We've been homeless, desperate, and forced to do horrible things to survive. Being here has made me see that others don't live like us. We're not living — we're existing. It's taken me a long time to come to my senses, but since we moved here, I've felt good, protected, and I have someone I care about. If you want us to stay together, you'll go along with me.' She shrugged. 'Otherwise, we're finished.'

The immediate effect of Shazza's declaration was for Kyle to storm out of the flat, slamming the door to indicate his displeasure.

A by-product of Kyle's reaction would have repercussions on their relationship that neither of them could have foreseen, and the knock-on effect would also be felt elsewhere — and would challenge Mike Nash's disbelief in coincidence.

Kyle's decision to leave stemmed from his wish to avoid making the situation worse. As he marched towards Netherdale town centre, he seethed with anger at Shazza's unwillingness to continue their life of crime, even at the expense of their relationship. Annoyance fuelled his stride, but as he reached the market place and his temper cooled, his pace slackened. Instead of walking through the crowded centre, he opted for the back street, a small ring road used by those wishing to avoid being caught up in the tangle of traffic, ever-present on market days.

As his momentum eased, Kyle looked around, taking in surroundings that were new to him. He soon realized the small yards and empty spaces were service areas for the shops lining one side of the market place, providing delivery and parking options for the proprietors. Some of these were uni-dentifiable, but others had their names and logos displayed.

Several doors along was the yard whose sign proclaimed it to be that of Jakeman's the Jewellers. It was there Kyle saw an unusual sight, one that caused him to stop and watch what was taking place. Two large SUV type vehicles were parked side-by-side in the yard, their tailgates open, as cages were transferred from one to the other. It was the content of those cages that intrigued Kyle and provoked a sad memory.

He had always liked dogs. One of the few happy memories from his childhood stemmed from the time when his mother brought home a puppy as his Christmas present. The joy he got from his new companion was short-lived. Less than two months later, the puppy absconded from their small garden and dashed into the road, and was hit by a passing vehicle. The car driver failed to stop and it was over an hour before the dog was missed, by which time it was far too late. When Kyle returned from school and his mother broke the sad news to him, he felt that all the joy had gone from his life, as if part of him had died along with the puppy.

Kyle's dog had been a curly-haired mongrel, but those in the cages were unlike any other dog he'd seen before. Their size suggested they were no more than a few weeks old, but their scrunched-up faces gave them the appearance of grumpy old men. Kyle was puzzled by what was happening. Whatever they had planned for those puppies obviously had nothing to do with the jewellery business. When the cages had been transferred, the recipient of the nine small dogs closed the tailgate, revealing the distinctive and memorable personalised number plate. It was clearly designed to attract and retain the viewer's attention, and this certainly worked with Kyle, whose recollection of the incident remained fresh in his mind, even as he returned to the flat in order to mend fences with Shazza.

It was only when she had threatened to leave him that Kyle realized how much she had come to mean to him. If this was the only way for them to stay together, he would give it a try. Whether it would work or not was anybody's guess.

Having such a goal in mind was one thing — achieving it was quite a different matter.

\* \* \*

The following day, it was the middle of Kyle's sister's shift at Netherdale General. As usual, Vicky spent the break in the rest room alongside the ward, indulging herself with a mug of coffee. As she sipped the drink, she scanned a copy of the *Netherdale Gazette* that had been left by one of her colleagues. She had reached page five when a photograph caught and held her attention. She gasped with surprise as she read the article under the headline, '*Woman sought by police in connection with mugging*'. The likeness was unmistakeable, but the name left no doubt in Vicky's mind. If Shazza had been part of the robbery duo, it stood to reason that Kyle had been her partner in crime.

Although Vicky had plans for when her shift ended, she changed her mind and went home. Kyle and Shazza were out, so she was able to search the empty flat thoroughly. In their room, she discovered an item under the bed that confirmed her worst fears.

Saddened by this, and despite her fondness for her young sibling, Vicky knew what she should do. She picked up the phone with the intention of calling the number listed in the newspaper, but then changed her mind. Whether her alternative plan would work was open to doubt, but she resolved to try it anyway.

As Vicky waited for the couple to return, she paced the floor of the sitting room, the kitchen, and the hallway, as she tried to work out how to broach an exceedingly difficult subject. It was with a mixture of trepidation and relief that she heard them enter the apartment. When they reached the lounge, Vicky was standing alongside the sofa clutching a copy of the newspaper. In her other hand was Muriel Croft's bus pass. She held it out to them, saying, 'I think you owe me an explanation.'

Half an hour later, after Vicky had listened to their tearful confessions, she managed to persuade them to a course of action they dreaded. Shazza picked up the newspaper and walked over to the phone. As she dialled, Kyle took her hand and grasped it in support. After a few moments' wait, Shazza was put through to a woman who told her the person she needed to speak to wasn't available, and asked how she could help. Shazza took a deep breath and explained why she had called the police.

\* \* \*

When Pearce arrived at work, the CID suite was empty. He went to the reception desk and asked Binns, 'Where is everyone? It's like the Mary Celeste upstairs.'

'Mike's gone shopping. My guess is it's probably an errand for his lady-friend, a trip to the supermarket. As for Lisa and Clara, they're interviewing a young man and woman who have come to confess to an old lady's mugging.'

Binns final comment wasn't altogether accurate. Although the mugging was intended to be the sole topic of the meeting, matters took a slightly different course.

Having ushered the penitent couple towards the interview room, Lisa realized she had picked up the wrong file from her desk. She excused herself, only to cannon into Clara who had attempted to follow her into the room. Contents from the folder spilled onto the floor.

As the detectives scrabbled about, collecting the documents regarding the puppy farming, Lisa picked up a photograph of one of the puppies. Kyle gasped with surprise when he saw the image, and nudged Shazza. 'That's the one I was trying to describe,' he told her.

Something in Kyle's statement prompted Lisa to ask what he meant. He pointed to the photo. 'That dog, I saw nine of them yesterday, all in one place. I told Shazza about it. I know some people have lapdogs as accessories, but I didn't think they were replacing jewellery with them.'

Clara stared at him. 'Jewellery?'

'Yeah, Jakeman's jewellers, I think it was called.'

Lisa glanced at the image of a pug puppy that had cost the owners nine hundred pounds. An investment that had been tragically short-term, as the dog had died within a month. 'You saw a bunch of these dogs together? What age were they?'

'Only puppies, I guess. They were in cages, but they were smaller than that one.'

Lisa held her hand up. 'Wait a moment, please. I don't want you to say anything else until Detective Sergeant Mironova sets up the recorder. Everything you can remember about those puppies could be very important, and it might help us look more leniently on your misdeeds.'

Shazza looked totally confused, and even Clara seemed baffled. It was only when Kyle described what he'd witnessed that Lisa's intention became clear to her superior.

At the end of the interview, Lisa asked Clara to hold the fort and went through to reception to tell Binns what she had learned. 'I realize that this is technically a robbery, rather than theft. But in view of their confession, and especially in the light of some valuable information they've given us, I think it would be appropriate to release them on bail. However, as custody sergeant, that decision is yours. But I believe it would be to our benefit if we show leniency to the couple. Unless they're extremely good actors, I think they're very contrite about what they did. And they did return the victim's handbag,' she added, hopefully.

Having heard Lisa's description of what Kyle had seen, Binns agreed to allow the couple to be bailed.

It was much later, when the formalities had been completed, and the young couple had left the building, somewhat chastened by their ordeal, that Clara asked Lisa if her guess as to the reason for her excitement was correct.

'Yes. That young man has just provided us with a major breakthrough in the puppy farming case. Until now, all we've had are some false names and spurious addresses for the people who sold the dodgy dogs. But Kyle has given us two names that are genuine — or rather one name and a personalized car registration number that will provide another. I need to talk to Mike and see how he wants to play it before I do anything else.'

Lisa's decision to consult Nash before taking action on the information she'd received proved to be a wise one. As she repeated what Kyle had told her, with Clara providing backup, they saw Nash's expression change to one of astonishment. His reaction came when Lisa mentioned the names. When he explained, they appreciated why he had seemed so shocked.

'I don't want anybody approaching either of them for the time being. I need more facts before we move.'

Further confirmation of Nash's theory came when Pearce entered his office.

'I went to see the man who bought Craig French's car. He took some tracking down. And you were dead right, Mike,' Pearce began. 'I took photos of the invoice, the DVLA paperwork, plus this one.' He handed Nash a sheet of paper with a print on it. 'Luckily, the guy hadn't thrown the key away. In fact, it was still on the ring provided by the dealer. The serial number matches the one Tom was given by the local authority. This is clearly the spare key to Craig French's lockup, but I can't understand why you're so excited about it.'

'It's all to do with dates, Viv. We already know that French didn't commit the murders, so how did the weapon come to be in his lockup along with some of the stolen property? French had surrendered the other key to the council, and sold his car before the date of the Cumbria murders. There was no way he had access to the garage when those goods were stolen and that knife was used. Now, I believe we have a new prime suspect — or suspects.'

'How do you intend to proceed?' Clara asked, after Pearce had left them. 'I admit it sounds convincing enough, but then so did the case against Craig French, until you took a sledgehammer to the evidence.'

Nash grinned at Clara's comment but his reply shocked her. 'I need more information. I am particularly keen to know why the killer chose French as a scapegoat — and if my theory is correct, why he also framed Bobby Walker for those burglaries.'

Clara blinked. She had all but forgotten the lesser crimes. 'How do you intend to get the information? And, in particular, discover why he framed French — if that's what happened?'

'I think we have to start asking questions.'

# CHAPTER TWENTY-THREE

Craig was now convinced he knew the killer's identity, and was trying to explain his idea to Tiff.

Tiff was confused. 'Why do you think Harvey Swann committed all those murders and framed you?' she asked.

'When I wanted to sell my car, I went to Swann's used-car lot in Netherdale. The price I got was less than it was worth, but it was enough to pay off the HP and leave a bit spare.' He stopped speaking and stared at Tiff. 'I've just remembered. The spare key to the lockup was still on the ring when I handed the car over. I'd already told him I'd given notice to the council for the garage — Swann knew the garage would be empty!'

'That's not much to go on, Craig.'

'Maybe, but he also knew I'd been made redundant. I'll bet he guessed I wouldn't have an alibi for when the robberies were taking place. Then there was what happened at the cabin. You'd mentioned it to him, so he knew there'd be a chance I'd be hiding out there. I reckon he went along to check, and finish me off. That way, he could continue burgling people, killing them and putting the blame on me, assuming it would be ages before my body was found. He obviously didn't know about the loggers working nearby.'

Tiff was shocked. 'You're absolutely certain it was Swann you saw at the cabin?'

'I didn't actually see him. But I don't think there are many people round here who own a Porsche Cayenne with his personalised number plate, do you?'

Tiff was feeding their son when Craig realized that one aspect of his theory hadn't been accounted for. The idea caused him to gasp slightly.

Tiff looked up. 'What's wrong?'

'Why? Why did he do it?'

'Sorry, why did who do what?'

'Why did Swann stitch me up? There were plenty of blokes he could have set up, so why pick me?'

It was a good question, and one they couldn't answer at that time. Tiff suggested they needed help.

Although the idea scared him, Craig didn't dismiss her idea of contacting the helpful police officer.

'The snag is,' he said, 'we don't know why. Apart from selling him the car, I had no dealings with him.' He shook his head and sighed. 'What do you know about Swann? Didn't he live next door to your parents before they emigrated?'

'Yes, and he always seemed pleasant enough. In fact, he was rather too nice.'

'What does that mean?'

'When I was younger, I know he used to watch me coming and going from the house. It made me feel uncomfortable, as if he was stalking me. I bumped into him more often than seemed natural. It got so bad that I was considering reporting him for harassment. Then I started going out with you. After that, he rarely spoke to me. Now I come to think of it, he never had a good word to say about you, called you a deadbeat and a loser.'

'That sounds like he was jealous. Did he ever try it on with you?'

'He did, but I told him I wasn't interested.'

'Was that before, or after, I was sent down?'

'It was before we met.'

'If he was still hankering after you, it might explain why he fitted me up, out of pure spite.'

'That still doesn't explain who rang the police and informed on you.'

'I reckon it does. If Swann hadn't sold my car, then he was parking it outside Bobby's. He was probably the one shagging Bobby's wife. My guess is he got her to make the call. It got rid of both me and Bobby. If I could, I'd confront her, but I'm a bit of a hot property at the moment.' He sank back to his seat.

'You'd find it difficult to do that anyway,' Tiff replied. 'I heard she's got a job in Spain as "housekeeper"' — Tiff made the air quote finger gesture — 'for some bloke who has a holiday home there. She buggered off a few weeks back, and good riddance, I say.'

'Whereabouts in Spain, do you know?'

'Este . . . something or other, sounds like a horse.'

'Estepona?'

'That's right. How did you guess?'

'It isn't a guess. I know somebody who has a villa in Estepona, and so do you. It's a bloke by the name of Harvey Swann.'

'Oh hell, I've just remembered something.'

'What?'

'Swann is selling the car dealership. I heard someone talking about it in Good Buys. They said, "The lucky bastard is moving to Spain permanently." I think the comment was, "It must be nice to have that sort of money. I couldn't afford to move to Whitby." Mind you,' Tiff added, 'he won't have that sort of money for long if that gold-digging bitch has got her claws into him. It was her extravagance that got Bobby working all the hours God sends, going here, there, and everywhere.'

'I think your idea is a good one,' Craig said. 'Ringing that detective, I mean. If he's as good as they reckon, we might get out of this mess. Until that happens, we can't hope for a normal life together. Mind you, even if I am cleared,

I've no idea where I'll find work. The stain on my character won't go away easily. People will always have doubts unless something changes their opinion.'

* * *

Nash closed his office door, moved the Craig French file onto his blotter, and picked up his mobile. He was about to make a call when the device buzzed. He glanced at the screen and smiled before pressing a button. 'Good afternoon, Ms Walker,' he greeted the caller.

He heard a gasp before the woman stammered, 'How did you know it was me? How did you know my name?'

Tiff could hear the laughter in his voice. 'I'm a detective — it's what I do. Strangely enough, I was just about to phone you. Why don't you tell me why you rang? Then I'll explain what I want from you.'

'I called because we . . . er . . . I had an idea about who might have done those horrid murders. I hope the photo I sent you proves that Craig couldn't have done them.'

'I was already fairly certain that Craig wasn't guilty, but the photo will help enormously when I put his case to the Crown Prosecution Service. They might be reluctant to re-open the case without that image. I assume from what you just said that you've worked out who framed Craig. Can I make a guess? Was it Harvey Swann?'

Tiff's long silence was sufficient to confirm the accuracy of his question. When she had recovered from her surprise sufficiently enough to speak, she stammered, 'Yes, that was what we, I mean I, think. But how did you know?'

Nash couldn't resist the chance to tease her a little more. 'I told you, I'm a detective.' He relented and explained, 'It was the dates that gave me the first clue. We know when Craig sold his car and surrendered his key to the lockup — a month before the Cumbria murders. I sent one of my colleagues to see the new owner of Craig's car, and he told us he purchased it well after the Cumbrian murders. That means

Craig's car was still on the lot at that time. Even more important, the spare key to the lockup was still on the key ring. That left only one person who had access to the car, the keys, and lockup at the crucial time. That was the dealer, Harvey Swann. What I still haven't worked out is why he chose to frame Craig, and also your brother.'

Tiff was overwhelmed by the extent of Nash's knowledge. He could tell that her mobile was on speakerphone by the echo from her voice. He grinned when he heard another gasp of surprise that greeted his final statement. The voice was distinctively male.

'I think I know the answer, Mr Nash,' Tiff said when she had recovered. 'Swann used to live next door to me and he tried time and again to get too friendly, if you know what I mean. We think he got jealous when I took up with Craig. Knowing he wasn't getting anywhere with me, he switched his attention to Bobby's wife. We think she's living at Swann's place in Spain, and he's going to join her once the sale of his dealership goes through. We also think it was her who rang the police, pretending to be me, and tipped them off about the stuff in Craig's lockup and Bobby's workshop.'

'What else can you tell me about Swann?'

Tiff thought for a moment, then told him, 'Not much. Although he always seemed to have plenty of money, even before he opened the car dealership. Where he got so much cash from, I've no idea.'

'That seems to answer one of the questions that puzzled me. What I would really like to know is where that money in Craig's mother's loft came from. I also need something more concrete to be able to pull Swann in and search his properties. He is connected to another crime, so we may have to use that.'

'I think I might have what you're looking for, Mr Nash. There's something I haven't told you. It's about that poor man who died in the cabin fire.'

It was Nash's turn to be surprised. 'What do you know about that? The only definite facts we have are the identity of the victim, and that Craig had been using the cabin.'

'Yes, Craig was hiding out there until the day of the fire. He chose that place because we used to go there . . . er . . . when we were courting. He hid in the woods when the other man turned up, and when he realized he was staying, Craig had to move on. As he was leaving he saw a car stop near the cabin, before the fire started. Craig was close enough to read the number plate, and knew it belonged to Harvey Swann. The thing is, Mr Nash,' Tiff gulped with dismay, 'I was the one who told Swann about Craig possibly being there. Now I feel awful, because that poor man died because of what I said.'

'I shouldn't get too upset,' Nash responded, 'the pathologist's reported the man was in a pretty bad way due to his long-term addiction to narcotics. The fire only shortened his lifespan by a matter of months. We found some empty syringes inside the cabin, so I guess he died happy. What you've told me has supplied the final piece of the jigsaw. If Swann believed Craig was dead, he'd be free to commit more murders, pinning the blame on him. Now,' Nash paused, 'what about the cash in the attic?'

Tiff explained about Craig's reward for saving the industrialist from death or serious injury. Nash scribbled the name Lionel Birch on his jotter.

'Ask Mr Nash what that other crime is.'

Nash heard the stage whisper and smiled again. 'You can speak up, Craig, there's nobody here but me. I shouldn't say, but we're looking into a case of pedigree puppy farming. The local vet has identified several animals we believe were bought on the black market.'

Craig's voice was now clear; he'd obviously abandoned any attempt at secrecy. 'Do you know where they keep the dogs? Is it somewhere near Wintersett?'

'It could be anywhere. What makes you think that?'

'When I was looking for somewhere to hide on my way to the cabin, I found a remote barn. I opened the door and the place was full of cages containing puppies of different breeds. Some I recognized, like spaniels and Labradors.

Others I didn't know. The conditions they were kept in were appalling. The cages had no water, and lots of them were filthy. The place stank of dog shit, and in one corner there was a pile of corpses, all puppies. One of the inmates must have got free because it shot past me and ran off. I didn't try to catch it. I had a lot of sympathy with a runaway. I can give you directions if I have a map.'

'What sort of dog was it that escaped, did you notice? Could it have been a young black Labrador?'

'Yes, it was, but how did you know that?' Between them, Craig and Tiff were beginning to wonder if Nash was psychic.

'Her name is Teal, and I'm pleased to report that she's fit and well, and has now got a loving home.'

'What happens now?'

'When we've arrested these men, I'll need a statement from you. I'm afraid that means giving yourself up, but I'll square things with the CPS first. The only charge you'll face is breaking and entering the holiday cottage. I'm pleased to report that Barry and Shirley Dickinson don't intend to prosecute you for the theft of the food. In the meantime, I'll have to check out the information you gave me.' Nash was trying not to let the fact he was smiling reflect in his voice. 'Will you stay there until I contact you again? As long as Ms Walker doesn't mind harbouring a fugitive for a little while longer, that is.'

'I think I can put up with him, Mr Nash,' Tiff responded. 'In fact, once he's been cleared of those charges, I'm hoping to persuade him to stay — forever.'

They heard laughter in Nash's voice as he replied, 'That sounds good, but perhaps you should persuade him to change his taste in dressing gowns. That shade of pink really doesn't suit him.'

* * *

When the conversation with Tiff and Craig ended, Nash called Clara into his office. She entered carrying two coffees, and listened while he presented her with the new information.

'It all sounds good in theory, but you've no concrete evidence against either Swann or Jakeman, have you?'

'But what if an eyewitness has come forward who saw Swann's car close to the cabin minutes before the fire, and that the intended victim was French?'

'The chances of that are infinitesimal,' Clara said before she saw Nash's smile. 'I don't believe this. You have a witness, don't you? Who is it?'

'Who do you think?'

'Not Craig French, surely?'

'It certainly was. He told me just now.'

'Hang on a minute. If you've spoken to him, we are duty bound to go and arrest him. He's a wanted fugitive.'

'Yes, I suppose we should, but he didn't say where he is. Besides, with what we know, I think that would be the wrong thing to do, don't you?'

Clara frowned. 'I suppose, morally speaking, you're right. OK, then. What was Swann's motive for pursuing a vendetta against French? Had they crossed swords in the past, or something?'

Nash explained about Swann's pursuit of Tiff and his anger at being rejected.

Clara's retaliation was swift. 'Ah, unrequited love. I bow to your superior knowledge in such matters.'

'Clara, how could you suggest such a thing? I'll have you know I'm a contented man with a settled family life.'

Fortunately, Clara had swallowed the last of her coffee, so the danger of choking was avoided. 'It sounds logical, now you've explained the motive,' she agreed. 'However, I go back to the point I made earlier, in that it would help no end if we had some evidence that didn't rely on an eyewitness with their own agenda. If we could lay our hands on the latest murder weapon or some of the missing jewellery, that would strengthen our case no end. Even if we can nail Swann for the murders, tying Jakeman to them will be well-nigh impossible, unless he's caught in possession.' Clara thought for a few moments and then said, 'I'm surprised that Swann is involved in this. I'm not disputing what you say, but I wouldn't have thought he needed the money. I believed his motor dealership was flourishing.'

'What made you think that?'

'It was only a few years ago that he had an extension built to his showroom and offices. That must have cost a pretty penny.'

'When exactly did that happen, can you remember?'

'It was around the time you and Daniel moved to Smelt Mill Cottage, before you met Alondra. When you asked me to help choose furniture, carpets and so forth, I had to visit furniture shops in Netherdale, next to Swann's showrooms on the trading estate.'

'Can you recall the name of the company that did the work? Contractors usually put a board out to advertise their services.'

Although Clara knew Nash well enough to second-guess the way his mind worked, in this instance, his subtlety defeated her. 'It was that local outfit, the one that advertises as *Bob the Builder.*'

'That firm has been out of business for two years. It was actually a one-man band, and the founder, Bobby Walker, is serving a five-year sentence for robbery.'

'Really? What next, then?' she asked.

'I need to make arrangements for going to prison.'

Clara stared at him in disbelief until he explained. 'I need to think this over before deciding on a plan of action. In the meantime, I'm going to phone Sir Maurice Winfield and get Sir Lionel Birch's contact details. Then I'll phone Birch to get corroboration of French's account of how he got that money. Once I have that, I'm going to enlist the acting chief to help in persuading the CPS to review Craig French's conviction.'

Nash's conversations with Sir Maurice and Sir Lionel provided confirmation of French's story. Having elicited a promise from Sir Lionel to provide a written statement, Nash made another phone call, which he hoped might ensure his reception at the prison would be a positive one.

Moments later, he took a call from the forensic team leader. 'It's about the footprints at Kirk Bolton Hall. They were so blurred they could be anything from size five to nine.'

'That can't be right, surely.'

'It is, and I'm sorry to say I can't come up with an explanation.'

# CHAPTER TWENTY-FOUR

The official from the Crown Prosecution Service listened with growing impatience as Nash outlined the frailties of the evidence that had led to Craig French's conviction.

When he judged Nash to have finished, his reply was cutting, to say the least. 'I have heard nothing that convinces me to re-open the case, and I'm annoyed that you considered it worth wasting my valuable time with this fabricated nonsense and your wild theories.'

Nash was unruffled and persisted, despite the criticism. 'I take it you do agree that the recent murders at Wintersett Grange and Kirk Bolton Hall were committed by the same person as the Cumbrian ones?'

'Undoubtedly: Craig French is guilty of all the murders. I think you would make a better use of your facilities trying to detain him before he commits further atrocities, rather than wasting your time, and mine, with this rubbish.' He waved a dismissive hand at the folder Nash had given him.

'You don't think they might have been committed by different people?'

Ruth Edwards watched Nash lead the CPS official into the trap he had set for him.

The man almost laughed at what he thought to be a ridiculous idea. 'Are you thinking of a copycat? That is impossible, because that trademark signature was not made public, and is still known to only a few people.'

'And you've subjected the evidence to the closest possible scrutiny?' Nash asked.

'Naturally.' He stared at Nash, indignantly. 'So, if there is nothing more I will take my leave of you.' He stood up, and turned towards the door, but stopped when Nash barred his way, holding out a single sheet of A4 paper.

'Before you leave, there is one more piece of evidence I'd like you to look at.'

The official sighed wearily, put his briefcase down, and took hold of the paper. Ruth knew he was in for a seismic shock, and reckoned he deserved everything that was coming to him.

Nash continued, 'This is a recent photo of Craig French. You can tell it is him, despite the beard. The scar from the brain injury is quite distinct.'

The man glanced at the image, then glared at the detective — his anger patently obvious. 'You actually know where French is and yet you haven't arrested him. That sounds like gross dereliction of duty to me.'

Nash shrugged. 'No, I haven't arrested him — nor do I intend to.'

The official was apoplectic with rage. He turned to Ruth and snarled, 'This so-called detective is unfit to hold the rank of detective inspector. In fact, he is unworthy of holding a warrant card at any rank. If you don't intend to pursue this matter further, I will be compelled to report Nash to the IOPC.'

'As a leading investigator with the IOPC,' Ruth said, 'I regard it as gross dereliction of duty for someone who represents the Crown to claim they have inspected the evidence, when they have ignored what is glaringly obvious. Had you examined the photograph Inspector Nash just showed you in a proper, diligent manner, you would have noted one salient fact. Whether you missed it because of your blind stupidity, or deliberately ignored it because it didn't fit with your interpretation of the facts — or should I say, misinterpretation of them, is open to question.'

Without looking at the image again, the official said, 'I have no idea what you're talking about.'

Nash explained, 'That photo shows Craig French clad in his girlfriend's dressing gown, cuddling their son while they are asleep. In the top right-hand corner of the photo, taken on her mobile, you will see the date and time clearly marked. Now I would like you to explain how Craig French managed to get dressed, leave her flat, reach Kirk Bolton Hall, an eleven-mile journey, in the two minutes between that photo being taken and the victim's call to the emergency services. That would be impossible even if he had Lewis Hamilton as his chauffeur.'

The man was flustered. 'Yes, but what about the money found in his mother's house and the stuff in his garage?'

Nash explained where the money had come from and told the CPS official that Sir Lionel Birch was providing written confirmation. 'As to the murder weapon and stolen property in the lockup, I believe we know who planted it to frame French. But as that is part of the ongoing inquiry, I'm not ready to release the suspect's name yet.'

There was a prolonged silence that was broken eventually by Ruth. 'Well? Have you nothing to say, no rebuttal of what is clearly watertight evidence?'

In the end, they reached a viable compromise, which as Nash and Ruth Edwards agreed later was the best they could have hoped for. The official agreed to re-open Craig's case, but told them it would strengthen his hand immeasurably if they could provide a credible alternative suspect. 'I'm not certain how you can achieve that, because from what I've seen you have very little to work with.'

If the man thought their recent disagreement was over and done with, Nash had a further shock in store for him, one that surprised Ruth also. 'Having examined the evidence closely, I now believe there is an alternative solution, but until I am certain of my facts and can present a strong enough case, I will say nothing more.'

When the official had left, Ruth said, 'I thought you said there were no other lines of enquiry to follow up on? That's what you'd told me.'

'That was true, but Alondra told me something that set me thinking. She mentioned valuations for some paintings she's been invited to send to America. I wondered that as all the victims had expensive jewellery, they would probably need it valued for insurance. When I checked the paperwork, I found that the Cumbria victims and the couple from Wintersett Grange had their most expensive property valued by the same company at their local offices. When Clara checked the diary of the last victim, Alison Stokes, she discovered that Ms Stokes had taken it to a company in Helmsdale, but because their boss wasn't available on the day, she had to use another firm to conduct the assessment, in Netherdale. Now that might be coincidence, but I—'

'Don't believe in coincidence,' Ruth finished his sentence for him. 'So who is this company?'

'Jakeman's, and they specialize in expensive jewellery and high-end timepieces. What's more, they have branches throughout the north of England, including towns in Cumbria — their head office is in Netherdale. The proprietor is someone named Aaron Jakeman, and he seems to be a bit of a mystery man. The jewellery company's reputation is not exactly spotless.'

'Who told you that?'

'Jimmy Johnson.'

'Yes, I am aware of him.' Ruth smiled knowingly.

'Well, he installed the system at Kirk Bolton Hall, and has a vested interest in seeing the killer brought to justice. The strange thing is that nobody seems to know anything about Aaron Jakeman. I asked Tom Pratt to check him out and he could find very little, apart from the fact that there was someone of that name born in Birmingham. I doubt if it's the same man, though.'

'Why not? It isn't exactly a common surname.'

'Because the person Tom found would be over eighty years old now. However, just to be on the safe side, I asked Tom to delve a bit deeper and see if Aaron Jakeman had any siblings or descendants. I'm waiting for him to get back to me.'

* * *

The prison visit went better than Nash anticipated. As he waited for the inmate to be brought to the interview room, he wondered how he was coping with prison regime. As a self-employed building contractor, Bobby Walker would have spent most of his working week outside, so the adjustment to life behind bars would have been traumatic. Knowing that he had been convicted of crimes he hadn't committed would have heightened his bitterness. In circumstances such as those, it would have been natural for Walker to be deeply suspicious of anyone in authority, especially a police officer. Nash hoped that Tiff had done as he asked.

An officer escorted Walker into the room and took up position against the wall. Contrary to Nash's foreboding, Walker appeared quite cheerful as he sat opposite him.

Nash smiled at him. 'Before we start, I only want to talk to you. This is not a formal interview, and isn't being recorded, so you don't need your solicitor. Do you understand?'

Walker nodded.

'I assume you've spoken to your sister recently?'

'Yes, when I phoned her, she told me you believe I'm innocent, and might be able to get me out of this dump.'

'Did she explain why I think you didn't commit those burglaries?'

'No, we're not allowed too long on the phone. She just told me to listen to you and answer all your questions truthfully. She also said I could trust you. Then she told me you'd done something similar for a good friend of hers.' He lowered his voice and added, 'We don't mention names on the phone. From that I assume she meant that bastard French, although why she's bothered about that scumbag, after everything he's done, is beyond me.'

'Like you, Craig French has been the victim of an extremely cunning frame-up. Let me explain, before you go off on one.'

Walker listened.

'French didn't commit the murders he was convicted for. Neither did he kill the more recent victims. It's highly significant that the murders happened once French was on the run, and therefore, unable to provide an alibi — or so the killer believed. However, the murderer reckoned without your sister's sense of humour and her photography skills.'

Nash explained about the image that provided French with a cast-iron alibi and then continued, 'Moreover, French was not sleeping with your wife. Everything that you and your sister were told was a tissue of lies, designed to set you at loggerheads with French. Those lies were concocted by a ruthless and vindictive man, with a penchant for expensive jewellery and a flamboyant lifestyle. He also possesses a complete disregard for the people he slaughtered, and the lives he ruined, in order to achieve his goal.'

Walker stared at Nash, his disbelief apparent.

Building on Walker's astonishment, Nash asked, 'How well do you know Harvey Swann?'

'Quite well, or at least I did before I ended up in here. Why do you ask? Has he become another victim? I hope not, because I quite like him. I did a fair amount of work for him before I was arrested.'

'No, Harvey Swann is definitely *not* a victim. That work you did was a while ago, correct?'

'That's right, but why are you asking all these questions about . . . ?' Then Walker gasped, the inference at last striking home. 'Is that what you think? Is Swann behind all this?'

Ignoring Walker's question, Nash asked how he had met Swann.

'He phoned me, said he'd seen one of my adverts in the local free paper. Said it was the title *Bob the Builder* that had drawn him to it. Told me he planned to extend his show-room and offices, and invited me to quote for the job.'

'And I assume that during the course of the work he visited your house regularly, and it was there he met your wife?'

This time Walker caught Nash's insinuation immediately. 'Was it Swann who was screwing the bitch? How do you know he was giving her one?'

'Swann bought Craig's car from him, and it was later seen parked outside your house in the early hours of the morning. Swann was the only person who had access to the vehicle.'

Walker's face was becoming contorted as he listened.

'Tiff told me that your wife has gone to live in Spain, correct?'

'Yes, the cow wrote to tell me she wasn't prepared to wait around for a loser like me. Said she was leaving the house keys with a neighbour — in case I needed them,' he growled. 'Nice girl, she is — I don't think.'

'It seems rather coincidental that the place she's gone is Estepona, where Harvey Swann owns a holiday home.' Nash smiled slightly as he added, 'My colleagues would tell you I don't believe in coincidences. Property in Estepona is quite expensive, I understand. And I don't think the used-car market is buoyant enough to provide sufficient cash to finance such a residence. I already had serious doubts regarding Swann, and then I got to thinking about the building work you did for him. I guess that would have cost a packet, with labour and materials?'

Walker named a figure, which was more or less what Nash expected.

'I can't see the sale of used Renault Clios paying for that, can you?' Without waiting for Walker to respond, Nash went on, 'What I need is as much information as you can provide about Swann. If I can collect sufficient evidence, I'll be able to put him behind bars for life, where he belongs. In doing

206

so, I will also be able to have your conviction overturned. Of course,' he added casually, 'without financial support from Swann, your wife's luxurious lifestyle will take a rapid nose-dive towards poverty.'

Walker's face turned from anger to a smile. The idea of getting revenge provided the impetus for him to give his wholehearted cooperation. In the course of telling the detective everything he knew, Walker provided one piece of information that Nash knew could prove crucial.

'I'd like to get this down in writing,' he told Walker. 'That way I can present it when I'm requesting a warrant.' He glanced at the prison officer, who had been listening with interest. 'I'm sure our friend here will witness your signature.'

When he left the prison an hour later, Nash was confident that he now had sufficient background to obtain a search warrant — and, armed with what Walker had revealed towards the end of their conversation, he was equally hopeful that the search would prove extremely fruitful.

Nash's final comment before exiting the interview room made Walker's smile even wider, his mood more upbeat than for many months.

'One thing I can tell you, Bobby. If everything turns out as I expect, you and Craig will have set some sort of a record — because you'll be able to boast that, unlike most of your fellow inmates, you actually *are* innocent.'

\* \* \*

Nash called in at the Netherdale HQ, where he presented Ruth Edwards with Bobby Walker's statement. She read it through before looking at Nash, her face reflecting none of the satisfaction that he might have expected. 'That is fairly convincing.' She gestured to the document. 'However, after having spoken to the CPS earlier this morning, they refuse to re-open Craig French's case until you can provide an alternative credible suspect. Sorry, but I think we've hit a brick wall.'

Nash concealed his anger. He stood up and turned to leave.

'Where are you going?' Ruth asked, mildly perturbed by his abrupt departure.

'I'm going to find a bulldozer to demolish that brick wall. In the process, I'm going to blow the smug complacency of the CPS to smithereens. If you feel like it, you can warn them. And, in the process, tell them that I expect heads to roll in their department.'

'You really think that will terrify them? We haven't the power to enforce anything of that nature.'

Nash smiled. 'Maybe not directly, but I've been told that they're overstaffed, and their executives are looking to make reductions. Anyone with a less-than-satisfactory track record could be extremely vulnerable. I wasn't sworn to secrecy, so if you wish to pass it on, that's no concern of mine.'

'And what about the bulldozer? How are you going to get these cases re-opened?'

Nash sat down again to explain. 'Organize some searches, and if they yield results, we can charge Swann. Perhaps we should also ask the Guardia Civil to take a look at his holiday home in Spain. We can also arrest Jakeman, if we find evidence when we search the jewellery shops and Manor Farm.'

Edwards blinked with surprise. 'Any specific reason for involving the Spanish police?'

'Merely a matter of putting the cat among the pigeons. We believe Bobby Walker's wife is Swann's mistress, and has gone to live there, waiting for Swann to join her. Given what Bobby Walker and Tiff said about her, I reckon she might be wearing some purloined pearls, or dodgy diamonds, that might tally with the list of stolen jewels. Once she knows her sugar daddy is in the slammer, I guess she'll return to this country, and we can arrest her as an accessory, and for perverting the course of justice.'

'On what grounds?'

'I believe she made the initial phone call about the stolen goods, posing as Tiff Walker.'

'Go for it, Mike. I'll back you all the way. Now scram, because I'm going to be busy putting the frighteners on the CPS. I'm going to enjoy this.'

'One thing before I go. I'd like to make a big show of the arrest and search at the car lot. Maybe take along a Tactical Response Unit? Plus as many uniformed men as we can rustle up.'

'Is that necessary? Do you believe Swann will prove dangerous?'

Nash shrugged. 'Not that I'm aware of, but I thought I'd invite the media along and make an exciting show for the TV bulletins or newspaper readers. The reporters will want to know what the arrest is about, and I can tell them. That'll have the CPS squirming.'

'I get it. What about Aaron Jakeman?'

'That's the other part of the plan. We turn our attention to Jakeman, with the assistance of the RSPCA.'

Ruth stared at Nash in astonishment. 'Did you say the RSPCA?'

'That's right.' Nash repeated what Craig French had told him about the barn's contents, and also what Lisa Andrews had learned from Kyle. 'We have a sighting of puppies being handed over to Swann at Jakeman's Netherdale branch. And we've discovered that the barn is on his land. We raid that, and it will give us justification to search his house and shops. And I think we should arrest them both at the same time.'

'Swann and Jakeman?'

'Yes, that won't give them the chance to dispose of evidence, or make a run for it. We've had enough trouble with one escapee.'

Edwards laughed, but pointed out that searching two business, two homes, and a barn simultaneously would entail a lot of manpower.

'I think we could manage if we split into three sections, have a detective plus some uniforms at each site. The only drawback is the lack of senior officers to make the arrests and authorize the searches. I can take care of Swann, but I'd prefer someone of high rank to charge Jakeman.'

'I could do that.'

Nash smiled. 'I hoped you'd say that.'

'Mike, you could give Machiavelli lessons in deviousness.'

\* \* \*

As he was driving to Helmsdale, Nash reflected on the recent misdemeanours he'd committed. Not only had he failed to act when he knew the whereabouts of a wanted felon but he had just lied through his teeth to a superior officer, who he felt sure was about to utter an empty threat to members of the Crown Prosecution Service. If either of those worried him, it wasn't apparent.

Back in the office, Nash told Clara, Viv, and Lisa the outcome of his visit to Felling, and the plan he had concocted to bring justice for French and punishment for Swann.

'Ruth has promised to let me know when the arrest teams are arranged. Then I'll alert all the local media. Once they're on board, we can haul the suspects in and go through their premises with a fine-tooth comb. Viv, you'll be with Ruth Edwards. She'll be in charge at Manor Farm, to arrest Jakeman and conduct the search of the house. With luck, we might find some of the stolen goods there. Lisa, you and Jack Binns will go to the barn and meet with RSPCA officers. At the same time, I'm sending officers to Jakeman's jewellery shop in Netherdale to lock it up as soon as Jakeman has been arrested. We can search it later. Clara, you'll go to Swann's car lot with me. The tactical response team will split between sites — we don't know how dangerous these people are.'

The raids were to take place the following day, subject to there being sufficient personnel available. With their limited resources, that was by no means a foregone conclusion.

Nash had been back in his own office less than five minutes when the phone rang in the outer office. 'Mike, it's Tom Pratt for you,' Clara called out.

'Put him through, Clara.' He picked up the handset. 'Tom, what can I do for you?'

'Sorry I missed you when you were at HQ. I did that research you asked for and the results are extremely interesting — to put it mildly.'

Nash listened in surprise as Pratt revealed what he'd learned. When the call ended, he stared at the notes on his jotter. What he'd just learned had turned the case upside down. He called Ruth Edwards.

# CHAPTER TWENTY-FIVE

Nash watched as the officers took up position out of sight of Swann's car lot, awaiting the call to action. Nash was unwilling to order them to move until everything he'd planned had come together. He'd already scoped out the premises when the showroom was closed. After a few minutes he saw a Transit van, bearing the logo of the local TV station, pull up down a side street as instructed. Simultaneously, he watched a man get out of a saloon car nearby, a man he recognized as a reporter for the *Netherdale Gazette*, who had parked alongside the local radio outside broadcast vehicle.

'Stand by, just a couple of minutes longer,' Nash said into his radio, 'while the TV crew gets set up. That way we can be sure they get you looking your best. We wouldn't want to disappoint your fans, would we?' Nash saw the cameraman give a thumbs-up signal, and radioed Ruth they were ready to go. He gave the order for the search teams to move in.

They entered the dealership in two parties, one of them taking the showroom while the others went via the workshop. Nash, accompanied by DS Mironova carrying a clipboard, walked in leisurely fashion into the showroom, where two men stood with their wrists secured by handcuffs. He asked an officer if they'd been identified.

'This man says he's a customer, negotiating to buy a used Ford Focus,' the leader of the tactical unit told him. 'The other one is Harvey Swann.'

Nash instructed one of the officers, 'Take the customer outside, get his details, and release him.'

'Who are you and what the hell is this about?' Swann demanded.

'I'm Detective Inspector Nash and this is Detective Sergeant Mironova. This' — he slapped the warrant on the desk where Swann could see it — 'is a search warrant. It's concerning several murders and burglaries, plus a variety of charges relating to obstructing the course of justice. Let's start with the burglaries, shall we? Would you care to tell us where the stolen goods are, or do we have to search the place and your house? Mind you, we're going to do that anyway, so it doesn't matter whether you say anything or not. On the other hand, it might save time if you confess right now.'

'I don't know what the fuck you're talking about.'

Nash shook his head. 'Such language in front of a lady.' He turned to Clara and smiled. 'I apologize on behalf of our friend here. I think he's realized that his murderous, greedy, and short-sighted attitude is about to cost him his liberty — and a lot more. He could have closed the dealership, taken his ill-gotten gains, and gone to Spain, with less risk of being arrested. But he hung on, trying to get extra cash by selling the business. He probably needs every penny to fund his mistress's expensive tastes.'

The second officer had returned, along with the officers from the workshop, informing him there were no other people on site. One was looking round the sparsely furnished room. 'Excuse me, sir. What exactly are we looking for? It isn't that big a place.'

Clara watched Swann and saw the dealer's expression change dramatically as he listened to Nash's reply. Up to that point, he'd been calm and relaxed, confident of his ability to answer the charges, but when Nash spoke again, his defiance crumbled.

'Note the layout of the building. It isn't a big concern, merely Swann, plus a couple of mechanics. Given the fact that the building is rectangular, and the length of the show-room and the workshop are the same, don't you think it's odd that the office here' — Nash gestured to the sales room — 'is almost three feet shorter than the one in the workshop?'

'Why's that, sir?'

'Because the back wall is false, the man who built the new showroom told me. It disguises the place where Swann keeps the choicest pieces from his burglary career. That proves how stupid Swann is. Trusting the secret of his hiding place to someone — then framing him for burglary, while at the same time screwing his wife. The entrance to that secret compartment can only be breached using a special key, such as the one our friend here has on his key ring.'

Nash picked up a key ring the arresting officer had taken from Swann's jacket. He selected a thin, circular rod with a star-shaped tip, which looked unlike any key Clara had seen before.

'Shall we give it a try?'

Sure enough, the hidden panel in the wall opened to reveal the treasures within. The detectives looked at the items of silverware, and paintings. 'I admire your taste, Mr Swann. That Lowry would probably have looked good on the wall of your Spanish hideaway. DS Mironova, it's your turn now.' Nash gestured to the interior. 'See if you can match any more of those items to the ones on your list.'

Swann, who had been brought by one of the officers, watched the process, his expression one of dismay.

Clara emerged from the rear of the office. 'There are several items in there that tally with the list. There is also a bag with a bloodstained set of overalls, a balaclava, and a knife with what looks like blood on it.'

'Right, let's make an inventory, get everything bagged up and off to the station. Give us a hand, will you?' he asked the other officers.

He turned to the officer restraining the prisoner. 'You'd better take him to Helmsdale' — he indicated Swann — 'and ask the duty officer to deal with him. Before you go, however, Clara, will you issue the caution?'

As the officers helped Nash and Mironova catalogue and transfer the goods found in the secret compartment, one of them commented, 'I can't wait to watch this on the telly. Tonight's local news bulletin will be like an episode of *NCIS*.'

The process of cataloguing the stolen goods had just ended when Nash got a call on his mobile. 'How did it go?' he asked Ruth Edwards.

He listened as she explained what they'd discovered at Manor Farm, and informed him, 'I've arrested the householder.'

'That's someone Clara and I are most anxious to meet. We're going back to Helmsdale.'

When he'd ended the call, Clara asked why he thought she was anxious to meet the person arrested at Manor Farm.

'Wait and see. I think you're in for a surprise. I certainly was when the chief told me.'

As they returned to the station, Clara reflected on the events leading to Swann's arrest. 'I know we've seen some wickedness in our time, Mike, but this must be fairly high on the list. Six murders, all because two people were so greedy that they committed such dreadful crimes, purely for gain.'

Nash corrected her, 'I think that although four of them were certainly down to greed, the other two were motivated by self-preservation.'

Clara didn't understand his reasoning, but knew Mike too well to challenge it without all the facts.

When they entered the building, Jack Binns was waiting. 'Lisa's still at the barn with the RSPCA. It was horrendous. We arrested the bloke who was apparently in charge. He and his assistant are in the cells,' he told them. 'Superintendent Edwards requested my presence here to book them all in.'

'Where is the acting chief constable?' Nash asked.

'Upstairs in the office. The car dealer's in a cell. So is the one who hasn't deigned to provide us with their name.'

'OK, Jack, would you send their fingerprints through to Tom Pratt and ask him to run them through the PNC. Clara,

I'd like you to concentrate on identifying and labelling every item from the properties we've searched. When Viv and Lisa return, I'll ask them to lend you a hand. They can deal with the men from the barn. We need reports from the RSPCA before we know for sure what we're charging them with.'

'What about our other detainees?' Binns asked.

'Let them stew. I want all the facts available before I confront them.'

'You've only got twenty-four hours, and the acting chief might not be happy.'

'She knows the score. We're going to unload all the evidence and bring it in. Tell her we're back, will you? Then take her a coffee — assure her Clara didn't make it.'

Binns reported that both detainees had requested the presence of a lawyer. 'That's OK, Jack. I reckon they're going to need all the help they can get.'

It was an hour and a half later, as Nash and Ruth Edwards were sitting in his office discussing interview tactics, that his phone rang twice in rapid succession. The first call was from Binns, who announced that both prisoners had consulted with their legal representatives and were ready to be questioned. 'Well they can wait a bit longer.'

He had barely replaced the receiver when the phone rang again. 'Mike, it's Tom. I've run those prints as you asked and they yielded results — big time. I've emailed the file to you, so you can print it off immediately.'

Nash and Edwards stared at the computer in the CID office, their attention gripped by the details on the screen in front of them. 'I think that looks like game, set and match,' Ruth remarked as Nash pressed the print button.

'I agree. Now we can confront them with everything we know. Shall we start with Harvey Swann?'

'OK, but I think we should invite Clara to join the party, don't you? If you conduct the interview with her, I'll watch on the CCTV. Got any popcorn?'

Nash laughed as he and Clara headed for the interview room.

Swann's solicitor had obviously been busy trying to drum up some sort of defence. His attempt to protest about the detention of a respectable citizen was cut short by Nash, who said, 'I don't have time for that rubbish.'

Turning to Swann, he told the motor dealer, 'Harvey Swann, I am arresting you for the murders of Clive Burrows and Stuart Davies. You do not have to say anything, but anything you do say . . .'

As he completed the formal caution, Swann, his solicitor and DS Mironova stared at Nash in perplexity. Who were the men Nash had named as Swann's alleged victims? Next door, Ruth Edwards was unfazed by his statement.

Naturally, it was the lawyer who spoke first. 'What are you talking about, Nash? I have no knowledge of these murders, or the alleged victims. I was given nothing relating to these offences.'

'That's because I didn't know at the time.' Nash took a folder from the collection he had brought in and opened it. 'Twelve years ago, a security company depot on the outskirts of Leeds was attacked. One of the guards raised the alarm, but the raiders still managed to make off with over a million pounds in cash. As punishment for the guard's audacity, one of the raiders stabbed him, and his colleague, to death. Unfortunately for him, he left a bloodstained fingerprint on the desk where one of the men had been seated. That fingerprint matches the one taken from your client today. Now we've cleared that up, let's continue.' Nash went on to list six more murders, ensuring his solicitor had paperwork for each of them in turn.

Nash looked directly at Swann. 'I guess you'd like to confer with your legal representative before we continue this interview, so I'll leave you to it.'

* * *

'Now for the other suspect,' Nash said as they stepped into the corridor. 'This should be even more interesting.'

When they entered the second interview room, Clara stopped dead in her tracks. She stared in astonishment at the person seated alongside a local solicitor. Nash grinned at his sergeant's expression and told her, 'Clara, meet Aaron Jakeman, or as you know him, Hilary Bennett.'

'I don't understand,' Clara muttered.

'Let me explain, courtesy of Tom Pratt, whose work throughout has been crucial in unearthing background. Aaron Jakeman doesn't exist, or at least not nowadays. He was born in Birmingham in 1938 and was tried, found guilty, and hanged in 1962 for murder. The family then moved to Leeds.

'Hilary Bennett is Aaron Jakeman's great-granddaughter. Her father was a small-time crook, whose criminal career was curtailed because of his heavy drinking. He died of cirrhosis of the liver, leaving his family in extreme poverty — but not before he'd taught his daughter a few tricks of the trade.'

The extent of Nash's knowledge shocked Hilary and her solicitor, in much the same way as he had dumbfounded Swann earlier. Once again, Nash suggested they should confer, but before ending the first part of the interview, he advised the lawyer. 'If I were you, I'd ask Ms Bennett to explain the stolen jewellery we discovered in her home, plus the origin of the Patek Philippe ladies' watch she was wearing when she was arrested. The serial number of that watch matches one stolen during a robbery and murder in Cumbria two years ago.'

Nash was about to signal Clara to make the closing announcement, when he turned to the lawyer and added, 'You can also ask her to explain the presence of twenty-five pregnant bitches of various breeds in a barn on her property at Manor Farm, plus the fourteen corpses of dead puppies in the same building. Even if you manage to provide an explanation for all that evidence, you might struggle with the other item.'

'And what might that be?' The solicitor was obviously less than happy with Nash's allegations.

'The presence of her fingerprints, along with those of another person we have in custody, at the scene of an armed robbery and double murder in Leeds twelve years ago.'

# CHAPTER TWENTY-SIX

Having left Swann and Bennett to mull over the accusations with their solicitors, the detectives returned to the CID suite, where DCs Andrews and Pearce were waiting.

'I think you should update everyone,' Ruth Edwards suggested, after Lisa had presented them with the complete list of stolen property they had so far identified. 'That includes Clara, who still looks shell-shocked.'

'Once we knew of Swann's involvement, and that the jewellery in all the properties he'd burgled had been valued by Jakeman's jewellers, I began to wonder how the two were connected. I was already thinking that Swann might have a dodgy past because of something Tiff Walker told me.'

'What was that?' Clara asked.

'She said that Swann always had plenty of money to flash around, even when he hadn't got a job. That was before he opened the car dealership. That led me to wonder how he managed with no obvious source of income. Starting up the business must have been expensive, what with premises, tools, and stock to buy. Either he had inherited a fortune, won the lottery, or acquired a lot of money dishonestly. Given what I already suspected about Swann, I opted for the latter.'

'OK, I buy that about Swann, but how did you suspect Jakeman — or Hilary Bennett, as it turns out?'

'When you reported your conversation with Jimmy Johnson, you told me he referred to Aaron Jakeman as a real mystery man. That puzzled me, because someone who heads up a retail business needs to interact with their customers, so why was Jakeman secretive, unless he had something to hide?'

Nash paused. 'That was the first part. But then Craig French told me about the dogs he saw at Manor Farm, which confirmed my suspicions that Aaron Jakeman was a less-than-upright citizen.'

Lisa butted in. 'I get it. I reported what Kyle, the young mugger, had seen at the back of Jakeman's shop. He said the person handing those pug pups to Swann was a woman.'

'That's right. We had no idea of her identity until I asked Tom Pratt to delve into the Jakeman family tree.'

'So why did she have her lover, Alison Stokes, killed?' Viv wanted to know.

'Without a confession, we might never know. It's pos-sible that when Alison Stokes went to Jakeman's to have her jewellery valued, she saw Hilary there, or spotted her Volvo parked outside when Hilary was supposed to be in London. If Hilary knew that Alison had discovered the truth, or even suspected it, she'd have to silence her. Enter the Grim Reaper in the person of Harvey Swann, her hired assassin.' Nash paused and thought for a moment. A brief smile spread across his face before resuming, 'Or perhaps not, in this instance.'

He turned to Clara and said, 'Give Forensics a call, Clara. I want an urgent test done on the knife we got from Swann's place. I'm willing to bet that Alison Stokes' DNA doesn't feature in the mix.'

The others looked appalled. 'Do you think Hilary Bennett murdered her?' Viv asked, eventually.

'I reckon so.' He turned to Clara. 'Remember those muddy footprints we found? The ones where the CSI guy couldn't be certain of the size? What if somebody was try-ing to disguise the actual print size? When Alison made the treble nine call, the operator said the last word she uttered before she was stabbed was "you", and that was because she recognized the intruder. If Swann wasn't the killer, it had to be Bennett, because nobody else would know about the letter carved on the bodies.'

As his colleagues assimilated the theory, Nash said, 'Viv, I've got a job for you. I want you to go back to Manor Farm, and here's what I want you to look for.'

Having sent Pearce on his errand, Nash turned and listened as Ruth said, 'The ironic part of all this, of which I'm sure you will remind both of them, is that their own actions betrayed them and cleared Craig French, their scapegoat.'

'And when Harvey Swann tried to barbecue him at the cabin, French saw Swann's car, recognized it from the number plate, and put two and two together. What Swann and Bennett also couldn't have known, was that at almost the precise moment Alison Stokes was being murdered, Craig was having his photo taken miles away.'

'Didn't you wonder if the photo was faked?' Lisa Andrews asked. 'There's a lot you can do with technology these days, even forging a time and date stamp.'

'I don't know about technology,' Nash retorted, 'but I'm absolutely certain no man in his right mind would volunteer to be photographed wearing such a garish pink flowered dressing gown. It made him look like an Amsterdam hooker — not that I've ever been to Amsterdam,' he added swiftly, seeing Clara's mouth begin to open.

'I've got some good news about French,' Ruth interposed deftly. 'I had a phone call from the CPS as we were bringing the prisoners here, but I haven't had a chance to update you. They're prepared to have French declared innocent of all charges and will offer him £100,000 as compensation for wrongful imprisonment.'

'It's not enough,' Nash responded immediately.

'Why not? I thought £100,000 was quite generous.'

'No, it isn't. It's short by at least £50,000.'

'How do you work that out, Mike?'

'Following French's conviction, the money impounded from his mother's attic went into the Victim Compensation Fund. The CPS must repay that money, plus two years' interest.'

* * *

The lights in Helmsdale Police Station burned until late that evening, despite the protestations of the defendants' solicitors. The second part of the interviews had been deferred until Pearce returned from Manor Farm. When he did so, Nash examined the contents of the evidence bags Viv was carrying. 'I reckon that's all we need.'

Before resuming their interrogation, Nash consulted with Ruth Edwards, then spoke to his colleagues. He looked at each of them in turn. 'Clara, you and I will interview Swann. I want you to take control of the recordings. Make the opening and closing announcements and then leave the rest to me. When we interview Hilary Bennett, I will be with the chief. Whereas Swann is a wheeler-dealer, Bennett will respond better to a figure of authority.'

'What do you want us to do?' Viv asked, indicating Lisa as he asked. 'I'd like to come in.'

'Sorry, Viv. This needs senior officers. Besides, Swann thinks he's a ladies' man and will appreciate Clara's presence. Come to that,' he said, with a smile, 'so will Bennett. You two can watch the screen and analyse what's being said. Pick up on any body language, especially Bennett. I think she's the brains behind all this. Although I have got something I need you to do during that session.'

Their careful planning proved as successful as he and Ruth could have envisaged.

Despite his solicitor's instruction to make no comment, Harvey Swann spoke for the first time since his detention. 'You said Bobby Walker told you about that room and told you how to get inside. He grassed me up.'

'That's pretty much true,' Nash admitted. 'He did tell us, but his sister and Craig French told us even more. I

223

wouldn't blame them for being upset with you. Apart from sleeping with Bobby's wife, you framed him for robbery, and framed French for murder. All in all, I think you're about as unpopular as can be. The way Craig and Tiff feel, I reckon you'll be much safer in prison where they can't get at you.'

Swann seized on one of the names Nash mentioned. 'I thought French was dead.'

'No, when you torched that cabin in Thornscarr Forest you should have checked who the occupant was. You should also have made certain there were no witnesses who could identify you. The man you murdered there wasn't French.'

Swann seized on what he thought was a golden opportunity to involve French in his misdemeanours.

'Have you recaptured French? That little toe-rag was behind it all, no matter what Bobby told you. French went into those houses. He killed those people. He organized everything, insisting I stored the loot for him.' He paused, momentarily, before announcing, 'He's got amnesia — he just doesn't remember!'

Nash shook his head, pityingly. 'I'm not surprised you failed as a used-car salesman — you're not even a good liar. The plain fact is that French has a cast-iron alibi for one of those murders. We also know that he couldn't have put the stolen goods in that lockup, and we also know the source of the money he had stashed in his mother's loft. So you've lost out again. I don't know if you believe in poetic justice, but I think it extremely fitting that the eyewitness who identified you as the cabin murderer was Craig French.'

'French is a liar, I tell you! I was nowhere near the forest on the night that fire happened. I was in Netherdale all night.'

Nash smiled, but without humour. 'Really? That *is* interesting. Tell me, how do you know when the fire happened? Because the only way you could have been so positive is if you were there. Nobody else apart from me and my colleagues is aware of the exact time and date of the fire. I said earlier that you were a bad liar, and you've just proved it. If you were in

224

Netherdale all that night, how come your Porsche Cayenne was captured by a CCTV camera in Wintersett? And when we check your tyres, they'll match the tyre marks found at the scene.'

Nash's final statement was the last straw and Swann's resistance began to crumble.

When Nash told Swann that they were unlikely to proceed with the prosecution over the cabin fire death, and followed this by offering to remove the Kirk Bolton Hall murder from the charge sheet, Clara thought her boss was losing the plot.

However, when Nash outlined the comprehensive evidence against Swann for the other six murders, the response was such that the strategy seemed to have worked better than they could have expected. Having secured Swann's confession to those crimes, Nash nodded to Clara, who uttered the termination announcement.

As they returned to the CID suite, they discussed how Nash had broken Swann's resistance. 'He might be a poor liar, Mike, but you're a damned good one. There was no CCTV image of Swann's car, was there?'

Nash grinned. 'You know that, I know that, but Swann doesn't.'

'Yes, but you played him, didn't you? You treated that interview as a used-car deal. You offered him relief from two murder charges in part-exchange for his confession to the other six. He didn't even twig that he was still going down for a long, long time.'

Although Ruth Edwards was pleased with the successful outcome of Swann's interrogation, she had doubts over repeating the strategy. 'I don't think I'll be able to treat Bennett the same way,' she commented.

Nash responded, 'Your presence alone should be enough — added to what Viv's going to bring into the room.'

'If this proves to be pivotal in obtaining Bennett's confession, it must surely rank as the strangest item of evidence of all time,' Ruth said as they headed downstairs.

Ruth waited until Nash had given the introductory message and then asked, 'I understand you live at Manor Farm and that there are no other occupants, correct?'

The accused woman agreed, clearly puzzled by the relevance. Nor was her next question more enlightening. 'I also understand from your employee that he has never seen you face to face, and that apart from speaking to you over an intercom, he has never been inside the house. Is that true?'

Bennett said she was correct, and was prepared to deny all their allegations, but when Viv entered the room and she saw what was inside the bags, her resistance soon ended.

She was shocked when Ruth continued, 'Then would you explain why we found these recently worn size nine galoshes inside your house, when you take a size six shoe? Could it have been that you put them on and deliberately trod in mud outside Kirk Bolton Hall before you entered the building? Where you slit your lover's throat with the knife found concealed within them.'

The extent of the detectives' knowledge was too much. Hilary Bennett's last vestige of resistance vanished when Nash added, 'We already knew that Alison Stokes recognized her killer from the taped treble nine call and, to the best of our knowledge, she had never met Harvey Swann.'

The confession that followed was gratifying, and it left Ruth in awe at the brilliance of Nash's stage-management in manipulating the interviews. Not that she would ever dream of telling him so. She was shocked, however, when Bennett admitted, 'Alison saw my Volvo outside the shop and realized I was the boss of Jakeman's. From there, it was only a matter of time before she worked out the rest.' She shrugged. 'Apart from that, she was beginning to bore me.'

After they left the interview room, Nash nudged Ruth. 'She'll soon have a chance to make some new girlfriends where she's going. However,' he added with a grin, 'privacy might be a bit of a problem.'

'One thing puzzles me,' Ruth said when they returned to Nash's office. 'Why did they switch from burglary to puppy farming? It seems a world away from jewellery or used cars.'

'We can only guess, but I reckon they needed to find another source of income. With their two scapegoats, Craig French and Bobby Walker, behind bars, their revenue stream had dried up. One of them obviously came up with the alternative idea to offset the overheads from their businesses, which must have been draining their reserves quickly.'

Even when Nash and the other detectives had left, Sergeant Binns and two uniformed officers remained until transport arrived to take Swann, Bennett and the two farm-hands to their new accommodation in the holding cells at Netherdale HQ, prior to their appearance in court.

The high point for Nash had come when he informed Harvey Swann that French's alibi for the Kirk Bolton Hall murder had been provided by Tiff Walker, and that the two lovers were back together.

That had provoked a tirade of abuse from Swann against French. Nash had stopped this diatribe by informing him that he also had proof of French's innocence via the car seen outside Bobby Walker's house. 'You should take up cards, because you're useless with women.'

Proof of Swann's fixation with Tiff Walker was provided by a large collection of photos, recovered from Swann's house during their search. Evidence of his bitterness at her rejection of his advances was plain by the way each of the shots had been scored through with a red marker pen. Nash decided that the photos should be held back until after Swann's trial, when they would be handed over to Tiff, so she could be sure to have them all in her possession. She would doubtless enjoy burning them.

Before leaving the station, Nash reminded his colleagues that they would have to manage without him over the week-end. 'Alondra and I are going to visit Daniel, and introduce him to Teal. That will be great fun.'

# CHAPTER TWENTY-SEVEN

Muriel Croft had been visited by the witness care officer, who advised her that the scheduled court date for the mugging case would be in two weeks' time. The official had only been gone a few minutes when Muriel's doorbell rang a second time. She was surprised, as getting one visitor was unusual — two within an hour was all but unique. Her surprise turned to shock when she opened the door. The young man standing outside was a complete stranger to her. The girl alongside him, who appeared extremely nervous, was all too familiar.

'You!' Muriel gasped. 'What do you want?'

Her fear was slightly assuaged when the girl spoke. 'I'm Shazza, er, Shannon, and this is my boyfriend Kyle. I know this is probably breaking some rule or other, but we had to come and see you to say how sorry we are — and to give you this.'

As Shazza was speaking, Kyle held out his hand, containing an envelope. Muriel took it. The envelope was open and when she glanced at the contents, Muriel's astonishment was obvious. She barely heard Kyle's statement. 'That money isn't stolen. My sister lent us it. She encouraged us to go to the police and confess. I hope you don't hate us, because like Shazza said, we really are sorry. If we'd been able to think straight at the time, it would never have happened.'

They turned to walk away, but once Muriel had recovered from the shock, she called them back. 'Wait a minute.'

They looked at her and saw her smile.

'Would you like to come in for a few minutes? I want to talk to you.'

They obeyed the request, which was almost an order, obviously anticipating a severe dressing-down. It was more than half an hour later when they left, and once she was alone, Muriel remained seated in her lounge for a long time, pondering everything they had told her, and trying to decide on her next course of action. Eventually, her mind made up, she called a taxi, and when the driver asked her where she wanted to go, she replied, 'Helmsdale Police Station, please.'

DC Andrews was in the midst of typing a list of stolen goods recovered from Swann's premises, and on display in Jakeman's jewellers when her phone rang. She was surprised when Jack Binns told her the identity of the visitor waiting in reception. Keen to ease her aching back muscles from the wearisome task, she hurried downstairs.

Mrs Croft apologized for disturbing her and said she hoped not to take up much of her time.

'Don't worry about that,' Lisa responded, 'I'm glad of the distraction. How can I help? Not more trouble, I hope?'

Muriel explained the reason for her visit, going into details of which even Lisa was unaware, before asking her advice. 'It has nothing to do with the money, although I'm glad they've returned it. I don't want them to end up in prison because of one stupid mistake.'

She paused before explaining her motives. 'I've been very lucky all my life. I had a secure childhood, and afterwards, I had a long and happy marriage until Ronnie passed away. All of which leaves me with scores of good memories. I am sure that Ronnie would approve of my thinking on this. When I spoke to Kyle and Shannon after they returned the cash, I learned a lot about their background.' Muriel went on to give details of what she'd learned, before adding, 'As you can tell, they both had a rotten start in life.' Muriel took a

229

deep breath, 'I don't suppose it's possible for me to withdraw the charges against them, is it?'

'I'm afraid it's too late for that,' Lisa replied.

'I thought that would be your answer, so I wondered if there's another way that I could help them?'

Lisa was still pondering Muriel's question when Sergeant Binns, who had listened in to their conversation, interrupted. His suggestion, as Lisa acknowledged later, was a pivotal contribution to the outcome of the court case.

* * *

The morning after the hearing, Lisa wandered into Nash's office to report on the outcome. 'I think the verdict and sentence were correct,' she began, before explaining how it had come about. 'Defence counsel encouraged me to explain how Kyle had helped solve a far more serious offence, and that his information had been extremely useful. Added to that, Muriel Croft's evidence, highlighting the return of her handbag and the repayment of the stolen money was very impressive. But above all, I think it was her letter to the court, with its plea for clemency, that persuaded the judge to opt for a non-custodial sentence. Kyle and Shannon got 100 hours' Community Service Orders each.'

'How did they react?' Nash asked.

'They were very relieved, and extremely grateful to Mrs Croft. They accepted the order well. Shannon even joked about dyeing her hair to match the orange hi-vis jacket she'll have to wear. I think if determination to succeed is sufficient, they'll be OK. With luck, we'll have heard the last of them.'

* * *

It was several days later, following the first appearance in court and remand of Swann and Bennett, that Lisa Andrews reported progress on another aspect of the charges on which they had been sent for trial. 'Thanks to Viv and our cybercrime boys, we've successfully hacked Hilary Bennett's computer, plus the laptop hidden in Swann's secret room at the dealership. As a result, we've identified ten more potential breeding sites similar to the one we found at Manor Farm. All of them are on properties owned by either Bennett or Swann, and all are close to towns where there is a branch of the jewellery business.

'They've also uncovered a network of what look to be itinerant dealers. By that I mean people with multiple identities, who regularly advertise dogs for sale via a number of internet sites. That information has been shared with Ms Parsons, the vet, and with the RSPCA and local police forces. I expect there will be a considerable number of arrests in the coming weeks.'

'That is excellent work, Lisa. Pass my thanks to Pearce and the tech wizards. I'll let Superintendent Edwards know, and then she can advise the CPS of the additional charges to pursue against Bennett and Swann.'

* * *

Alondra was putting the finishing touches to her latest work, a portrait that contained two subjects. Although one of them was not available to pose, her memory was sufficient to ensure the likeness was accurate. She put her brush down, stepped back from the easel, and was examining the end product, her critical eye looking for flaws, when the doorbell rang.

The young woman standing outside was a stranger, whose opening words made Alondra wonder if she might be one of Mike's old flames. She stared at her a mite suspiciously until she identified herself, clearing up the misunderstanding by telling Alondra, 'I'm Faith Parsons, Teal's vet. We spoke on the phone about her. I came to see how she is and to thank Inspector Nash for his help with the puppy trafficking case.'

'Mike's out at the moment, but he shouldn't be long. He's taken Teal for her walk. Why don't you come in and wait for them?'

'I'll do that, if I may.'

Alondra asked if she'd like a drink, and as she prepared coffee for them, Faith said, 'I understand you're an artist. Are you working on anything at present?'

'I am. I'll show you in a moment.' Once their drinks were ready, she escorted Faith to the conservatory. The vet looked at the image of a black Labrador lying fast asleep and using a boy as a pillow as they sat beneath a tree. Faith smiled and gestured to the painting. 'That's Teal, isn't it? But who is the boy?'

'That's Mike's son, Daniel. He and Teal are already good friends. We weren't able to visit him earlier, with everything that was happening for Mike at work, so we kept her secret. He didn't know about her until we visited him last weekend. He was so excited. I saw them like that and couldn't resist capturing the moment on canvas. Now he can't wait for the summer break to start.'

At that moment, they heard the door close and a scampering of claws on the kitchen tiles.

For the first few minutes, Faith concentrated on updating him with their success in smashing the trafficking ring. Her attempts to do so were severely impeded by Teal, who insisted on greeting her enthusiastically, and prolonging that greeting for as long as possible.

Eventually, however, Faith managed to tell Nash that as a result of a series of raids carried out by local police forces, accompanied by vets and RSPCA officers, a further fifty-seven people had been arrested and were awaiting trial. In addition, over two hundred dogs, comprising stud dogs, breeding bitches, and their offspring, had been released from captivity and were in the process of being examined prior to possibly being re-homed, unless their condition was beyond redemption.

'In the computers, we found reference to a young black Labrador with a high pedigree. It had been sold on for breeding to Jakeman. We know it wasn't microchipped, and there was no such animal found among those rescued. Although it might have escaped,' she added with a smile, patting Teal on the head.

'I actually have some information that verifies that statement.' Nash said. 'The barn door at the puppy farm was opened and one of the animals escaped at around the time I found her.'

'Really? Well, that closes my file,' Faith responded.

* * *

It was almost three months later, and normality, as far as a detective's life could ever be normal, had resumed. Daniel, now turned twelve, had started a new school year. During the summer break, he had spent some weeks in France with his aunt Mirabelle, who had raised him as a baby when his mother was ill. Following his mother's death, Mirabelle brought him to England to the father he had never met, but knew everything about. To the father who knew nothing of his existence. During the long summer holidays, Daniel always stayed with his aunt, a necessity when Nash was working. However, this time Daniel had insisted he should return earlier to be with Alondra and Teal, causing his aunt to be upset.

Mike and Alondra settled down for a quiet evening and were discussing how they could resolve the issue. 'Now you're here,' Mike said, 'it isn't really necessary for Daniel to go France at all, but it would cause more upset should Mirabelle not see him. Besides, I owe her a lot for her help over the years, but Daniel will be a teenager soon, and she is quite elderly. I don't know if she could cope. And then, there's the house.'

'What house?'

'Daniel owns the family home.'

'He does?'

'It was where his mother lived. It's held in trust for him, with Aunt Mirabelle as resident caretaker.'

'But I have my house in Spain as well. If I am to stay here, should I sell it? I thought it would make a good holiday

233

home, but it seems you already have one in France.' She shook her head in confusion. 'We need a family meeting, to include Daniel. I think next summer we should all go to France together and you can introduce me. Then Daniel can still visit for a shorter time. And, if she likes me, she would know he is safe with me.' Alondra looked at him, waiting for his response.

Nash shook his head. 'I doubt there's anyone who wouldn't like you. But I think she would be happier if she knew we are in a settled relationship.'

Alondra looked crestfallen. 'Oh, Mike, I thought everything was OK. Aren't you happy I am here?'

He smiled at her. 'Of course I'm happy. But I think it would prove so to Tante Mirabelle if you were wearing this.' He produced a small box containing a solitaire diamond ring from his pocket.

Their plans for celebration were scotched almost immediately, though, when Nash's mobile rang. He glanced at the screen. 'It's Jack Binns. That can't be good news.' He pressed a button and listened.

'Sorry to disturb you at home, Mike, but they've found a body in Netherdale Cemetery.'

Nash's buoyant mood was reflected in his flippant response. 'This might come as a surprise to you, Jack, but I already knew that. In fact, I'll let you in to a little secret, as long as you keep it between us. That place is actually full of bodies. It's what a cemetery is for.'

'Yes, Mike, but they're usually inside a coffin. This one isn't.'

## THE END

# ACKNOWLEDGEMENTS

On this occasion, I owe a great deal to my reader Wendy McPhee for bringing to light an error in my thinking. Spotting a flaw in the plot involved a minor rewrite, making the storyline far better. My other reader, Al Gowans, also deserves my thanks.

As always, there's my wonderful partner in crime, the wife, who keeps me in order, reading every word I write until she is satisfied.

I must also thank the great team at Joffe Books, Jasper, Emma, Steph and Nina, who are so supportive and encouraging, and my editor Jodi for keeping me on the right track.

**Thank you for reading this book.**

If you enjoyed it please leave feedback on Amazon or Goodreads, and if there is anything we missed or you have a question about, then please get in touch. We appreciate you choosing our book.

Founded in 2014 in Shoreditch, London, we at Joffe Books pride ourselves on our history of innovative publishing. We were thrilled to be shortlisted for Independent Publisher of the Year at the British Book Awards.

www.joffebooks.com

We're very grateful to eagle-eyed readers who take the time to contact us. Please send any errors you find to corrections@joffebooks.com. We'll get them fixed ASAP.

Printed in Great Britain
by Amazon

34115103R00138